I0534273

WILD

GOLDEN

OBSESSION

A Wright Series

Book 3

Linda McKown

WILD GOLDEN OBSESSION

ISBN-13: 978-0-9997357-2-5

Author:
LindaMcKownAuthor LLC
11574 E Running Deer Trail
Scottsdale, AZ 85262

Any names of people and entities are fictitious in this story having been created by the author's imagination.

Front Cover Photo of the book is copyright through Shutterstock. Book title manipulation was done by Joseph McKown

Dedicated to my husband, Joe, and a beloved Tonkinese male show cat. The cat was named after Muir Woods in California. The reason for the name was his size. At four-months, our kitten was huge. At ten months, the cat was awesome. When he was young, Muir loved to go to the cat shows. He enjoyed riding in the car, staying at motels, and didn't mind taking a bath. Once in the ring, he sucked up to the show judges and knew which ones liked him. It was those judges that carried his favorite toys on their table. Anything that moved was fair game. His aqua eyes lit up and his platinum mink fur stood on end. The toy to him was worth a leap or jump.

After the judging, Joe carried Muir upside down from the show ring back to his highly-decorated cage. The cat, of course, was holding onto his rosette ribbon, much to the delight of the spectators. His tail flicked happiness. A person could almost see the grin on Muir's handsome face. He also knew the ribbon represented a treat of baby food meat once he was returned to his cage. Muir was very special and walked like a king. He knew there was a closet full of ribbons at home.

Later, our cat would win his crystal award that read, The Cat Fanciers' Association, Inc, National Award 2003-2004, Third Best Tonkinese, Grand Champion, Regional Win, Conamorecats Muir Illusion.

He was by far the sweetest and smartest cat ever. We greatly miss him. Memories of Muir are included in my writing as I compare him to Felidae.

Contents

1   Goddess and Felidae

TIGER BLACK, AN African businessman, brought the magazine with him and sat down in the small café. He peered around the magazine and looked across the street. His eyes rolled when he recognized Santan Chesin's former flunky, Stew Avery, who was sitting in a green shirt at the coffee shop. His hair was short and slicked down with some type of hair cream which made the hair look shiny.

Tiger shook his head in disgust and sniffed the air. There was the smell of pine or wood. The green shirt of the tourist across the street intermingled with the sun. The light against shade created a camouflage fabric. The forest-type smell from the hair cream intermingled with the coffee house smell and the arborvitae. Tiger knew that his senses were heightened as well as his eyesight. He remembered that Santan had called his subcontractor creep a weasel. But then Santan called most people a weasel. He believed that there sat a shiny weasel in plain view across the street. The camouflage didn't work for Tiger, nor the man's beard.

Why are you in Fort Payne, Alabama? This is not your normal tourist attraction. There must be secrets or strange happenings involved. Let me think about the underground vibrations. "Aah, yes. I remember that you screwed Santan on a deal involving a fake diamond necklace and there was something about a diving venture. There is a woman with you that looks familiar. Of course, she was once a guard for a woman in Miami."

Thoughts of Miami and the woman he knew appeared to him, adding fuel to Tiger's ire. Yet, the man's face was quickly calmed. There was no time for self-absorption on this project. His business reasoning kicked into play.

"Are you stalking the same person that I am?"

The businessman took a bite out of his whole-wheat sandwich before speaking to himself and the air. "Yes, I'm correct. You figured out that she is the person who stole my gold antiquities. You somehow know auction houses and how things work. Interesting job for a weasel, but priceless and rare is the name of my game. Money is your draw. I do think it was very clever of you to find her. But finding her won't matter. You will remain only a creep, con artist, and slimy weasel with no moxie once the dust settles."

Tiger Black continued holding the magazine so that he didn't have to see the obnoxious couple. He pretended to read an article when the café waitress refilled his cup. She took away his sandwich plate and was glad the man stopped talking to himself. The bacon, lettuce, and tomato sandwich with cheddar cheese was amazingly good and thick for a small-town cafe. He noted with relief that the lunch crowd was dispersing. They wouldn't remember him. However, he wasn't too sure about the waitress. Then he saw her heavy soled, beige shoes. He knew that she wouldn't be a problem. There wasn't any excitement in her life. The reason for this was that the waitress wouldn't and couldn't afford to get involved. Beige meant safety.

Tiger concluded that the man and woman at the coffee house were here to steal from his target. He poured cream into the coffee and stirred. He used to drink the stuff thick and black. The cream now soothed the acid in his stomach. He threw an antacid pill in his mouth just in case. He hated the pills because they reminded him of a judge he once knew in Dakar. He frowned, threw the pills in his mouth, and crunched. Pretty soon the pills did their job. Slowly drinking a sip of the refilled coffee, he almost felt human.

Suppressing another laugh of disgust at the two people in the coffee shop, he said, "I will beat a weasel and his female guard every time. The two golden objects are mine to hold and obsess over. The permanent damage to the holder is all arranged and will happen shortly. She will be but a memory."

All three knew the Fort Payne young married woman's schedule. She did the once a week beauty shop, a check on her business coffee shop, and finally, walked into her bank. They knew she wore a gold chain around her neck always. The bank keys were probably there.

Every one of the con artists gathered knew that her husband, Scott Barrow, and his magnificent horse estate was a veritable fortress with high-tech security to protect his prized polo horses and their lucrative stud juice. If illegal trapping was going to take place, it

3

would be outside those gates. Scott failed to protect his wife. She was left wide open. The tiger man laughed even more. He loved failure, especially loss this massive. Scott Barrow wasn't very smart. Tiger Black was the king who would reign today.

"My business is more longstanding. Also, I'm extremely experienced at tracking her. The scales will slide in my favor. You, slimy weasel, and your girlfriend are like minor, tiny gnats swarming toward the light. Dare to interfere and more than squashed disaster will follow you. Go hide, weasel. In the meantime, I can wait for an important phone call."

Tiger Black smiled evilly. To the patrons, he looked nice, rich, and comfortable sipping his milked-down coffee. He was another average tourist in town having a leisurely lunch. If anyone looked closely, they would see his eyes contained smoldering vengeance. The inner orbs were turning to empty black holes. The gold objects were only part of the justice he would take away from the young woman.

XXXXXX

The Alabama countryside spread before her on a beautiful blue-sky day as she drove out the tall impressive wrought iron black gates which were etched with *SB* in huge imprinted gold letters. These gates were the release into the normal world from their exquisite paradise. The gates represented richness and extraordinary people inside. Only correct society was allowed entrance.

4

Mrs. Barrow stepped on the gas of her red sports car. She loved her car, because it was in her name only. It would take her only twenty minutes to reach town. Suddenly, there was a large and dirty tow truck blocking the private gravel road. The license plate was obscured. She slowed down. The huge beast was an ugly dark black-green. She hated green except in plants. The color made her skin look olive.

Impatient, Mrs. Barrow honked and received no response. The no response irritated her. She didn't have time to mess with workers today. There didn't appear to be anyone in the truck. She stepped out of her car and walked over to the tow truck. Opening the door, she was surprised the truck was truly empty and, of course, even more dirtier inside. The keys were missing from the ignition. There was a minor crack in the windshield. This scenario was unusual. The private road wasn't heavily traveled this time of day and no one from the estate called a tow truck. She would have been informed, or at least her husband would have told her.

"Who could these people be and where are they?"

She checked the ditch and thought she could drive around the stupid truck. It was an unwise decision to drive her stunning red car today and not the heavier, high-wheeled, black vehicle that was her husband's. Mrs. Barrow thought about calling Scott for help and decided to make her own way out of this situation. She would have to clean the dirt and grass off the muffler, but it would be all right. Her husband had special hoses in the horse barn for washing the animals. If the tall grass and swaying top stickers scratched the paint on her red, sweet sports car, then it would mean a day at the body shop. She could handle herself and her car.

The young woman listened and didn't hear or see anyone. She quickly made her decision. Walking back to her vehicle, she saw an ominous apparition. It was almost as if the vile thing appeared from nowhere or dropped out of the sky. Or perhaps the creature arose from the earth? It was standing on the earth. The apparition looked like a man, but not a normal man. It was a jungle man in full war paint, feathers, loin cloth, and adornment holding a spear. He looked out of place in the Alabama open countryside.

"Were there movie people in town with a film crew?"

Her life was busy, but surely someone would have told her, especially if the film crew were close to the Barrow property line. She couldn't believe she was seeing correctly and blinked in confusion. Not sure why he was in this spot in time, Mrs. Barrow thought perhaps the man was lost. She raised her hand to say hello in a hand message.

The jungle man bared his teeth. She figured the hand message wasn't working.

"Where was their property line?" She should order the man off if he was trespassing. He had to be trespassing.

Mrs. Barrow remembered a distant conversation about a jungle man. The man's name was simply, Midge, except he was the opposite from his name. There was no simple anything to the vision he represented. Instead of being a small man, he towered over six feet nine inches. He was an anthropologist's worst nightmare from some lost indigenous tribe. An African man she lived with a while ago told her about this type of creature. The jungle man was a hired killer and sometimes was a cannibal when he chose. He was not part of anyone's future film.

"Who hired you, devil man?"

The young woman wasn't sure if that part was true, the cannibal part, but no sane person would wait to find out. It was not a good time to be sociable. His spear contained bones from his kills.

"Why did he have his spear now?"

Then she understood. Full comprehension hit her in the stomach. The jungle man was here because of her. He was hired to do a job. She was the one in danger. Her revolver and cell phone were in the large designer leather purse inside the red sports car along with her car keys.

"Were the car keys still in the ignition?" Mrs. Barrow kicked off her expensive high heels and reached for her knife. The tiger name tattoo showed on the tops of her feet where her shoe strap had been.

She turned to her sports car. There was another woman who looked exactly like her, standing a short distance from her rigid, frightened body. The woman carried a large gun. The gun was aimed at Mrs. Barrow. It was an old waylay trick and she unwillingly stepped into their sinister devil trap. There were two assassins. Her sports car was fiberglass and wouldn't stop a bullet.

The young woman screamed and panicked because the other woman frightened her more than the jungle man.

"Felidae! Where are you?"

This scene was more than someone's cruel trick.

There was no help anywhere. She knew that she needed time for her tiger to find her. Her Felidae was the only one she thought about as she pulled all her energies for the next task. The young woman turned to run to the nearby trees. Run were the only thoughts in her brain. She sprinted, her agile body leaping across the ditch. The trees would cover her while she made her way to her pool house. Scott was somewhere on their property. Once she reached the pool house, there was no way the odd jungle man and his bold assassin woman could get inside. Mrs. Barrow was scared, but knew that she could call her husband for help from their private phone. His security people would race to her rescue. The timing was a matter of seconds.

Just a few more steps and she would be to the shadow edge of the trees. Three to five seconds were all that she needed. She miscalculated the distance and a sound came screaming toward her. It was a sound she hadn't heard before. The young woman slowed in her stride. She saw orange fur in the weeds.

"Felidae."

The calcified, clapping bone spear hit her in the back. The bones swung and stopped their evil dance motion. The pain from the sharp spear caused white light with fire to roll past her brain. Warned that the man was fierce, she thought of her tiger. Her tiger was fierce.

"Feli, Feli..." Her speech slurred and stopped. The young woman was delirious with pain, but smiled. She blew a soft and lasting fragile kiss to her beloved tiger before blacking out. The young woman gave up. There arrived for her blissful, immediate unconsciousness. The goddess-like woman collapsed into the dense weedy ditch with arms outstretched as if she were reaching for something. The protective trees were close, but not quite close enough. The heavy weed growth on the edge of the field cushioned her fall. There would be no way to contact her husband, Scott.

The strangely-dressed man approached where she lay. He was satisfied that the young woman was no longer moving. He nodded to his female partner on the road to make the phone call. The female partner pocketed the expensive heels on the road. They would look stunning on her feet and they were free for the taking. There was no need to waste good designer shoes. The evil woman with the gun touched the fur on the shoe. The fur and leather were real. Inside the shoe was a message, "Save the tiger from extinction."

The female partner cruelly laughed. "Who cares about extinct?"

"Mrs. Barrow, trust me, you won't be needing these heels anymore." The female partner threw the shoes into her large bag along with the gun.

The jungle man dragged the body.

A tiger paced in its cage.

2   Earlier Time in London Streets

THE YOUNG WOMAN'S earlier life started with a mistake. Her poor judgment parked her on the streets.

She wiped her eyes so that she could see, because the light was dim in the underworld of London's East End. Underworld was the name the current poor residents called the place. If misery had a color, this side of town would be called wretched greige or gray cemetery-stone. Underworld meant *the other place* to the local British who were being polite.

The rest of the people spoke their true mind, "Don't go there! Dangerous, insane souls rule the streets day and night, tormenting visitors with their schemes. A person would be safer on Mars."

The poor wished they could take a bus or train to Mars every day, but they realized it would never happen. There wasn't enough time. They would be dead before countries built the right spaceship or passed legislation allowing them entrance. The borders were clearly defined. So, they blamed parliament, the police, their neighbors, and anyone within reach. They screamed to the passerby that they could be dead in an hour in their underworld. They yelled that no one cared. It was true.

The poor didn't flip-a-coin to find a solution about which direction to take or where to go in the morning, because a person might get mugged.

Therefore, they were resigned to stay and ambled off with all known assets well hidden from view. It was rare that anyone helped another person. There was always a trade-off required. The young woman encountered the trade-off scheme every day.

She wrote her name in the dusty broken glass of her dingy room.

"Redeen."

She drew a crown around the words. Then she felt sad because her face barely showed in the glass reflection.

"Still blurry."

Taking the palm of her hand, she erased the writing. "No kings in shining armor today. At least the window looks a little better." She was hungry and must find food plus fresh air. Walking past two male beggars in the street, she had no money to give them today.

The young woman stopped and turned to listen to their first song. The older one had the scratchy, perfect pitch voice and his instrument, the harmonica. The harmonica doled out its sexy twang while the younger male played on a handmade bongo drum and stringed shaker. He did a little two-step dance while strumming and pounding the drum. Each instrument was strapped to his body which allowed his hands free to play.

Their sound this morning was fast-paced and catchy. A small crowd began to form, entranced by the levitation feeling of their own souls. She swayed with the beat and could feel the incoming tide of elation. The young woman was glad to see a man drop a dollar bill

11

into their jar. Others dropped in coins. A worker gave them bottled water from his wheeled tower of stacked containers. There would be enough money for tobacco and food tonight for them.

The two beggars were called The Happy Dylan Jacks. It was an appropriate name. The younger son was called Dylan. Their street music brought jacked-up relief every Monday and Friday. The older beggar tipped his hat to the young woman. She curtsied before leaving the area. She had called him Jack of Diamonds once and he laughed, enjoying her compliment more than anything. The young woman thought they were good enough to play in a blues bar in the city.

The happy music resonated in her head during her leisurely stroll. She had walked five miles and arrived at the specific location. Having laid on the flat rooftop, she saw where the truck stopped. In the truck's backend, open framework were crates of vegetables and fruit. The food was for delivery at the farmer's market. An older bag lady told her about the place. This place was a distance from the food kitchen. She brought her netted bag to capture some of those free items. Or, rather, a person should call the items stolen. It depended on your point of view.

She was tired of the soup at the kitchen and the unclean, half-sane people that talked to themselves. She was beginning to talk to herself. The young woman wanted to get enough food for both to eat. The bag lady told her the market was near two tall towers which were housing for the working poor. She told her about a possible social worker person who could help her get a job and maybe get her into the towers to live. First, the young woman would have to bring a bag of food from this market to the bag lady. The bag lady told her to be aware of the bobbies which frequented the market.

The young women knew the word meant the police. The British called them bobbies, especially the older crowd. She liked the shortened American word which was cops. The young woman looked longingly at the buildings which were five blocks away. From a distance, they looked better than her current accommodations. She could see herself on the tenth floor where there was sunshine and more air. If she had a job and money, she could buy a real sandwich with meat and live there.

Easily reaching the tarred rooftop, she could smell the diesel fumes. The air usually smelled of dust and recently-moved garbage. This time it smelled of vegetables and fruit mixed in. The young woman followed her finely tuned nose. She crouched down low and readied her tool.

This market was busy with people mingling and talking. It was crowded, and she saw money exchange hands. The vendors pocketed the funds quickly. There was no way to steal from the vendor's hands. They were skilled artisans in their own territory. Her vantage point was a perfect place. The young woman could steal other things. She also had skills.

She moved fast to pull out the white tape she found earlier in the hospital dumpster. She bit into the tape with her teeth, tearing a strip, and wrapped a small piece around her finger. Next, she put a second adhesive tape attached to her finger and pulled out about thirty inches to serve as a swinging contact point. Her finger was the fulcrum.

"The tape will work."

The young woman waited until the worker left the truck and she swung her tape over the highest open crate and pulled a carrot into her bag. Next, there was a tomato, an onion, and an apple were secreted away in the sack netting which was belted securely to her waist.

A sickly, thin rat scurried onto the roof. She stopped her theft movements and stood slightly to retrieve the bottle. She pulled her half-filled water bottle out of the left pocket and clicked on the plastic. The clicking compression scared the competitor rat away.

Suddenly, the man unloading the truck saw her and yelled, "Thief!"

She saw the cop look toward the roof where the man pointed. Her bag bulged with stolen items. Dropping her tape, she ran across three rooftops and down the fire escape, jumping to the ground, and wove in and out of the alleyways. The young woman ran up another fire escape to get the lay of the land. On top of another roof, she saw the bus turn and stop. The young woman fumbled with the roof eaves-trough to reach a spot, jumped down onto an open balcony, and ran down the decrepit stairs to ground level.

Her lithe body raced for the bus which released its brakes while at the stop. The bus was going to move. She saw that a car pulled in front and blocked the bus's path. She sprinted across the street and pounded frantically on the bus door. The driver shook his head, but opened the door. She was relieved and glad to catch a ride. Dropping her coins into the small glass enclosure for her fee, the coins clinked to the bottom, and the bus swung away from the curb. People on the bus didn't look at her. Their thoughts were far away in their own space.

Pulling the high cord above the cracked window, the bus stopped at her designated pullover. The bus dropped her in front of the two buildings she saw in the distance. It would soon be dark. She looked at the bag of vegetables and fruit. It would have to be enough. There wasn't any money to waste on a return bus trip. The bus would have been the faster route. Counting the time on her fingers, it would take too long. If she walked, it would be dark. She would arrive at the soup kitchen too late and the place would be closed.

The risk wasn't worth it. She hesitated and stood near the wooden bus bench with the black and white advertising obscured by black and yellow graffiti. The young woman was glad she found an escape route, but now she would need to find an empty vehicle to spend the night or hide behind a dumpster.

Her plans weren't working too well. She realized, too late, that she was at the end of her world. The darkness brought forth the inhuman dregs of society. There was no escape. Her freedom in this place was limited.

"My cld dingy room is non-existent this evening."

15

The message flashed repeatedly in her brain. "You are nowhere tonight."

The image of her erased name on the broken glass flashed across her thoughts. The place was empty, i.e. devoid of anything. If she stayed there, she was *nothing*. She didn't want to be nothing. The train to that place had been bypassed a long time ago. The young woman faltered. There was the solid wood bus bench. Someone drew a simple bird on the wood in acrylic. The young woman traced the stick design, curious about the artist.

"Were you young or old? Did you give up or did you win?"

She saw the tall man approach. He appeared out of nowhere. She hadn't seen anyone like him for a while. But, she was out of her normal environment. His shoes were new and polished. His clothes didn't have any holes. The blue shirt and slacks looked recently pressed plus he wore gold cuff links. His hair was brushed and neatly trimmed. Polished, no holes, and trimmed meant money. Gold was a statement. She was sure the cuff links were gold because the items gleamed. She was fascinated and saw a diamond ring adorning his finger. The image on top of the ring was a tiger. She was fascinated, but unsure if the gold or diamond were real.

"Are you lost?" It was a logical question. Her voice sounded hoarse to her as she hadn't spoken to anyone in some time. She glanced again at the ring.

The man assessed the wild creature in front of him. "No, it is not I who appears to be lost. The ring is real gold as are the diamonds. You like tigers? Yes, you do. The ring is special to me. My wife bought the ring for me. She is now gone, but that is another matter. Are you waiting for the bus or are you resting before you go back to your building?"

The man assumed that she lived in one of the towers. His voice was smooth and deep with a foreign accent. She was confused and stepped closer. He smelled clean, a fresh-water smell like a waterfall in a misty forest. He smelled of good living and there was also a hint of sweet aftershave.

"Are you legally old enough?"

The young woman stepped back like a frightened cat. He wondered at her feline movement. She drank from her water bottle and eyed him. The tall towers didn't look so nice up close. She could see broken down furniture and hanging, not-quite-clean laundry on the outside balconies.

Meanwhile, the man was assessing her. He was again reminded of a cat he used to own named Tunes. He called the cat that name because it was always looking for the next opportunity. The young woman was the same way, except there was an element of underlying nervousness. The man knew how to handle those emotions. He corrected his thoughts. Her nervousness wasn't fear. She was as cautious as a wild jungle cat. The man let the brief thought go. A wild cat was not a good thing to own.

She knew what he meant by legal. The young woman turned her head to make sure no one was in the area. The space only contained the two of them. He

17

extended a piece of wrapped beef jerky to her. She immediately pocketed the strange gift like the vendors at the market did with their money. The young woman was almost legal age, just a month away. He didn't look like the police and, therefore, wouldn't be able to check her records. She lied.

"Yes."

The young woman fidgeted with her other pocket. The man was on immediate alert.

"Is that a knife?"

She kept a secret knife in one of her worn shoes for the ultimate protection package against threatening vagrants. If she showed him her knife, it could bring unintended consequences. He looked like a man who carried a revolver. A gun could kill you.

Would he use his gun? Her mind worried. She weighed her options.

"No, there is no knife." It was her second lie. The young woman willingly brought forth her empty hand.

The man noticed a piece of tape on the end of her finger and figured she was covering a cut. He was distracted by the tape and thought that was smart of her. He decided to ask the next question, because he was liking the young thing in front of him. He knew she had lied.

After her response, the expensively-dressed man told her that he would get his car and pick her up in ten minutes. That was all the time she would have to get her things or change her mind. He wanted her to think about his proposal.

The bodyguard figured that the young woman would either steal away, like her other pursuits in life, or she could possibly be there at the curb waiting for him. It was a gamble. There was something about the woman that attracted him. He hoped that he was not wrong. He saw the lonely hunger in her eyes.

"You will do just fine."

He saw a brief nod from the cat creature as she licked her dry lips. He had accomplished his mission. The man would look forward to leaving this filthy and poorer part of town. The young woman was riveted to the spot after he walked away. Stealing had gotten her to this very spot. She saw the cop car drive by and look at her suspiciously. She sat down on the hard bench. The car drove out of sight. She was again relieved. Capture was a tad too close today.

"Was meeting the man a good consequence or not. He wore the tiger as a symbol. She loved the animal. Was it fate that she met him? How could she decide? Staying meant the opposite," were her thoughts, spoken out loud to no one. The only items near her were the painted stick bird on a desolated bus bench. The bird couldn't help her. She must help herself.

She looked at her bag of food and the two buildings. Nothing, but extraordinary sensational, was going to stop the young woman from hitching a ride with the man. She believed it was her day for good fortune after all. She dropped her netted bag of food into the trash bin next to the bus stop, feeling guilty for not being able to give it to the old woman who waited.

There were pop sounds in the distance and the cop vehicle tore down the road with the sirens and lights blaring to the world, "Gun fire, disaster happening in the next alley."

She stood close to the curb looking in the direction the police vehicle left her. Other residents were doing the same.

In fifteen minutes, a shiny black, elegant car arrived at her feet. The car was expensive. It was so far out of her monetary capabilities that she stared at the huge thing. Finally, she touched the gleaming body in front of her. The vehicle appeared solid. She was surprised. The man hurriedly came around to the passenger side and opened the door for her to his elegant black vehicle. It took her a minute to understand his words.

"I apologize. I had to chase scumbags. They were trying to steal rims from my vehicle. A gun is always a handy tool, don't you think? If you agree, I need you to get inside my vehicle really fast."

The young woman accidentally touched the tiger ring and nodded before entering the vehicle. Her fingers felt warm from where she touched the ring. That was a good sign. She must be headed in the correct direction. The shiny car meant escape. She would follow her heart and follow the bodyguard. This area was no place to hang around. The neighborhood was better, but still, not safe.

Safe was where she needed to be right now. The cop car and shots were messing with her deprived body and mind. She was tired and hungry. Safety was high on her list. The young woman would have to fake things for a little while longer. A bed was where she wanted to reside after eating something. It could be anything. The man was apologizing to her.

"What did you say?"

Apologies were a new one. She was intrigued and had no clue where she was headed.

"Please fasten your seat belt."

She wrestled with the belt. The bodyguard was surprised there were no pieces of luggage with her. Once the woman was inside, he returned to the driver's side. A fast U-turn put them in the opposite direction. She was glad that she put the seatbelt on. Before exiting the slum streets, he looked at her.

"Call me the bodyguard. That is what my boss calls me."

"My name is Q. Redeen Pyra. You can call me, Redeen."

Her life was about to change in three hours. She would have a month and a half off before the boss returned from a vacation. The bodyguard told her she would have time to rest, get strong, and receive excellent medical care. He would teach her the manners of the house and buy her necessary clothes. A beautician would do her hair for the first two weeks.

The young woman sank into the plush leather seats and watched the scene out her side window. It was another trade-in scheme. This one looked better. She relaxed and fell fast asleep after eating the jerky. The treat filled the empty space in her stomach.

21

He told her it would take a couple hours to arrive at his boss's owned flat. The bodyguard didn't say apartment. An owned flat meant wealth. Rich was what she dreamed about. She was on her way finally. At least she was going somewhere? This could be another nothing-rut in the road. She hoped not. Tomorrow would wait for her ten thousand questions. She wondered if there was an agent to hire for her type of strange business. It was something that she would think about.

"No white stones should be left unturned." It was an idiot motto, but she had heard it all her life. She felt her mother, or some preacher mentioned the phrase wrong.

"What about all the other colored stones?"

Eventually, she would throw most sayings away for better ones. Her new motto would be, "Good enough, was for the poor and illiterate." She would select money and intelligence from now on. Therein, lied the golden path. It was the only avenue she would choose. Her dreams were going to come true.

Redeen captured the *me-ism* vogue of current times. Anything less would be thrown away and she knew when to walk away. The streets taught her smarts. The bodyguard would teach her more. If problems arose, she would be gone before the dust settled, richer, and wiser than before. She learned to close doors. The past became a distant memory, which she became skilled at parking away. Her story was just beginning but the inescapable past would follow her.

3   Louisa Renaliere's Drawings

JESS WRIGHT CONSIDERED the research she completed from an enchanting love story found in a deceased friend's notebook. It was regarding Louisa Renaliere's great-great-grandmother who married into royalty. The family was from Rome, Italy. The notebook contained drawings of old gold antiquities that her family once owned. If the items were still in existence, she very much wanted to see them.

The Wrights would do well with Louisa's additional hidden knowledge in the notebook. Louisa carefully wrote down and drew the drawings that were stored in her head regarding her family's heritage. Her mother explained every single detail to her as a child and drew the partial drawings to show her. Louisa wished she kept those old drawings now. They somehow were lost. But her mind had not dulled for a minute and she drew exceptionally accurate drawings.

The notebook contained descriptions and drawings of the family's riches. The items were sold to pay for mercenaries to fight the warlords a long time ago. Louisa drew a picture of the gold crown which showed an eagle carved into the gold with the wings wrapping around the head. There were no jewels in the crown in the drawing.

The design of the eagle was very clever. By artistic standards, the design was ageless. It fit into

23

elegant society then and looked modern today. Louisa did not list any engraver's name. The name was never provided or else she forgot. Louisa wished her mother were there to ask questions.

Louisa knew Jess was talking about designs for some dresses she was experimenting with. Jess wanted to enter the high-end fashion world. The children were older and didn't need her total supervision. She told Louisa that she needed to feel useful. Louisa loved that expression. Louisa believed the notebook would give Jess some grand ideas. She certainly hoped so. The notebook was also a good history of her family's collection. The drawings would be in good hands.

Jess held the notebook. The Wrights were at home in Los Angeles. It rained earlier in the day and the sky turned into a beautiful golden hue. She touched the arm of her favorite black velvet highboy chair. It went well with their white leather sofa where Derek was sitting. He unbuttoned his shirt and looked relaxed. It would be a good time to talk with him.

"The scepter appeared to be approximately three and a half feet long with a large eagle head on the top. The metal artist again cleverly put engraving of eagle wings and feathers which wrapped around the scepter in a spiral fashion to the bottom. The design was perfectly beautiful, almost exquisite. I'm getting inspired by them."

Derek glanced at the drawing. He could see what she meant.

"Under the head were two rows of small diamonds. The eagle's eyes were emeralds and it carried a gold branch in its beak with a large ruby on the end. She used colored pencils to draw an enlargement. She must have viewed pictures of stones online to get the angles right. Or perhaps that was the way her mother drew them originally. The scepter came apart in the middle of the staff and then at the head. That makes sense; a person could pack it away properly for travel. A secret compartment within the head opened with a special mechanism. The compartment was large enough to store the stones. There was another easily accessible compartment in the upper part of the scepter exactly like the head part."

"Didn't Hades, the God of Death and King of the Underworld have a scepter with a bird on top?"

"Yes, but the Renaliere's scepter contained the more majestic of birds, the eagle. In Greek mythology, Hades also was known as ruler of the very fertile earth plus its gold, silver, and metals, not just the underworld."

"I vaguely remember those facts. Was the embellished eagle design on Louisa's drawings a part of the family crest or emblem?"

"Yes, it was. Two of the last pages in the book show a beautiful cape or cloak drawing with a gold clasp. It is the full regalia costume of the Renaliere leader during his days of glory. The gold clasp appeared to hold the fur part of the garment together at the top. Louisa drew the clasp in two pieces. The eagle head was positioned on the left clasp with the left wing, and the right clasp is the other wing. The object was in gold with the same carving as the crown and scepter."

Jess held up the book for Derek to view the page. He liked the leader's cloak and was impressed.

"The ring drawing showed the eagle design and the ring did contain small diamonds. It matched the other items flawlessly." Jess turned the pages of Louisa's notebook back to the scepter.

"The collection together would be an impressively rich find."

She glanced at Derek, "Do you remember that day in Rome in Louisa's apartment?"

"I do. Louisa kept whispering things to you. I felt left out."

"She forgot to mention something."

"I know the something word always means trouble in our lives. What now? It probably was a profound something," said Derek.

"I can't tell you about the scepter because I did promise."

Derek was a bright detective and guessed. There weren't many places to hide things back then, so subtlety worked. "The bottom of the scepter may contain the real jewels."

Jess nodded, "Absolutely correct and if so, we might have a problem with others wanting the gold objects. If there is a third storage within the scepter, it must be difficult to find the opening. It could be another case of obsession, with the gold and jewels fueling the chase."

Museums contained no such items as the ones in Louisa's notebook. Therefore, the collection was one of a kind. She hoped the beauty of the valuable art objects helped keep them in existence in some private collection. Whenever those collectors passed on, the next generation could sell the collection. Young people were more interested in money. Then they could go on vacation or buy new furniture.

Derek recommended, "You should create some drawings to give to the major auction houses in case the items come up for sale. That way, we will be contacted before the auction takes place to preview them."

"It is definitely worth a shot and will add credibility and further salability to the book I want to write."

XXXXXX

After a couple of months, the Wright's auction friend called Jess. He told her the crown and eagle clasp were coming up for sale. He was sent a photo by the woman who owned the objects and it looked amazingly like her drawing. He did not have authorization to release the photo to anyone though.

The price was high for the two items. After talking with Derek, she called the auction clerk. The Wrights requested a preview of the two items to validate their authenticity. However, before the preview date, the woman who owned the valuable objects withdrew the items from the sale.

Jess was very disappointed. She managed to retrieve the person's name and location from her auction friend. Derek tracked the information to reveal a person by the name of Queenie Redeen Pyra in

Miami. He ran a background check on the person and found there wasn't a whole lot of solid information. Derek's meaning for solid meant the same as Judge Daken. The woman's paper trail was thin. A better example of thin was *not legitimately verifiable or on the normal sc*ale.

Derek didn't want to mention anything to Jess, but he couldn't avoid the conversation. He waited until they were alone in the family room.

"Queenie's apartment building guard supposedly committed suicide. The young woman hung herself and the police found the death suspicious. What if the valuable items she had were stolen? I think we might be entering another firestorm of trouble."

Jess looked out the window. It had clouded over again. She grabbed the fur throw to cover her tanned legs. Derek was disappointed. He liked looking at her legs. He came over to sit beside her.

"The situation doesn't sound very promising. Suspicious usually meant murder in the police world. Stolen is another word that breathes of massive heat. We seem to run amuck with that word. Or rather, we run into the criminal element. Firestorm may be literally the correct vision. There's also golden, charged-up emotions, heavy undercurrents, and obsessively fierce people who come to my mind. I don't know why I said fierce," mentioned Jess.

Derek looked at his wife. He knew his wife was unwinding some vision she saw in her frame of reference. *His wife usually accurately assessed the situation.*

He moved off the couch and flipped the switch to ignite the fireplace. It would warm the room in a short time. It also gave him something to do. Derek counted, "One, two, three, four, and five." He needed a few seconds to catch his breath. He wasn't ready for fierce or obsessive. He wasn't sure if he wanted to meet violent and unfriendly people this soon.

This current situation was rolling toward crazier than a loose cannon. Bat shit also came to his mind. He wished his wife said *amicable* or *tame,* instead. He knew their life would be like a calm before the raging monsoon storm. Derek could see the bats flying for cover. Their beady eyes and claw-like hands skipping the food hunt for the night and flying to the trees or elsewhere. He wanted to go with them and live in a safe cave. The shit there couldn't be as bad as what might be headed their way. He voiced his own images.

"Bats, that's what I'm seeing, and you know what bats do a lot."

He ran his hand through his brown hair, his tall frame pacing the room. His eyes turned a darker brown with sparks emanating like the pilot ignition he might have just touched. He was agitated by her vision and turned to face his wife. "We step slowly through this problem."

Jess saw his eyes and nervous hesitation. They had been here before. Slowly she removed the fur cover and thought about her words. She shouldn't have spoken. Her speech conjured up evil images for Derek. She was familiar with his look of resistance.

She would have to be more careful how she spoke in the future. Her mind was also racing, trying to keep a step ahead of her talented, investigator husband. She tossed her blonde hair and spoke, "Agreed." There, she had said the words, but her gray-mist eyes gave her away.

Her husband knew the shielded look of non-compliance. He saw it all the time with Jess and other criminals. There was a slight twitch. His wife was too clever for him, but this one facial change he knew. Derek walked out of the family room mumbling to himself, "Not again."

Jess sighed and talked to the empty room, "Yes, they better hang on. You're thinking bats. It wasn't bats at all."

She wished their problem was birds. A person could take cover or hide from them. Bats were mammals. He had been close. Her vision showed mammals and humans. A strangely-dressed man was in her vision. His face reminded her of the masks they saw in an African museum. It was daylight, so the creature man wasn't nocturnal like a bat. She thought she heard a tiger's low growl when the man's face showed fear. She touched her fur throw and wondered. That was the reason why she was thinking fierce and fur.

"Who was the man? Which one was the fiercer?"

There was complication disturbing the air. She could feel it come in waves. Derek felt the same disturbance. They were a perfect team to pursue the golden antiquities, but they would need to be cautious and patient. Patience was not her strong suit.

"Neither was caution."

Derek came back with a glass of iced tea for each of them and a plate of microwave popcorn.

"Oh, goody. I love this stuff."

He sat close to Jess. He didn't like being distant with her and brought a peace offering. He clicked on the television. There was no need for talk. He wanted some time to calm down. Jess, however, looked serene. Derek couldn't help, but laugh.

Jess threw popcorn at him. It started the popcorn fight. They were laughing later when they picked up the pieces off the floor. They didn't want their kids to see the mess two grown adults could make in the family room. They would think they were out of control.

4   Q. Redeen Pyra

REDEEN THOUGHT SHE had killed before. A person might categorize her as an extreme killer. She was not your normal person, but someone whose face to the world was currently false. Their unconscious mind was silent. There was no self-examination and no effort made to reorganize their life away from the dark side. Redeen believed she was born there and couldn't change her circumstances.

Was she born with evil or did opportunity surround her, and present itself? Perhaps opportunity was not the correct word.

What made a person continue the evil? Was it self-destruction or self-preservation? More than likely, the situation created a little bit of both. She felt that the line had been crossed and there was no way to break away from the past. Mistakes put her here.

"My first kill was an old boyfriend. Yes, this event was necessary because he wasn't kind and wanted to leave me. Or should I tell the situation exactly how it happened? He wanted to dump me. But first, he needed to be cruel for the world to see. Or in my tiny world, cruel destroyed a person."

First, he beat her so bad, she was in the hospital for a week. When she got out, Redeen told a gang member what her boyfriend divulged to her one night. He stole from their gang. The gang took care of her boyfriend for her.

"Now you are where you belong, in some never-world. I hope the monsters and creatures there are huge." She had obtained her revenge. She felt better except scars remained, mostly on the inside.

Then there was a girlfriend who also left her. She felt loved or, so she thought. She almost went crazy about that loss because the girlfriend stole all her clothes and money. She ended up on the streets in London's poor neighborhoods.

"I learned to never date women again."

There was mass confusion and starvation for a few months on the London streets. Then she thought her luck returned when a man offered her a job with his boss, who would certainly take care of her. She would need to also become his lover. The young woman looked at the gutter in London. It was swirling with litter as the air flow was disturbed by the heavy truck traffic.

The traffic in her part of town was the only reason air reached the underground hell-hole. The restricted air became filled with dirty garbage. She didn't want to become part of the end scraps of the earth. Redeen rubbed a tear from her smudged face. Her hair was a tangled web from living in the cobwebs of an empty, musty building. Stealing water and food were becoming more difficult every day. The shops called the cops immediately upon seeing her. Redeen had to run most of the day, burning valuable calories which her young body required.

If she stayed there much longer, her percentage survival rate would diminish.

The weather turned cold suddenly. The next day, an ambulance took a dead street girl away. The dead one had been there awhile because the stench squeezed a person's lungs. Again, more diminished air and strangulation sounds hit a person's throat. Illness brought fear to most people. Death was the permanence thing. It was the thing people feared the most. She was no different in her feelings. Redeen became afraid and looked for an escape. Any escape would do. Her options were slim. She shivered. When the opportunity approached, she wouldn't waste any time holding on. Street life wasn't fit for anyone.

Therefore, the young woman went willingly with the bodyguard when he told her that things would be all right. He would be there to help her. She saw trust in the bodyguard's eyes. It was a new experience. The carrot and food were gone for good. She wouldn't need to eat ugly carrots again unless they were specially washed and cooked.

In the bodyguard's car, she dreamed of steak. The young woman could almost taste the meat in her mouth when she stepped into the elegant London flat in a nice neighborhood in the evening. She smelled the clear night air and a slight grin reached her lips.

He told her again, "See, this should work for you. I will show you the room and bathroom that will be yours for your stay here."

The room was elegant, and she relaxed. Desperation slowly left her body. She never had her own bathroom before with a large, clean mirror. She touched the fluffy white towels fearing she might get them dirty. There was a hair dryer she could use. The soap had a French name impressed in the bar. It, too, smelled good.

The bodyguard brought her a tray with a ham and lettuce sandwich. He sat it on the small table. Redeen sunk into the soft, rose colored chair. There was hot tea and ice water. It had been a long time since she touched ice. There were clothes in the closet and shoes that might fit. He left her alone and told her to be ready at nine o'clock in the morning. He showed her the nightstand with the clock and showed her the buttons to turn for the music stations and the alarm. He gave her the television remote and explained how to turn the volume and channels. She was pleased.

During the month and a half, the young woman checked the flat out secretly. The refrigerator was full as was the bar. She ate steak, baked potato, and salad. Fruit was always available. She was in heaven. The young woman wondered about her boss's name changes. He was a man who had changed his original name to Mann Nisee and then to Charles Mann. She mouthed his first name parking it in storage. She wondered why the name change? People hid things when they were on the wrong side of the law. It was the smoke and mirror theory. A name change was the smoke to hide what was in the mirror.

She spoke to her bathroom mirror, "My boss may be illegal as all get-out. He must be in deep stuff to the very bottom core."

How did she know this information about her boss? Her bobby pin opened the metal file drawer. There was only a small two-drawer file that was half empty. She worried about where his other documents were. She found the folder with the typed letter from the manufacturer of the safe codes. Once she found the safe, she tried the combination, which worked, so she remembered the stops. She snooped through Charlie's private papers hidden in his safe.

She wasn't going to waste this opportunity to learn more. She was going to pull into her world all advantages to enhance her life. She was told to call her corrupt boss by the name of Charles. The young woman decided the man must be a Charlie person. It was her way of taking a small piece of control at the beginning of their strange relationship.

She would later change the "Q" in her name to Queenie. It wouldn't really be a name change is what she thought. The change would just be an addition that her parents forgot. With her allowance money, she eventually bought a small recorder for her own security.

Once she was cleaned up, the bodyguard thought she was the prettiest blonde girl he ever saw. She was also bright and very smart. She told the bodyguard her wishes and dreams. He would call her the name she had chosen when they were in private. He brought the queenie-girl to the library while he went to the market. They talked about tigers and became friends. She studied everything. Books were checked out and hidden from her boss when he finally arrived home. The bodyguard took her to discount shops for clothes. It was where she learned about name brands. She selected expensive tags. Her education wasn't wasted there either.

Then one day, he took her to the beauty counter where she bought cosmetics and a gold-plated compact with a mirror. She kept looking at her reflection and the shiny, sleek hair which was devoid of tangles. The white adhesive tape was lost previously. There was no need for tape, because the compact mirror now held the favored spot in her right pocket.

5   Unintended Consequences

AFTER A FEW weeks, she saw the old girlfriend eating lunch at an outside restaurant. Redeen couldn't believe it was the woman who robbed her. She stepped closer to be sure. Charlie's bodyguard was across the street buying coffee lattes. A normal person would have dismissed the scene playing center stage. The young woman wasn't going to let pass this moment to extort a little payback. She saw the girlfriend who wanted to impress the well-dressed young man at the restaurant table. The young man would be the major catalyst for her enemy's doom.

"Ivy league, good looking, moderately wealthy," acknowledged Redeen. She would file the male type into her brain for future use.

There appeared to be a dead sparrow in the potted planter out front of the restaurant. Redeen smiled because there was a second minor catalyst which might play into her hands. Using a tissue, she scooped up the little bird and deposited the scrimpy thing in the young woman's soup on the tray held high by the waiter as he passed her.

The timing was right. It was before the waiter set down a bowl at the restaurant table. The waiter noticed the lump which looked like overcooked croutons. The only thing was that the man forgot the croutons. How could there be croutons? Checking the waiter's restaurant tablet, he noted this table ordered soup. The tablet was new. This waiter messed up on occasion and accidentally hit the delete key. Food orders became mixed up. The notebook computer had a devil mind of its own. There should have been more classes for the inexperienced. The waiter didn't let anyone know that he was technologically illiterate. The younger waiters would sneer.

The waiter looked at the alien soup bowl and frowned. But it was too late. The woman at the table picked up her soup spoon and had a look of sheer delight as she dived in for her luncheon meal. The computer was correct, the soup was what was ordered, but no croutons. The waiter was unsure how to intervene. Perhaps the lumps were large tomatoes. They had a new chef, didn't they? The waiter grabbed his large napkin off his white, clean uniform. The napkin was a good defense mechanism just in case.

Revenge was Redeen watching the girlfriend scream her head off as the supposed croutons moved. The soup bowl tipped onto her nice sweater, turning the white yarn to an ethereal red tomato hue with orange-yellow undertones from the onions and peppers. Suddenly, the bird wasn't dead after all and came to life, flapping its wings, revived by the cold.

The sugar and salt in the tomato gazpacho tasted good to the small bird. It was the pressure of the spoon that pushed air into the little thing. Oxygen flowed, and the spirit of the bird moved. The critter flapped its tony-brown feathered wings more. It was full of renewed vigor. The wings almost reached supersonic speed and chirping sounds gurgled forth. The bird rose mercifully higher in the sweet air. The wings splattered the woman's sweater more, moving upward onto her face. The new spray hit a very shocked waiter as he bent over.

The expletives coming from the girlfriend's mouth were earth shattering. A nun would have been shocked. The tomato splatter did land on the waiter who stopped his forward motion. After hearing the customer's horrible words, he wiped his shirt with the large napkin instead of offering the item to the distraught woman. The small bird flew away, miraculously free at last to visit his teammates in the trees.

Redeen watched the young man's face turn beat red, like the tomatoes, and his mouth opened in an appalled expression. He slowly handed his date his napkin, because he was a gentleman. The young man further shuddered when a photographer walking by took a snapshot for his local newspaper. The young man's face fell further, worried his mother would probably see the article.

He texted another woman friend on his cell phone. Redeen saw the name, Celeste, appear on the man's cell as she walked past him. She figured that he was getting a new lunch date for next week. The young man probably was ditching the foul-mouthed, hysterical woman in front of him.

The other patrons of the restaurant went back to their conversations, not focusing any more on the belligerent woman. A person shouldn't go nuts in a public place. It meant disaster to your reputation. The waiter left the scene to find the manager of the restaurant. There would be unpleasantness and a free check at the *bird table*. The waiter clutched his tablet computer for verification that he did everything per restaurant code with this establishment. He would now love the notebook because it would save him.

Redeen felt great to be alive. "Unintended consequences happen. I count this mission successful in saving a life or two."

It would take a little more time before the young woman named Q. Redeen Pyra learned to control her childish anger.

The bodyguard reappeared with two cups of steaming licuid.

"Here you go, Queenie, the best vanilla latte in town."

She sipped the hot vanilla warmth. He didn't call her Redeen. "This is the best show in town."

The bodyguard couldn't tell what was going on in the young woman's brain. He thought he heard a ruckus at the restaurant when he was buying the coffee. The streets seemed normal. The bodyguard tucked her arm in his like he would with any lady entering the opera. He guided her to the distant parking spot. Redeen couldn't help but glance one more time at the empty table at the restaurant scene. All players were fighting their own cause.

"I love the best."

He thought she was talking about the coffee and nodded his approval.

XXXXXX

Things went smoothly at the apartment flat once her boss arrived. She was allowed the selection of her contract. There was a companion or enhanced clause that held more pay. There would be no emotional or permanent attachment. She signed the contract which also stated that there was no claim for her to the boss's property.

Redeen searched the flat for the man's bank accounts and couldn't find anything. The man's computer was impossible to crack. She asked the bodyguard about Charlie's financials and he told her the man did everything online and memorized all passcodes. Charlie's mind was a minefield of numbers that only he knew. She needed to give up on finding any information, because the bodyguard tried, and failed.

After six short months, Charlie became bored with her. His bodyguard was told to bring more blonde women to the flat. He brought some new young blonde women over to the house. Then Charlie began having dreams. He called out in his wet dream some other woman's name or a place in his sleep. She never heard of Calypso. She would read the age-old story later.

Redeen thought, "I don't know who this Calypso person is or the other ones that came the other day. But you told me about your diamond smuggling jobs and arranged murders which I secretly recorded. I hid the tapes for my protection because I'm afraid you will kill me. Even without the recordings, I know too much."

Her life, again, was in imminent danger. Imminent meant she was running out of time. All she could think of about her future was a continuation of more dead waste. Redeen didn't want to return to the streets. She would never go there again.

When an African businessman, Sphinx Reeker, approached her about a small job, she was ready to destroy everything behind her. Poison was the kill method used. Her elderly, former diamond smuggler that she called Charlie, abruptly died. Having brought the poisoned bottle into the house, he greedily drank it. She thought he would because of his insatiable thirst. Charles Mann had been her lover and planned on dumping her permanently. He asked his bodyguard to do so. The bodyguard let Redeen know she was supposed to drown in the river. He recommended she run. The bodyguard was her ally and would help her out. She wanted more than out.

"You shouldn't have trusted your bodyguard who was smitten by my beautiful blonde hair and young body. He liked to watch me and talk about lots of different subjects. Your bodyguard didn't want to kill me."

She justified her boss's death, "You met your demise with the help of the strange, murky liquid. The choice was either your final gasping breath or mine. I didn't want it to be mine. I was the smart one. You, Charlie, were the crazy, heavily demented one, unable to wait for your trusted bodyguard. Your arrogance and hatred killed you. Somehow, the Americans were your enemy and I knew nothing about them. I wonder who they are? It sounds like they are rich. That is where I'm headed. Your bodyguard and I have already forgotten our life with you. The contract between us is now null and void. See, there is no emotion."

6   Africa and Choices

Q. REDEEN PYRA went to Guinea-Bissau, Africa, with the man called Sphinx because dead bodies piled up around her. London was left quickly behind. He became her new lover. The Sphinx also kept many other women around and lied to her about his business. He wasn't in the diamond business but was a drug trafficker.

She just substituted one bad situation for a worst one. It was another mistake. The mistake was huge and would cost her. She needed to leave, but again, couldn't. Thinking the police would help her, she threw those thoughts away when they appeared at his friend's night party. The man owned the police in town.

The Sphinx controlled her life. She was his prisoner. She was alone. Help didn't exist. She believed she would create that shortly. With her legal name change to Queenie, the old Redeen was gone. A changed woman appeared. She felt stronger and almost invincible. She watched warrior princess stories on the television. She wanted to be fierce, just like them.

"I will scheme to kill you and want to do the same to your other women. Your other women shun me because I'm your new, pretty girl. They have tried to undermine my relationship with you. I don't mind but feel disdain for their loyalty to you."

Queenie took horseback riding lessons to get out of the house and away from his women. She became an expert rider, loving the horses who nudged her back to get the precious carrot. Sphinx gave her the lessons, so she would stop wanting to buy a tiger. The desire for the tiger never went away. She secretly read all about them. Queenie studied hard, learning other major important things.

Working on her plans for escape, in the mornings she watched the clock for the time to arrive. She made trips to the next town to buy perfume. He let her buy an expensive bottle. Her clothes were inexpensive. She didn't need much and wore simple khaki's and white tops. He left the house the same time every morning when he went out to do his drug business. There was never any deviation in time and he drove alone in his car. His car was the expensive one with special plates. The other cars were for his bodyguards. She memorized his plate number.

"It finally has become my time to activate my escape plan. The weight of your domination will end. If I miss any part of my plan, the stakes are high. My life will be in peril."

Sphinx's car was stopped on the road to town. He was placed in a locked crate and would be taken to a place in the jungle. A second crew would pick him up and drop him in the Congo River. Her hired men quietly let the women in the Sphinx's house go. She then stole the bank accounts of money that Sphinx told her were in Guinea-Bissau.

In the last five minutes before she left, Queenie remembered his room that contained his private collection of antiquities. Keying in the unlock codes, she entered the special room. The Sphinx told her that only a very few select group of people knew about the room. He had taken her around and explained the objects to her. He showed her two very precious antiquity items, the gold eagle crown and beautiful two-piece eagle clasp. He told her those two items were the oldest and the finest pieces of perfection in his collection. Their rareness made them expensive, and were his favorites.

The crown he owned was not as ornate as the French Imperial crown that belonged to Napoleon III, but at least this majestic crown had not been melted down and destroyed. He told her there was still another smaller crown at the Louvre which belonged to Empress Eugenie. He couldn't understand why the National Assembly voted to destroy the Imperial crown, other than Raspail hated the man. Raspail obviously must have been obsessed or deranged. In eradicating the man's crown, Raspail thought he defiled Napoleon III's French coronation regalia and all that his royalty had stood for. You see, they didn't want the monarchy anymore.

She picked up the two objects and put them back down. They were heavy gold. She knew a little bit about Napoleon, but not much.

"Heavy was important in the gold market."

She remembered gold was the 79th element. There was no purity mark or maker's mark on either item. The gold was probably not 24-karat because that was too soft to manipulate in jewelry. Now, 22-karat was usually used for gold leafing. She did read about gold and that in France an eagle head stamped into an object meant the worth reflected about 18-karat since the late 1830s. So, she concluded the gold was more than likely 18-karat or lower. A person more knowledgeable about the history of the item would better clarify the purity. She needed to talk to either auction people or investors.

"Why are you standing here, girl? These two objects are a goldmine and will fit in your carryall. What did they matter? The man would be dead soon and not have a want for such objects."

Her indecision was taking too long. Slowing touching the cold metal and tracing the eagle design gave her confidence. The eagle head felt beautiful under her fingertips. She picked up the crown again and put it on her head. The mirror showed her reflection and Queenie smiled. She wondered if there existed a smaller crown for a queen or a favored subject. She removed the crown.

The clasp was nice. Queenie touched the golden object. It made her feel good. Some person long ago wore this item on a cloak or coat. She wondered how a person could make the clasp into a necklace without destroying its value. Or she could have the clasp sewn into a nice fur capelet jacket. The gold would sparkle in the moonlight on dark sable.

"It must have been a king who wore these items long ago."

She could imagine how the royal man looked wearing the crown in a heavily-tapestry filled room and sitting in a large chair in his castle. He was a man who probably sacrificed much to save his valuable treasures. She wondered what his name was and if there were any family still living. It would help in determining their worth or value.

"The king who originally owned this crown would want me to take them away from this horrible, monstrous place. Besides, the money from the antiquities might be needed in the future. I could enjoy them in the meantime."

She danced a little in the room with the crown on and holding the clasp to her breast. Queenie began humming a song she liked. The mirrors encouraged her with the rainbow fire shooting rays in all directions. The gold went nicely with her hair and skin. That did it. Reason and logic left the building. She was overcome by golden obsession.

"Gypsy girl, you are a wild thing and can build your own ivory tower."

Queenie placed the two works of art in her large handbag. She quickly ran out of the room and shut the special door one last time. She didn't want to change her mind.

"You owe me the money and the antiquities for my time spent here. Even celebrities get money when they leave someone or become divorced. They hire smart lawyers who see right through the disaster and, hence, rake in millions for their clients. I don't need a lawyer to steal for me. Endless emptiness happens,

49

Sphinx. Just like shit, you aren't going to exist for long. The only gold touching you will be the flames of your dark hell. And by the way, here's to my darling millions."

Queenie also recorded some of his drug trades and packed those small tapes. She wrote down names of his many contacts and hid them in her handbag. She would remove the recordings and client list, placing them in one of her private off-shore accounts later.

In her youthful quest, Queenie thought she had won. Unfortunately for her, the worst thing happened. The Sphinx eluded the hired killers.

XXXXXX

"Rage doesn't die. It grows stronger by the hour," exclaimed Sphinx.

The dissonance began in the man's heart. His love for her was turning into a violent sleep. His behavior would become distorted. It would take some time to find her, but she was easy to track. He only needed to find rich people and their playgrounds.

Sphinx sent a hit man to snuff out Queenie. The only problem was the hired person would hang the wrong female in Miami. The hit person would kill one of Queenie's look-alike guards and set the scene to appear as a suicide.

Meanwhile, the Sphinx would burn his house down and move to Dakar, Senegal, removing all remains of his former life. He would buy Santan Chesin's former home with negative edge pool overlooking the ocean. He would change his name to Tiger Black. The Sphinx would disappear. However, he couldn't change his looks, other than his hair was becoming grayer. People would see a successful business man. Unknown to Queenie and other people, there were his hundreds of other accounts full of drug money. He was a very filthy rich man. Rich people have all the time in the world to change the game.

Having gotten out of the drug business, his plan was to look like a professional investor. Secretly, the man wouldn't forget the woman who took advantage of him. He remained provoked. He would inflict his anger and malice upon the real Queenie later. His valuable objects would belong to him again. They were temporarily lost.

In the meantime, he would undertake to find the other eagle antiquities. He knew friends in the market that showed him the drawings the Wrights gave to an auction house. Joining the search for the large scepter and eagle ring, he would create major conflict for the Wrights or anyone who got in his way. He was on more than one mission.

7   Miami Life

QUEENIE BELIEVED THE Sphinx was dead and she was safe because there were three dead bodies found at Sphinx's charred house. Unknown to her, those bodies were some of the Congo truck drivers she hired.

She became proficient and capable traveling the series of islands around Miami. She drove the many bridges or causeways and past the mangroves to her destination. There were white sand beaches, fruit and palm trees dotting the land with glimpses of crystalline blue water. She loved the names of streets like Venetian, Hibiscus, Star, Palm, Ocean, and Conch.

Queenie hadn't been to the Riviera, but thought Miami was her Riviera. She partied and played in the Miami night scene spending her money. She especially liked all the new bands at the posh hotels with fast-paced, kicky beats. Her heart released itself in the exotic wonder of Latino pop sound.

Mediterranean and Italian Renaissance-inspired architecture dotted the boulevard as she drove her car toward expansive hotels. She walked quickly mingling with people on the hotel waterfront terraces. She was a known figure among the rich young elite men around Biscayne Bay.

Beautiful Biscayne Bay separated Miami Beach from South Beach. She relaxed in her element at last.

She was part of the young entrepreneurs and *Very-Important-People* crowd attending poolside soirees. She walked with a rhythm and each step made a beautiful cadence of sound in her designer high heels.

International fashion shows were attended with Caribbean and Latin American designers. Sub-tropical swimsuit competitions brought her into the daytime fashion world of South Beach at art-deco hotels. The hotel's architecture showed the interesting stepped-back facades which kept the hot sun away.

Her connection with the rich introduced her to the celebrity world and their lush estates. Outside cafes on Ocean Drive overlooked the Atlantic shorefront. Seafood consisted of stone crabs, Florida lobster, snapper, Mahi-Mahi and shrimp. She ate ceviche, paella, and crawfish. Sushi bars were abundant.

"My young gorgeous men, whose daddies own large, splendid mega ships in the port, will take me out to play."

She listened to the men's conversations about shipping cargo and the new homeland security rules. Riding out of Biscayne Bay on the state-of-the-art ships with the playboys to the Bahamas was a great way to get beautifully tanned. They indulged her with their time and expensive gifts just to be seen with the exotic creature.

Diving lessons brought her close to the breathtaking underwater scenery of coral reefs around Key Largo. Afterward, the diving team went to restaurants that served conch fritters and key lime pie.

She loved the white quartz sand beaches where she could jog and let her mind wander.

The vacationers and tourists provided wonderful cover for her on the Miami streets during high season which was March through August. She could blend into any crowd if needed.

Clothes and diamonds were luxuriant designer league styles. She hit the boutique stores and pedestrian-only mall on Lincoln Road.

As soon as one of the rich men became serious, she moved onto someone else. Being young and beautiful opened doors for her and further released her from the past. Miami was a perfect place for her steps forward. Her spirit was moving toward something. She felt it was moving in the right direction.

The evening sky started to look brighter. She wanted to be a part of that beautiful mauve-blue skyline. Queenie no longer felt locked out or constrained by her world. She wasn't a prisoner anymore.

Telling herself, "I'm strong and capable. My life is balancing and coming into harmony." The personality was changing and rejuvenating. The makeover put a pretty dew on her face and suntan body. Anything and everything could be hers.

"Correction, everything will be mine."

The next day the weather man blared from her car radio that the day was a balmy 89 degrees with humidity at 76 percent. It currently was clear, but would rain later that evening. Queenie always went to a wonderful massage and spa treatment at this modern, chic hotel. Today she decided to check out another piece of property in Miami with her realtor friend.

She now paid several guards to look like her with some minor enhancements. The guards were heavily trained fighters with weapons. Extra security was to fool any future enemies. Her guards were perfect robots who pleased her. Queenie acquainted herself with a favorite guard named Bri who ran most of her errands. Rather than throw away her spa appointment, she decided to let Bri have her scheduled fun day.

XXXXXX

The African businessman couldn't get away for several months to kill Queenie in Miami. Instead, he called in a marker and hired a hit woman called Snake. Bri went to her fun spa day and didn't know the masseuse was a different girl. After her steam and sponge bath came the next part which was a glorious massage. Bri relaxed even further. The neck area was smeared with a special bottle of hand-warmed substance.

The masseuse wore special gloves because she would drop gold flecks on Bri's neck and back. The masseuse showed her the wonderful gold-fleck and precious liquid bottle. She put the warmed stones on her muscled back. The warm stones felt good. The Black Mamba snake's venomous poison worked fast from the bottle. Cheap disposable acupuncture needles were inserted around Bri's neck.

The virulence of the lethal liquid raced through Bri's bloodstream. The Snake woman was working on a different method of killing. But she hadn't quite perfected it yet, so this was the old way. She told Bri she would come back to remove the wonderful metal and then the client would be completely done. Soft music played while the unconscious mind slipped away.

The poison worked in less than an hour. The young woman named Bri would never get up again. The masseuse retrieved her empty bottle of liquid and put it in the black bag. A piece of the dry brown/olive snake skin was placed upon the woman's back. It was her calling card and people would know to special handle the body. Gloves were placed in the black bag and the bag was thrown in the cleaning woman's garbage. The Snake woman put some newspaper on top. The gold-fleck bottle was put back in her pocket.

The masseuse followed the cleaning woman out of the hotel to the garbage dumpster, making sure it would be disposed of properly. When the cleaning lady went inside, she left the area believing she killed the Queenie person whose name was in the computer for the scheduled massage. The Snake woman would call her contact to let the man know the transaction was complete.

When the police arrived, they thought the dead girl was R. Queenie Pyra until the coroner saw all the implants in the body and injections in the face.

"I'm surprised by another call from the police. I have no information other than the girl's application form for employment. Her name was Bri Stannon," said Miss Pyra.

She thought it odd and wondered what her employee, Bri, was into that caused her strange death. Then it dawned on Queenie what might have occurred, "My world is closing in. I know who was behind this second death on my premises."

Queenie became extremely agitated, "I must quickly formulate different plans."

The poison should have scared her. She liked her newly-found freedom. Not wanting to leave her new life in Miami just yet, her compound was prepared for trouble. Installing a better security system upgrade for her floor with a secret elevator and a small private hidden space allowed her to easily travel between two floors. One by one, she removed the two precious gold items from her warehouse in her large handbag and put them in her hidden space. She kept the warehouse in case she needed it. There was a knife strapped under her clothes.

One of her tenants left a newspaper behind when Queenie did the move-out inspection. Her eyes captured an article about a retired circus tiger that needed a home. She remembered when her mother took her to the circus. There was the show tiger who had a small cub with her outside the ring in their haul- trailer with bars.

The child stopped and approached the cage. Her mother was talking with someone. She touched the bars of the cage and the small creature approached and smelled through the bars. The girl looked at the little tiger and smiled. The tiger rolled on its back. She knew the little animal was a good guy. He was very sweet. She blew him a kiss before the large mother tiger roared.

Her mother quickly dragged her daughter away. The little cub caught the smell from the blown kiss and remembered. Reading the article, she reached for her cell phone. The tiger was familiar. She would check his history. She wanted to believe it was her cub. She told herself to not expect much.

Queenie called the phone number in the article and told them, "I want to buy your tiger. It will be a private transaction."

They informed her the sale must be cash only.

"That is no problem, because I specialize in that concept and can bring loads of cash. I will take exceptional care of the precious golden tiger as if he was a rare antiquity." They accepted her offer to purchase the animal. They liked the young woman.

Meeting the tiger, Queenie knew it was important. The tiger sat up instantly when she approached the cage. The tiger smelled her, and the woman looked him directly in the burning-bright golden eyes. Queenie saw the tiger's ancestors standing behind the tiger. She was not afraid. The tiger in the cage laid down. Queenie smiled.

"It is you."

The tiger rolled again so that she would know that it acknowledged her. The tiger licked the bars where she had touched and waited. She remembered. Queenie couldn't believe it. He was a good soul. It was her baby tiger, older, now diminished by years of work. She touched the bar on his cage and the tiger approached, rubbing the bars. She knew not to touch him yet. There would be plenty of time. She was pleased. The animal stayed close to where she was. Slowly, Queenie walked away and turned back.

"I will return, my love. It won't be long. It is now our time." She blew him a kiss. The animal seemed to understand.

She looked back one more time. "We will be good together."

The tiger laid down as if acknowledging her one more time.

"Yes, I love you, too." Queenie left the area to complete the purchase transaction.

After having bought a large crate, Queenie put the beautiful tiger with the golden eyes in it. The cage was delivered to her warehouse.

"I know it is illegal to own a tiger in Florida. I don't care. Rules can sometimes be broken. I will experience my dream. I will save this one endangered species. The beautiful cat is more important than rules. Besides, let the lawyers handle the rules. They work for money, too. Let them manage the bureaucrats and fallout."

Sphinx taught her anything could be bought. Ownership of the cat and warehouse were put under a fictitious corporate name out of Alabama. That way she wouldn't need a permit nor be charged with possession.

She hired an animal caretaker to feed and clean up after the large feline. His name was Hamm Roe who recently helped take care of the animals at a traveling circus show. Queenie had one last item to explain to Hamm.

"There is something that you need to know. If the correct code is not keyed into my security system, the animal's cage will open." She pointed to the buttons on the wall.

8   Hamm Roe's Appearance

FOR SOME REASON, the con artists were congregating around R. Queenie Pyra. Hamm Roe was a supposed lesser one. He used to be called Stew Avery, the son of a butler who worked for Louisa Renaliere. He tried to steal one of Louisa's diamond necklaces, but old lady Renaliere was smart and replaced the necklace in her wall safe with a fake. Louisa set up a video camera to record and catch any thieves. That's why his name change was done to Hamm Roe. The police in Italy were looking for Stew Avery because Louisa told them the necklace was real. He was considered a criminal in Rome.

Stew had a run-in with Santan Chesin from Dakar, Senegal, Africa. Santan wanted Stew dead for selling him a fake paste necklace and some sunken ship coordinates that didn't pan out. Back then, Stew knew nothing about diamonds or diving for treasure. He sold himself to Santan as the real thing. He wasn't anything. He was a sad story of a criminal mind in its younger stages. There were other criminals in the game. The red tribe member who accidentally purchased the fake in the underworld market for his boss, Santan. The red tribe leader couldn't clear himself of the deceit to his boss.

Then, there was the police in Curacao who also wanted Stew for questioning in a space party shooting when his girlfriend was accidently shot. Santan was at that party. There was a knife guy, hired by Santan, who tried to kill Stew later. The knife guy was caught in time by the police. Hamm barely escaped with his life from a book signing held by the Wrights in Los Angeles, California. He also was wanted by the Los Angeles police for stealing an old telescope. At the book signing, he evaded the police. He managed to crawl away like a chameleon from the stupid mess of a bombed van in the street. He hid in a metal locker in the building until everyone left. It was a good thing the wounds he received weren't too severe.

Hamm laid low for some time working as an accountant at one of the auction houses. Lying low was his specialty. All types of information could be retrieved from the unknowing. The garbage can did contain rich client's addresses. He perused the can daily. When he picked up the ad from the garbage can and saw the photo of two golden antiquity items, he wondered why they were withdrawn from the sale. He saw her name and address. Her phone number could be useful. The ad was about *gold and diamonds* which were his favorite subjects. He wrote down the address and information of the owner and left the auction house. He picked up with a traveling circus to hitch his ride to Miami because his cash was limited.

He was an opportunist. He also learned from his mistakes. While in Miami, Queenie's ad in the paper for an animal caretaker was a perfect entrance for him.

He rehearsed his resume to fit the ad. She carefully interviewed him. She gave him the job when she found out he was almost broke. In her business, desperate people were usually quiet about illegal activities. Hamm looked desperate. She was a good judge of desperate and the man would fit her needs. If not, he was easily disposable.

Hamm thought for sure the two valuable golden objects would be in her locked, secured warehouse. It was the only reason to respond to her ad. He checked the entire large space of the warehouse out and the gold antiquities were not to be found. Hamm would need an assistant's help, someone on the inside.

He was positive Queenie must have the two rare gold eagle antiquities in her apartment building. Hamm found the old diagrams and permits for the building. No changes were made for a long time. Yet, out back stood a dumpster of old wallboard and a new elevator company's box. Hamm figured if there was no permit for the elevator, she must want its existence hidden.

Hamm would need to get into the apartment and find the elevator. He felt confident that finding the elevator was key to finding the objects. Queenie didn't know he existed as an eligible male. Knowing he was out of her league, he tried to figure which one of her female guards was the stupidest. He chose the newly-hired girl, Karine Kline.

Once a week Queenie went to talk to her beautiful tiger boy in the warehouse. Hamm watched the two wild creatures bond. He was amazed to see the likeness between the two. The two wild things liked each other. He thought that was plain screwy. But then his cousin was odd, too. This job would be his cover for some time if he played her correctly. He played his cousin most of the time. Stew felt confident. To each his own were his thoughts. He could mimic his cousin and guide the poor slob if it didn't cost him.

After a few weeks of work, he realized that the tiger knew that he was a suspect in the animal world. Even stray kittens didn't like Hamm and had hissed at him in Venice Beach. The golden tiger knew evil because the cat had a finely tuned nose. Hamm wondered how the cat knew and always was in the office when its cage was opened. He didn't trust the cat at all. Hamm's movements would show caution because he worried about his boss. She wasn't normal either. He wore more disguise, growing a beard. Disguise was the key. He wanted the real key to riches. He watched the cat and his boss.

She would bring treats for the animal and wouldn't give him the treat until he sat for a long time. The tiger learned to sit and wait while she paced back and forth. Then Queenie would give him the treat. The longer he would sit, the more treats he received. Hamm couldn't figure out what she was training the cat for. He didn't care. There were other fish to chase.

Had Hamm known Queenie was also a cat with nine lives, he would have run for his life. Having entered a much more dangerous game, Hamm changed. More greed enveloped him and then a deeper, darker evil strolled in. Evil entrapped his puny weasel heart and forced him to yield and do bad things. Queenie would get caught in the foray.

Queenie also went to see the tiger on Hamm's day off. She didn't want him to see her accelerated training. She taught her tiger boy more. She bought the cat at a cheap price because it had been a circus animal that wouldn't always behave. They said the cat had attention problems. It was too easily distracted. The only thing the heavy creature required was a ball. It liked any kind of ball. Queenie could understand the attraction to balls. They bounced. Capture was the tiger's desires. No ball was left behind. Each one was played with. The ball was like a little mouse. Same thing, balls bounced and so did the mice, or at least, it appeared to.

She carried with her a heavy gold chain which she would clink when the cat wouldn't behave. She also owned a knife and carried it secretly. She would show the cat the knife and clink it on the chain when he would not do her bidding. The tiger learned.

Then she let the tiger out of its cage a few minutes at a time and the cat would walk with her among the huge plants she brought in and would drink water out of a small pool she installed before the cat arrived. The cat loved the water and rock waterfall. She couldn't tell if it was the water or the balls that were first. Both held the allure. The animal learned to wait for Queenie's commands which was what she planned.

There were two contraptions that would eject out of a glass-walled room in her warehouse. One of the boxes was to place a plastic bin of fresh meat for its supper. The other box was a bin of the treats she used to train the cat. She told Hamm only she could run the treat box.

There were three buttons in the room and these three buttons on the main floor did start, stop, and activate the boxes. The tiger knew when the boxes were activated. He would come out of the cage if the open button was pushed and wait for Queenie and his treats. Or the door remained closed and his meat would be delivered. The cat would wait for its gate to open or close. There were no mice scampering in the warehouse to distract so the cat followed the routine.

9   Investor David Dunker

THE OLDER INVESTOR, David Dunker, was notified by the Auction House of the possible sale of two gold antiquities. Then he saw the removal of the items and wondered. He owned the head and top part of a gold scepter with an eagle design. The scepter contained no jewels, but he thought they probably did a long time ago.

There also was a diamond ring that looked like they matched. He bought the two objects from another investor in the secret market a long time ago. He would have liked to see the newly placed auction items. But suddenly they were removed. It would have been an investor collector's rush of love. It was love for the extremely one-of-a-kind, exceptionally rare object of beauty. David sighed and was crushed.

He collected his two objects one at a time over many years. David bought them because of an odd story about royalty. The family of royalty sold them to pay their mercenaries to fight a war. He wanted more information about the family. David thought he found the bottom of the scepter once. But it was part of something else and the wrong size.

David wanted to see the other items. His auction friend divulged her name and address. He contacted

Queenie via a polite note and he received a polite note back. She refused to show him the objects. He used this auction person in the past. He pleaded with the young man for her phone number. David left her a voice-mail and explained his profession and desire to purchase the items.

Sending her a packet of his own credentials, she could check him out. He had plenty of money and a whole room of exquisitely valuable antiquities in his mansion in Miami. He wanted the items or the ability to see and touch them.

He was a man who also knew people. He was experienced and dealt with unlikely characters who walked the thin line of good or bad in the past. Some collectors were ruthless in their pursuit of a beloved antiquity. David knew obsessive collectors, but he was not crazy obsessive. He lost people he loved and planned on giving his antiquities to his favorite museum. He wanted the items to be seen and treasured after he passed on. David was alone right now, unmarried.

If this Queenie person didn't want to show him the items, then he would walk away and pursue other ones on his list. David also wondered if the items were stolen. He would ask one of his ex-detective friends for any help in checking her out.

David Dunker headed out for two weeks to play polo and cards with one of his male friends who owned a nice horse ranch in Alabama. They were good friends and sometimes went on trips together. His single friend sold his valuable polo horses all over the world.

When David's marriage didn't work out, he found some nice lady friends who went out with him to an occasional party, charity, or other function in Miami. He played in the older social scene. His world and Queenie's would never collide unless she contacted him. He hoped she would call again.

Fortunately for David, a horse would throw him, and he would break his leg at his friend's ranch estate. He stayed at his friend's house for three months in the pool house until he was out of the cast and could maneuver around. David called his mother, an antique dealer in Walnut Creek, California, to let her know where he was located.

His mother always liked Scott Barrow having visited the Alabama estate one time with her son. She knew Scott would take good care of David so there was no need to come to his aid. The mother was extremely busy with the antique business. David liked the polo horses and wouldn't be bored. He helped Scott write some stories for the Polo Magazine.

Paying his bills online was easy. David wouldn't see Queenie's invitation to lunch until he returned. The lady who picked up his mail thought the card unimportant. The woman knew David wouldn't be attending parties for a while, so it was not forwarded to him.

10   Bottom of the Scepter

THE BOTTOM OF the old golden scepter rested in a broken-down box in a dark old attic that was shaded by a huge oak tree. There was an old woman who lived in the rambling blue house with white trim and shutters. There was a single car garage that held rusted old gardening tools. She owned one of the larger lots in this subdivision. Her house was beginning to look run down. The shingles looked bad, too. A few of them already littered the lawn.

The inside begonia-flowered wallpaper in the dining room told everyone she hadn't redecorated in years. The linoleum flooring was worn in places the braided rug didn't reach in the kitchen. She looked one time at new linoleum, but decided the old stuff kept the dirt out just fine. There weren't any holes in it yet. The old woman didn't care any more about such nonsense. She hadn't been able to get into her upstairs or attic for years.

The long wood stairs were a huge problem. Underneath the beds upstairs, a collection of dust-bunny threads blew across the floor whenever the downstairs front door was opened. The old bed springs creaked in the dead of winter from the cold. There also was a pecking sound. It gave her a fright. She called the fire department, because she thought there were ghosts in the house. She was surprised to see the fireman was her neighbor across the street. The old woman thought that he was nice because he always played ball with his children.

The fireman told her there was a bird under the eaves that pecked its way almost through to the inside and the wiring. Her house could have burned down if the bird frayed the wires. It was a good thing that she called them. The fireman gave her a card of a carpenter who could fix the outside. It would be sealed so the bird couldn't get in. She ordered the repair job.

The thought of fire scared her. There were no battery-powered sprinklers in this house. Her memory was going, but she knew there were a few valuable items in her attic because her great-grandfather had been a collector of war memorabilia. The house was owned by her and was in her family a long time. She thought about bringing those items down to the main floor. She made the mistake of telling the other neighbor. Her neighbor volunteered to help clean out the attic, but she didn't trust her.

Her neighbor was an antique dealer in downtown Walnut Creek, California. The antique lady told her how she bought items cheap from people and made a lot of money. Her only son in Miami built a wonderful collection of items from her treasure finds.

The old woman decided no way was she going to allow that antique woman past her kitchen.

The real jewels were still in the secret compartment in the bottom of the gold scepter. They were there since the Renaliere family put them there for safety many generations ago. The jewels remained hidden for several centuries. The jewels shouldn't have been in the attic.

The large oak tree swayed on a light breeze. The green leaves were the largest she had ever seen. It hadn't been trimmed for years. When the occasional light snow hit the area, the branches touched the ground. The old woman began to worry about that tree. She wondered which one of them was going to break down first.

She checked on the tree every day. All she needed were some ghosts trying to make a tree fort and it would go down. People thought ghosts were lighter than air. She believed they were heavy. She wondered why she was thinking of ghosts lately. She started talking to the tree and told it to wait. The old woman knew she had no relatives and was no longer young. She told the tree it was no longer young either and was looking bedraggled like her. It needed to just hold on.

The old woman felt bad about telling the tree that information. The tree finally gave up. When a storm approached, the wind blew down the gnarled old oak tree. A large branch hit the corner of the house where the broken-down box resided.

Workers came to clean up the tree and mess. One of the workers found the scepter and put it in his jacket. The old woman saw him take the object while she was standing in her window. She immediately called the police. She was sorry that she hadn't trusted the antique lady. The valuable item was gone. The only thing that remained were papers.

By the time the police caught the correct man, the valuable bottom half scepter was sold to a jeweler for one hundred dollars. That store then was hit with a robbery. The thieves stole the valuable object and sold it for two hundred dollars to some underling auction clerk in the underground world in Walnut Creek. The underling auction clerk gave the scepter to his brother to deliver to a Miami investor for a potential, profitable sale.

The underling auction clerk paid his brother to deliver the package to a man named Mr. Dunker. Mr. Dunker was a valuable client who displayed interest in a scepter bottom in the past. He knew Mr. Dunker would want to see if this one fit his piece. The underling auction clerk hadn't been able to get hold of David, but felt confident in sending his brother to Miami. He needed money and the fee from this item would be almost a year's salary for him because he was going to keep all the money and cut his company out. Besides, he believed the need to share any money with the auction house shouldn't happen. He brokered the whole deal. Illegal, of course, but no one was looking.

Queenie also wondered why she did not hear again from David Dunker. She did receive his credentials and she wanted to talk with him. She drove her new expensive white sports car to his house, leaving her limo at her apartment building. Her guards were busy with other tasks. As she was walking up to his steps, there was a package in a young man's hands who was knocking on the front door.

The young man turned and there stood a beautiful blonde woman in a designer red and black dress.

"Are you looking for Mr. David, too?"

"Yes, maam, I brought an important package that I must show the investor who lives here to see if he is interested in purchasing the item. I traveled a long way from Walnut Creek, California, and I'm disappointed Mr. Dunker is not home today. Do you know him?"

Queenie looked around the street and there was no one in sight. She said, "Why don't we check the back, because sometimes Mr. David was outside."

She would play along with the game. What could it hurt? Queenie looked at the young man demurely. Actress mode kicked in a notch higher.

The young man vacillated, but her serene, sincere quality changed his mind. He followed her.

"My name is Queenie and a person might compare me to a temporary secretary. I'm very good at my job. My personality fits perfect in this wonderful world of old items and intrigue. Your object is full of intrigue. That's how I know Mr. David. He loves intrigue. I can tell when an item is the original. That's why he hired me."

She bent over to whisper to the young man, "There are a lot of fakes out there."

His brother told him about the problem with fakes. The woman wasn't a fake. He could trust her.

"Why don't we go through the patio gate into the small courtyard between the garages and large house? Evidently, Mr. David is away today. You can show me the package. We won't need to bother Mr. David. I can accept the package if what was inside is credible."

She noticed on her previous visit there were no cameras in the courtyard.

The young man thought everything would be fine. He opened his package and laid the bottom golden scepter on the glass patio table.

Queenie saw the object and was instantly fascinated by the gold and carving. It was the same eagle design as her two antiquities. She knew to remain calm. What a small fortune in gold weight alone was this item? The fool in front of her had no clue. The beautiful object landed in her lap. Queenie touched the cool gold, tracing the design. The object was stunning, way beyond anything she ever saw in her life. She thought of pharaohs and dynasties filled with earthen gold.

She quickly formulated her next plan. She was pleased and knew there must be a smile. As an investor's protégé, she must remain cool. Only thing, she wasn't an investor's anything. The young man didn't know that revelation. Did he even understand the value of this object? There should be an armored car surrounding this thing. She smiled.

The young man smiled. The deal would happen if he played his cards right.

She turned to the young man and asked him, "What is this precious object because I will not know how to describe it to him. Usually, pictures of kings show a top part or whole staff." The lie of being unsure was thrown out there to see how the young man would respond. She was toying with him. Queenie held out her hands in a helpless gesture.

The young man beamed. He knew information that his brother entrusted with him. The young man wanted to gain her trust with his new intelligence. He puffed up his chest like an African Crowned Crane attracting a mate. Queenie touched his sleeve to encourage the young man, secure in the knowledge that her con-job was working, and the scene was moving into her court.

He thought it was all right to tell the woman or anyone who asked. What harm could there be in explaining the contents and his reasons for the trip? None. It was an item up for sale to the first buyer. He would be glad to disengage from the final sale and go home. He wanted this woman to purchase the object.

He said, "It was the bottom part of a rare scepter. The object could fit to the top piece that he owns. Mr. Dunker has the top piece and head. He has been looking forever for the rest of the thing. He wasn't sure how Mr. Dunker knew there existed this piece. But, somehow, he did. The other bottom scepter we found for him didn't fit at all. It is gold. There are fakes, but this one is real."

"Mr. Dunker didn't tell me how long he was looking. That is a new surprise. Thank you for telling me. It will help me in my job. Why do you believe this one will fit? There must be many of these old things out there. I bet there were many copies made just to confuse people. How do you know this one is real or will fit?"

The young man said, "Because we took precise measurements. Not us, but the investor did. He hired an expert draftsman to do the measuring part. My brother said our piece has the same, perfect dimensions. My brother knows gold. He used to sluice-box gold in the Colorado hills and streams. He spent his younger life looking for the stuff. I'm sure he took the object into his good buddy friends for verification. He wouldn't send Mr. Dunker anything fake."

"This piece and if there are any other similar objects would make a valuable collection."

The young man shook his head, "Yes, most certainly. It is the one-of-a-kind collection that investors pay large sums of money. I'm not sure why. The gold stuff never turned me on."

Queenie told the young man confidently, "We will need to go to this warehouse where you can leave the package. I can pay you cash from the safe at the warehouse location. The receipt should be addressed to the Alabama company name. I will give you a receipt with the company name. I know he will be pleased and you will be happy that you are no longer detained. You can begin your journey home with your money."

She made a lot of sense. They needed money. His brother was waiting. He took too long to reach Miami. He was sidetracked by a boat show he snuck into and met a girl. The young man followed Queenie and parked by the back dock where she pointed. He brought the package with him into the dimly-lit warehouse. She told him to wait because she must get the money from the office upstairs.

The cash was given to the young man and he put it in his jacket pocket. She handed him the receipt and he placed the package on a small table. As he walked back to the side door, he accidentally pushed on the wall button. The tiger cage door moved upward. The tiger stepped out of the cage.

The young man dropped the receipt and ran toward the locked side door. Queenie would have to open the side door for him with her key. It was part of the security system for the large cat.

11   Miami Report for Derek

DEREK READ THE murder report he received from Miami regarding Queenie Pyra's guard. Bri Stannon died from snake venom at a local hotel spa. The police remembered this killer who was on their wanted list because she left her snake skin calling card. The calling card was left at the scene in Miami. The Snake woman was well known by the police who were unable to catch the crazy hit woman who traveled across continents as if she were some diplomat or secret spy.

"I can't see anything strange about this person to require a hit. Or they murdered the wrong one."

Derek shook his head.

"I know the person was after Queenie." What did she do to engage a murderer near her door? The murderer will possibly try again were his thoughts. He wondered about the strange suicide of her other guard, too.

Next the Miami boys turned their report over to Derek about the Queenie woman. There recently was construction completed on her apartment building, but they weren't sure what she put in. It looked like an elevator. Huge boxes were at the back of her building near the dumpster. Next, she brought trees and put in a pool in her warehouse. A large truck came one day with a huge crate. They weren't sure if there was anything in the crate. The woman came twice per week to the warehouse and stayed a couple of hours. Cortez asked Derek to look closely at their recent photo of the woman.

There was always some sort of traffic in and out her warehouse back dock and side doors. Meat truck, garbage, water, plastic bags, soda, pizza, and sandwiches were the main items they could view. There also was a cleaning company that delivered bleach one day. She just recently bought a white sports car and was still going to parties. The Miami boys shot a close-up picture of her at a rich investor's house.

Derek did a double-take, "You look like my wife. No way. That is unbelievable. The other women that died were bloated a little, so it was hard to compare."

He had seen early, grainier distance shots of Queenie, but this photo was unreal. He thought Jess owned the same designer dress, only hers was white and black. He knew how much that dress cost.

"You will be an expensive woman for a man to keep. You move in high circles of the rich."

Per the Miami boys' report, Queenie was seen at a collector investor's house, but the person wasn't home. She waited out front and eventually left, as did some delivery boy. They were not sure if she kept the antiquities at the warehouse because she always carried this large handbag. She canceled the second night security company which seemed strange. They gave Derek the name and address of the investor collector.

Derek ran a check on David Dunker. He found the guy was wealthy and thought he knew why Queenie was at the guy's door. The man was a mark to wealthier circles in case she needed more.

Jim Michaels called him from Los Angeles and told Derek about the strange theft in Walnut Creek, California. The old woman, Constance Olsen, claimed her great-grandfather had been a war memorabilia collector. She said there was the bottom of a gold scepter stolen by one of the tree removal crew. The box fell out of her attic after a storm. Her tree knocked it out when the wind blew down the huge oak tree.

Derek asked, "Did the police catch the guy who stole the scepter?"

"No, also the scepter was ripped off again from a jeweler who had purchased the object. He hadn't taken any pictures of the scepter. How unlucky for us were those set of circumstances?"

"This robbery scene went from bad to a worse one. Thanks, Jim."

Derek talked with Jess. "We need to interview this Constance Olsen and pay her a visit. More information is required to find out what kind of scepter is missing? Perhaps she kept pictures or can describe the object for us."

Jess made some fake top and bottom drawings of a scepter to see which one Mrs. Olsen would choose. She didn't want to get her hopes up. It would be worth the trip if they could ask her questions. The old woman was a lead they didn't dare pass by.

They flew to San Francisco and drove to the home. After talking with Constance, the woman went to her bedroom closet to get something. Jess looked at Derek and shrugged her shoulders. She had no idea what would be presented to them. Derek ran his fingers through his brown hair and wondered if this visit was another bad idea. He was feeling edgy. Jess bit her lip.

One of the tree workers saved the old box that once held the bottom scepter. Constance proudly brought the mangled, medium-sized box out into the living room. Constance explained her grandfather was a draftsman and decided to do a drawing of the gold object. He wanted to impress her great-grandfather for his birthday. The great-grandfather was the one who originally purchased the item long ago. She removed a drawing from a cardboard tube and then gently unrolled the drawings.

"He drew the scepter to perfect size. The actual drawing is right here of the scepter that we owned."

Jess didn't need to show her fake drawings. "Here is the drawing of the bottom of the golden eagle scepter." Jess smiled.

Derek looked at the drawing and couldn't believe it. The stolen object was the same close-up drawing that Louisa formed in her notebook.

She told Constance, "This drawing is identical to Louisa Renaliere's drawing. Louisa's family once owned the scepter. She was from royalty, but is no longer with us. We have been trying to find the objects from her notebook."

Jess showed the old woman a picture of Louisa's drawing.

Constance was thrilled. She excitedly told them her grandfather wrote down the estimated age for the gold and metal engraving. The time-period for the items matched the Renaliere's notebook history. She allowed Jess and Derek to keep the drawing if that would help find it. Derek assured her they would make their own drawings from the old paper. They would also photograph her document and needed her signature approval to use it in their book. Then they would mail the drawings back to her. Constance willingly agreed.

Derek talked with Constance's insurance company and paid them a check to bring her account up-to-date. Then her roof could be totally repaired and shingled.

On the return flight to Los Angeles, Derek showed Jess the new photo of the real Queenie.

"Oh, doesn't the woman absolutely look like me and she has purchased from the same designer? How odd? She has good taste in clothes, however."

"Whoever was hunting Queenie could mistake you for the same person. You might be a target in Miami when we hold our annual party. That is a huge problem," said Derek.

"You believe Queenie is in grave danger from a potential murderer. I know about that experience. Being the target of an evil con artist was never a good place. Having been there, I personally don't want to participate in that type of game again. I hope the woman finds protection soon."

Jess thought about her husband and Dean's wonderful protective crony families. Those families were now her keys to safety.

She looked at Derek, "What if I wear a wig or something?"

"They might think you are trying to disguise yourself. The murderers would not really care, because the money is always exchanged beforehand."

"We need to put some thought into a different plan. Our motorboat may be the only safe place for me during our party. We can do a limited, family-only guest affair this year. What do you think about that idea?" asked Jess.

"That idea is fine with me. You can inform the dignitaries that we will donate money to one of their charities or museums rather than have them in attendance at our party."

"What about the fireworks? Dean Crain always loved the noise and explosive lights that set the night ablaze. It is such a part of my wonderful memories of him."

Derek debated. "Let's skip the fireworks this year and throw an edible lei in the ocean water. I know Dean would laugh at the idea, but he liked fun. He would help the children throw the lei's if he could."

Jess liked the idea, "I found the perfect place the other day to purchase such a product and the lei's will look pretty. I'll contact the hotel and bands to cancel those plans."

Once their group was onboard the motorboat, it would head out of the Miami Beach port and go north up the coast some thirty or so miles to Fort Lauderdale. Jess would work with the chef on box lunches and the change in dinner plans. Derek would work up the protection teams for their party. She ordered special feather masks for everyone to wear when they stepped onboard.

They would hire no extras nor crazy waiters that could cause anyone on the boat harm. They loaded more music to their stereo system.

Their people were excited about the cruise as it would be a different party this year. They all agreed to pitch in to help stage the party. Jess created a signup list for their group of different tasks, breaking items down by team. Their group loved teams. Derek ordered inexpensive remote helicopters for the games when they dropped anchor. There would be drone demonstrations, too.

They discussed Queenie. "There is something very wrong with her and the warehouse. We know she is in danger. We have no clue who has been tracking her nor why? The woman provides no information to the police. She has kept them at a distance."

Jess volunteered, "There may be a reason for her lack of trust."

Derek said, "The second strange death of her protection guard is too coincidental. The activities surrounding this woman were not normal."

"You are right. The food delivery truck is disturbing. What if Queenie might have some version of exotic animal there?"

"We should steer clear of her. The perimeter surrounding her is a very hazardous arena. A bad con artist game has begun called let's-kill-your-circle-of-protection. Stalking evil fills the Miami air. I can feel it. Maybe the evil will kill each other. The police could then relax if those events occurred."

Delighted about the lower half of the scepter and its existence, they felt there must be the upper part as well. Jess and Derek looked hard at the new drawing and Louisa's drawing. Jess and Derek smiled because Louisa had done an excellent drawing. They wanted to talk to the David Dunker person to see what was in his collection or what he knew. From the report that Derek pulled, there were no red flags.

They thought they should warn him about Queenie, but decided the police ought to do that. Their cover must stay as book authors who wanted to write their story about gold antiquities. They were a rich family playing in Miami. It would be only Derek who met with David. Jess would remain back on the sidelines. Derek would call their auction friend to check around for them. He wanted to see if there was any talk about the lower half.

Jess thought about an idea to lure the investor out who might have the real bottom half of the scepter. She would move forward with that part of her idea. Planning their annual party for the motorboat would take priority and they would work on the rest of their venue later.

12 Underling Auction Clerk

HIS BROTHER WAS missing, and the bottom half scepter was missing. Their supply of money dwindled, but he didn't think his brother would run away and not share the money with him. The brother's car hadn't been found anywhere that he knew. He tried the Miami hotel several times, but there was a no show of the brother.

The underling auction clerk panicked. He wasn't sure his brother arrived at David Dunker's house because he never called him from there either. He couldn't go to the police because he knew the two guys probably stole it from the jewelry store in Walnut Creek. He didn't think the two hundred dollars he paid for the golden scepter bottom was worth going to jail.

Remembering David Dunker's mother worked at an antique store in Walnut Creek, he called all the antique stores until he found her. She told him about David's broken leg and where he had been and was still. She gave him the friend's cell phone number in Alabama. Now the underling clerk must make some decisions. He called David and told him about the lower half of the golden scepter. David was extremely interested. David would send him a preview check if required to hold the precious item.

The underling clerk trusted David and told him he already sent his brother with the package to David's residence. David checked with his mail lady and no one left a note or anything there. So, the clerk assured David that his brother would show up. Perhaps he stopped in Reno, Nevada, to do a little gambling or drinking on his way to Miami.

Now the underling auction clerk was worried. Something unforeseen happened to his brother. He should have gone with him. He was now out four hundred dollars because he gave his brother gas money.

Then one day the clerk thought he was being followed. He started feeling creepy and getting nervous. One evening the underling auction clerk saw his brother's car parked in his dark driveway. He ran over to the car and peered in the front left side window. The keys were in the ignition. He opened the door. He felt a slight hot feeling on his neck and saw a dark shadow as he fell.

Five days later, the two bodies were found in the trunk of the brother's car. The one brother died of a knife wound recently. The other brother was dead for some time. There appeared to be a small animal bite to the neck which wasn't the cause of death. His neck was slit, and he had bled to death.

They figured the small streak which was just a scrape from a large tooth was probably from a large wild cat of some sort. The other brother was killed by the same type of knife. The two guys that originally stole the bottom part of the scepter from the jewelry store read about the two brother's deaths in the newspaper and left town permanently.

Jim Michaels sent Derek a note about the strange deaths and which auction house the one clerk worked. Derek flew back to San Francisco. As soon as the police checked the boy's phones and the files on the auction clerk's home and work e-mails, they would get back with him. The auction house refused the search, complaining about their private data base of clients. The police must obtain a search warrant.

Derek told Jess and the Miami people about the murders. The Miami group were told to back off for a little as the police would be watching the warehouse and Queenie from now on.

The Miami boys were glad to take a break. Knife marks were from the murderer. They thought about the small scratch mark and figured leopard or tiger for that. That's what the crazy woman wore. All the cops needed to do was look at the Queenie girl's shoes. No snake or crocodile leather there. Just cat fur on those very expensive heels.

She also wore red most of the time due to her blood-thirsty nature. The Miami boys weren't fooled by that cat broad. They privately called her Cat Queen. They knew there was only one way to bring her down. But then the boys liked the way she walked in her tight knit dresses.

They knew if she owned a tiger cat in her warehouse, it was a gentle soul because there was only one small scratch and not very deep on the one dead body. A bad tiger would have maimed or killed the unfortunate brother in a heartbeat.

13   Tiger Black Arrival in Miami

TIGER BLACK SENT his wife and two children to London for a month while he did business in Miami. He needed to make sure Queenie was dead. He somehow missed the article about the snake venom murder and the name of the victim. Tiger walked off the airplane into the terminal and picked up the rental car. He felt the heavy moisturized air from the high humidity.

It was a beautiful day with full sun. He drove to her apartment building, parked his vehicle, and watched. He saw several women that looked like her, only they didn't look like her. They didn't walk just right. Queenie swung when she walked, very model-like, because she practiced watching many videos online of fashion shows.

"I figured and know what you have done. You made clones of yourself, disposable minions."

Then he saw the woman in the white sports car.

"You do exist and look better in your designer clothes. I wonder if there is a boyfriend." There was no doubt in his mind the person in the car was Queenie. She developed a bad habit of always checking herself in a mirror. None of her minions did the mirror move.

She frequented some of the expensive hotel restaurants. Life wasn't passing her by. She was living it up, having a blast with his money. He was going to fix that real soon. He would tear her world down. One time, he hid behind some massive sculptures in the fancy hotel lobby to get closer to her. Queenie didn't see him because she was going to happy hour at the Oyster Bar. They served mini-plates of oysters from Apalachicola.

Tiger followed her to a blues bar where two musicians, Diamond and Dylan Jack were playing that Friday evening. He didn't know them, except Queenie did. She talked with them at length after their first set. He couldn't figure the connection, except she sometimes chose strange people for conversation. He thought it odd that she would know such plainly-dressed entertainers. They didn't seem to fit in the upstart of more glamorous Miami players. He did, however, admit their harmonica style of music was very good. The older musician man bowed to Queenie before she left. It caused them both to laugh. Tiger wasn't amused.

Tiger kept getting close to her to catch any glimpse he could. He knew he was taking too long watching her. He needed to get about his business, but he still felt strong emotions around her. Tiger hated her, but he still loved her somehow. It was confusing. He thought his wife knew what was going on in his brain better than he did. He saw Queenie moving around the corner, a ray of sunshine in the throng.

She went to the symphony at the arts building with a young man, but Tiger didn't see her with him again. She drove back to her apartment building alone. Tiger watched her go out with another stud to a dance club to listen to their vibrant music. There were always other places like bars with blues and Caribbean music. He watched her dance and wanted to dance with his Queenie, but knew he messed up long ago. He wished he could undo the mess. She went alone again to her building.

"It is probably a good idea that young man did leave, because he touched her a lot. I know I'm obsessing about you. I must keep tracking you until I have my plan."

Watching her drive to the warehouse, he saw the garbage, frozen meat, and water trucks. He figured she bought her tiger. She wanted one and he refused to buy her one. Tiger told her the orange, black and white-striped cat didn't belong in Africa. They belonged in Asia.

"Would you have stayed if I bought you the cat?" Tiger should ask her.

He remembered, "It is the one thing you told me you truly wanted."

Queenie hadn't asked for the material things like his other women. She liked the horse lessons and he could see her passion for animals. He wished she felt that passion with him. Sometimes, he felt she locked him out of her world.

"Correction, that's exactly what you did. No, I shouldn't go that route in my stupid brain. I already did that once."

Tiger took the heart medication his doctor gave him. His doctor told him he was seriously ill, but Tiger must fix the Queenie problem first. He saw her car coming and Tiger ran to a side door of this shop to avoid her. He would have to come up with a disguise.

"Which method to use to kill her? The method should be easy. Which of my clients scared you the most?" He remembered which one. Then he changed his mind.

He stopped and smiled, "The answer just drove past me. I can rig your brakes or put a bomb under the white car or both."

The phone call was made to one of his bomb friends. He would change his rental to a sports car when the time was right. Tiger would need to find where she parked the white machine, or it might be easier to get a job where she serviced her car. Her license plate would show the name of her car dealership."

Tiger read her license plate number, "Felidae1".

He laughed, "I can't believe you, girl. The tigers belong to this family of mammals."

"Why didn't you use PTigris1? Your panthera tiger name seems more appropriate. The number was more than likely taken by some other crazy bitch."

Next, there was the thought process that she may have clone cars as well. He watched for her white car and found there were two. She would alternate driving them with no set pattern.

"Felidae1 will be the brake problem and Felidae2 would be anything I can accomplish."

He would have to figure out a way for the cars to fail, like a broken windshield washer, missing gas cap, or tire cut. She probably had a car alarm, but no one paid any attention to them, because they were always going off in the streets or parking lots.

That was it, "You like to shop at the expensive malls."

XXXXXX

Queenie was upset that Mr. David hadn't called her back regarding her invitation. She wondered if he was a snob or already kept a lady friend. She found out he was rich with money. Her money dwindled fast. She began checking out all the almost-eligible or eligible men she could marry. Perhaps they would accidentally die, leaving her everything. She could steal again. Divorce never occurred to her. It had flickered in her brain briefly, but she decided it was too messy and took too long. Judges seemed overworked and underpaid, so a person couldn't trust the outcome of a divorce.

She would need to be very good at rounding someone up. Queenie looked in her mirror and liked what she saw. She knew she could pull everything off with Mr. David. If not, then she would find a way to get everything he owned.

While she was making plans, there was someone else in the game whose sinister eyes were focused out the window of an airplane. Mrs. Tiger

95

Black was on a flight from London. She left her children with the two hired nannies and her parents. She told them that she was going to Miami to be with her husband. She was going to Miami to kill that stupid Queenie girl that her husband was so obsessed about. She could go places that only women could go. Her husband made the mistake of telling her Queenie's location with a selfie photo he sent. The two street signs were easily visible.

Mrs. Black would be a pretend decorator and offer her services to gain the woman's confidence. If that didn't work, she would talk about antiquities as an investment to get her foot in the door. Or there was Queenie's vehicle that she could destroy. Mrs. Black didn't know about the knife Queenie carried. It didn't matter. Mrs. Black started running, lifting weights, and working out to get stronger. She knew her husband would be there in disguise. She would have to create her own different look. Mrs. Black needed to fool both.

14   Lunch, David and Queenie

DAVID CALLED THE auction place and was told that the underling clerk didn't work there anymore. He was disappointed because he wanted to see the fine object, the bottom scepter.

Then he found Queenie's invitation for lunch in Miami Beach at one of his favorite waterfront hotels. He called her back and explained that he took a fall from a deranged polo horse. He could finally walk without a cane. He hated that cane. It made him feel decrepit.

Queenie tapped her foot on the marble floor of her luxurious apartment. "I would love to meet you for lunch." They agreed to meet at her favorite hotel in two days.

The rest of his mail was sorted and completed. Invitations were accepted to several parties indicating two guests would attend. One of the functions was a mayoral fund-raising party which he accepted. David would call his lady friends after his luncheon date with Queenie. The mayoral party was the same evening as Jess and Derek Wright's annual party.

He drove off to get a new tuxedo ordered and a haircut. He enjoyed buying new clothes and shoes.

David went later to his favorite shoe store at the mall because he needed a larger softer pair of shoes.

The day arrived, and Queenie went to the shop for her beauty appointment. Tiger parked his car behind hers, quietly unlocked her vehicle with a special device, and turned on her windshield wipers. He bent and twisted the metal wiper. He put a long scratch in her door by the lock that could easily be buffed. He relocked her car. Tiger did everything so fast, no one saw him. Then he drove off to his new part-time job at the car dealership.

Queenie came out and saw the scratch. She looked apprehensively around the area. Stopping a woman with a baby, "Did you see anyone near my vehicle?"

The young woman said, "I haven't seen anyone. Who would do that to a car and drive away? Probably young juveniles."

Queenie climbed gracefully inside her car. The windshield wiper turned on and the blade scraped on the glass. She called her guard to bring her second vehicle and requested they drop her first car off at the dealership. When her second vehicle arrived, she checked it for scratches and tried the wipers. Everything was fine. Therefore, she drove to the hotel for her lunch date.

Tiger placed Queenie's car on the hoist and took his knife out. The other workers left for their break. He examined the brake line for where to place the cut. He put his knife in his pocket and lowered the vehicle. There already was a cut in the brake line.

"I am really curious. Who did that one? There must be someone else anxious to do you harm."

He still wanted to get her other car in the shop soon in case the other person's job failed.

XXXXXX

Entering the ladies room of the hotel to view her image, Queenie wore a scowl on her face. She went into her actress smile.

"There, that is much better."

She spritzed on a little more perfume and moved her lips into a kiss shape.

"You, girl, are hot, hot, absolutely the best looker in the building. Go get and rein your man into your snare. Use and dispose as soon as possible is my motto. I'll see how it goes."

Queenie frowned again, because she reviewed her security tapes of her apartment building. One of her guards, Karine, brought Hamm into her apartment to retrieve a package Queenie left there. Hamm walked around looking at things. He also touched stuff, but hadn't taken anything. Karine received instructions to never let anyone into her apartment unless she obtained clearance. She would need to dock some of the girl's pay and watch her animal trainer.

An older man approached her table and the actress smile returned. His face matched his credentials that were sent. David Dunker saw the beautiful blonde woman at the table. He suddenly felt young and vital. She made him feel that way. It was going to be a lucky day and he would certainly add this exquisite woman with beautiful shoes to his collection of woman. David belonged to the group of rich men that the ladies wanted. Queenie would make him feel wanted. He could tell by the sparks that were rocketing off between them.

David held out his hand to her, "Hello, I am glad to finally meet you. You are an immensely intelligent beauty that is important to meet on any day and you are a collector as well."

Queenie thanked him, and he sat down. They immediately got along.

"I once went on safari in Africa and must tell you a story about tracking the lions. It took three days to find them. Then we ran into some northeasterly, very dry Harmattan wind for another a day. Finally, we saw our tribe of lions again. I did hire a photographer to take some authentic close-up pictures for my den. Fortunately, the photographer visited the place before. There were special bags for his photographic equipment protecting them from the fine dust particles that blew in from the Sahara. The last day of the safari we could get splendid shots. You should see my pictures in my den."

She told him she also experienced the cold dry wind in the morning and hot dry day wind of the Harmattan around Sierra Leone. Once, she went on safari but was disappointed.

"Tigers are my favorite animal, and there aren't too many in Africa."

David thought she looked melancholic talking about Africa.

"I like your candor about tigers. I have great affection toward tigers as well and believe they are exotic creatures. As a child, my father took me to the circus for amusement, too. The tiger species, many million years ago, descended from a smaller animal called the miacid. Their form hasn't changed much for over sixteen thousand years. I find that extremely comforting. People of long ago enjoyed the same beauty and bone structure in the animal that we do. They did roam for food and water. I believe they migrated from Turkey to Asia. Asia was probably a better place for them than Turkey. I'm not fond of that country. Bad memories. I was robbed once while visiting friends. They stole my wallet. Nasty business trying to get back home."

Queenie appreciated the fact that he was a bright man. Glad that the woman in front of him had brightened after talking about the tiger species, he asked her to be his date at an upcoming party. He wanted to know more about her.

Queenie looked out the restaurant window down at the boats in the harbor and knew that this next date was too easy. She accepted the date.

The next day she drove her second car to the pricey mall to purchase a new dress for Mr. David's party. It took her an extra-long time because she met this African woman while they were getting coffee lattes. She sat down and talked with the woman who was an interior designer. The woman smiled at Queenie

101

a lot as if she knew a secret. The designer gave her a business card to a place she just started working. Queenie accepted the card. She didn't currently need a decorator, but you never knew when a project would arise.

She parked her car in the underground parking earlier. While she was in the mall, another rental car parked next to her. A tool was used to puncture two front tires, so it would appear as if Queenie drove over something and cut them. Exiting the mall, Queenie drove slowly home. Her mind replayed recent events. A phone call interrupted the process. The first car was done and one of her guards would pick it up from the shop.

15   Queenie's Car Wreck

IT WAS A warm balmy evening as Queenie drove her Felidae1 vehicle toward David's home. Her other car developed two front flat tires and it needed to be taken into the shop. He invited her into his spacious modern home and showed her around.

David did not show her his special antiquities room that was built into the hill. He wanted to tell her about the thick cement walls, but held back the information. David calculated in his head the potential prices. He owned very rare items that were now worth a lot of money. His hesitation on the room's disclosure probably saved him from danger.

They talked over drinks on his back patio. He opened the inner gate and walked her through another patio area.   Then through another gate out to the driveway and her car. Queenie noted again where the security cameras existed. They left his home and went to a dinner party.

"I need to be gracious this evening, so I'll be able to have another meeting with this person."

She noticed the home was stunning and opulent. The dinner party woman incessantly talked, "My ancestors are from a long line of prestigious stock. The family tree can be traced forever. My side is longer than my husbands because we bore large families. Yet, his side of the family owned more land and factories. Hence, that was where our money came from. My husband reminds me all the time that he is richer."

She didn't know these people. The trivia exchange at the table was boring her. "You act as if your ancestors are some mythical blue-blood gods. Perhaps they are?"

The woman responded, "Oh, but they are, and most people are jealous."

Queenie had no clue who her ancestors were. It wasn't a common subject in her small circle, and she certainly wasn't jealous.

The hostess looked at David as if to let him know his date was obnoxious.

Queenie believed the woman's husband was worse and a total snob. She wondered how David could talk with him so long. The only conversation the man knew was golf. Or it was about all the championship games he attended as a spectator and which celebrities played. The man shook hands with champions.

She found David's friends dull and arrogant. Party meant excitement, drinking, and dancing. All this group drank was wine and cognac. She was shown their wonderful wine cellar. There was no dancing.

David saw her reluctance to join in the conversation and drove her back to his home. He hoped she could stay the evening. Queenie told him she must keep an early appointment but maybe next time she would stay. David kissed her a friendly good night.

Driving to her warehouse, she played with her tiger upon arrival which put her in a better mood. She had been surprised her tiger bared his teeth at that young man with the package. She was glad there was only a small scratch. After she paid him for the package which contained the gold bottom scepter with the eagle wing carving, he tried to run.

That was when it happened. He shouldn't have run. The tiger wanted to catch him. He thought the man was a mouse or ball, playing with him. Her tiger was re-caged quickly. The young man came back from his fainting spell. She gave the young man some antiseptic and he left the warehouse in a big hurry with his receipt.

She looked at the African woman's card and thought they should meet for lunch some time.

There was something David said about his friend. It was the one he stayed with while the leg healed. His friend lived in Alabama on a private ranch with his champion line of polo horses. She remembered the picture that David showed her.

She was told the Alabama friend sold his two-year old polo horses all over the world and traveled with them until they were delivered. In the picture, she remembered there stood this good looking young man. His friend was younger, single, and richer than David. He was from old money and lived off his inheritance on this large ranch outside of a small town.

Queenie saw tonight all the pretty things old money could buy. The friend did have a girlfriend that was an on-again and off-again romance. She hoped it was in an off-state. Her enthusiasm toward meeting Scott rose.

"Scott Barrow, from Fort Payne, Alabama, is your name. I will remember."

She thought of her tiger and transportation to her Alabama warehouse. She already contacted a company. Renovations started on the warehouse in Alabama to accommodate the tiger, just in case.

On her way to her apartment building, Queenie approached a bridge and drove across. She always drove a little too fast. Moving down the curved cement ramp, her brakes failed. She screamed. The car flipped over the curve landing on the engine first and rocking the sunroof on the cement pavement with a sharp crack of fiberglass and metal. Another sports car already drove past the curve and looked over at the damaged car. No one in the damaged sports car moved so the occupant drove onward. When the fire trucks arrived, they cut some of the twisted, smoking metal to get a young woman out of the crumpled vehicle.

Queenie awoke in a hospital bed and a nurse came into her room. The nurse explained she was in a bad car accident. Then she drifted back into unconsciousness and did that for two days. Finally, the swelling on her brain subsided and she was fully conscious. She broke her left arm and a deep cut existed on the left side of her face, and now her brain showed a mild concussion. The doctor told her she was very lucky. She could leave in another day or two, but may want to convalesce at home a few weeks.

The doctor gave her a card for a plastic surgeon he would recommend. He wrote her a prescription for pain pills. He told her she might have headaches for a long time. They found her health insurance card in her purse, but didn't call anyone, because they did not know who to call.

The hospital gave her cell phone back and keys. A nurse owned the same model and they charged the battery for her. Her clothes and shoes were thrown away due to the blood and their having to cut them off. Her vehicle was totaled, and the police would want to talk with her about their accident report. They asked her if she needed them to call someone.

"I will take care of things." Queenie was headed in the direction of negativity named revenge.

After the doctor and nurse left, she called one of her guards to bring clothes, shoes, and to pick her up. Her body felt stiff and sore. The guard drove her to the apartment building. She sent an e-mail to the delivery people that it was time to move her crate in the warehouse to Alabama immediately. Queenie would meet them there at the warehouse. She packed in boxes her valuable antiquities herself. Her guard helped put her clothes and shoes in boxes. A move-it same day company would pick up the boxes to transport them to her warehouse in Alabama.

Both her attorney and accountant were used to handling unsavory characters, and they liked those clients because they paid their bills on time. Queenie called her attorney to handle the sale of her apartment building and the sale of the warehouse a week later plus the limo.

She called her accountant to handle notification to her employees that their jobs were terminated and to provide their final checks. She gave both men a bank account to wire her money. Leaving Hamm, a voice-mail message, she let him know he could take the day off. She didn't want him to see her moving the cat. She didn't trust him.

Then she drove her second vehicle to the warehouse and fed her tiger a large meal. She filled a special container for him with water and another timed container of dried meat and bolted them inside his crate. Queenie gave him some sleeping medicine after he did his business.

She hugged him, "Goodbye for now my sweet exuberant boy," and locked his door.

She bought a special breathable cover that went over his cage. The special air-conditioned truck picked up her crate and boxes. She got back in her sports car. Selling her car at the old dealership, she walked across the street. A new red sports car with new plates under a new name was purchased at the different dealer. She drove in and out of different exits at one of the malls to lose any tails. At the bank, she withdrew her money and closed the account.

By noon, she was half way to Alabama before she stopped. She now knew the Sphinx still lived and she would take care of him later. Queenie changed her name. Her lawyer worked on her name change a month earlier.

Her new name was Elizabeth Banks. She previously picked up her filled prescription. Finally, she checked into a motel after eating a sandwich. She set her alarm for early and took some pills. Elizabeth rubbed her head trying to make the terrible headache go away. Her body and mind felt trapped in her predicament. She would go to this unknown place, far from Miami, where she could disappear. She was still alive.

When she arrived at her Alabama warehouse, she walked around.

"This will be our home for a while with my tiger boy."

A couple of weeks ago, the men installed a pool and three freezers. They also brought some large potted plants and some hoses attached to the water. She stepped into her office and looked through the glass. The couch would do for now.

"The place doesn't look as nice as the other one, but it will work."

The delivery truck unloaded the crate and then her boxes. Everything was in order. She stopped at a grocery store and stocked the freezer. She picked up her bag of treats. Elizabeth took her arm out of the sling and uncovered the cage. There sat her beloved tiger. He came to the door and she gave him a treat. She touched his paw and let him out. She filled his pool which he went to first and looked at her. Elizabeth broke their routine because sometimes things were difficult. The tiger awakened to unfamiliar surroundings. She was also in familiar and unfamiliar territory.

"I will relent this one time."

She gave him the release command. The tiger ran to the pool and drank the water.

Then she called him, and they did their routine and walked around his new environment. After an hour, he went back to his now washed cage. She refilled his water for him. Then she gave him a large roast to eat. She put a few jerkies in the upper device.

She looked at him and his tail was flicking back and forth. She would check on him daily until she could find a suitable caretaker. She looked in her mirror at the scar and knew she would get plastic surgery. Elizabeth researched information about Scott.

"I must find a permanent place for my tiger."

Then Elizabeth Banks would visit the polo playboy, Scott Barrow, in Ft. Payne, Alabama. Her skills had been honed, and the actress was ready for an impressive new show.

16   Disappearance of Queenie

TIGER BLACK CALLED his wife to let her know his job was almost complete and he would be in London in a few days to visit her and the children. Then they could go back to Africa. His wife mentioned that she would like to fly to Miami and be with him those few days. She heard high-end Miami clothes stores carried the height of fashion.

"I can meet you in The Glades Bar at the airport."

"I will be delighted to meet you in the bar at seven in the evening and take you shopping," said Tiger.

Tiger drove by Queenie's apartment building and saw the For-Sale sign. She fled the area. He knew she had been in the hospital from a bad car accident. He talked to one of her cleaning maids. Destroying his remote for the bomb on Queenie's second car, Tiger knew he didn't cause her accident. The bomb would fall off the second car and not detonate as the glue was a temporary type which would eventually dissolve. He hoped it would roll into a ditch He wasn't sure if she ditched the second car, but he couldn't take a chance.

Tiger was glad his wife joined him. He took her to some of the hotel restaurants that Queenie frequented. They toured for three wonderful days in Miami visiting all the tourist sites. She wished that she brought their children. They flew back to London and then Africa.

One day, he was trying to find an outfit top for his wife that he bought her in an expensive shop in Miami. He thought it would look good on her for their dinner party that he hadn't told her about.

"I will find the top and lay it out on the bed for my wife."

His wife hid her passport in the beautiful rhinestone knit top. Curious, he opened her passport and saw the two sets of stamps to Miami. She was in Miami the same time Queenie incurred her accident."

"What is it that my wife did?" His face and eyes grew dark when he remembered Queenie's bad car wreck and her injuries. How dare you try to kill my beloved woman, thought Tiger.

"I never gave you the right. You did it without my permission? Why? I gave you everything and improved your designer business. This is another insult. It was one too many."

His woman was out of control. He knew his wife was in an illicit affair with the bodyguard at his home. He ordered his wife followed in Africa, but not England. She planned the brake failure after he left. His separate loathing for her grew into a silent hatred. Silent hatred was the worst kind. It festered quicker than a wildfire in California fanned by el Nino winds or the Harmattan in Africa.

The police also saw the For-Sale sign on Queenie's building. The police tried to find information from the tenants who knew nothing. They watched the warehouse and there was a plant company picking up potted ferns. Then a cleaning company came. A week later the warehouse went up for sale.

The police contacted the realty firm and all they knew was that the person left the state. There was no crime committed so the police would keep their investigation into Queenie Pyra open. Unless more information was yielded from another source, they were at a dead end. They let Derek know.

"Where have you disappeared? What did happen to the gold antiquity stolen from Walnut Creek and do you have the two items you advertised and withdrew from the auction?"

Derek went with the police when they contacted David Dunker to find out any information regarding a bottom scepter that the underling auction clerk might have obtained. David told the police about the item and how the clerk called David. He called David on his cell phone while he was alive. David never saw the bottom part of the scepter and was horrified the two brothers were murdered.

David explained that he owned the top part of the scepter and a ring that he thought matched. The police asked him if he knew Queenie Pyra and he told them he went on two dates with her. The police wanted her for questioning due to the two young men's suspicious deaths. She disappeared before the police could talk to her. If David heard from her again, they would appreciate a call.

Privately, Derek asked David if he would sell his gold eagle antiquities. David did not want to sell them because he wanted to donate them to his favorite museum when he died. He would allow Jess and Derek to view and photograph them for a fee for their new book. David would let them have full copyright to their photos. Derek and Jess already copyrighted the designs from Louisa's notebook. A brief synopsis of the Renaliere story was presented and David was fascinated. Derek set a date, so his wife could view the objects.

Derek knew Jess would be ecstatic.

Meanwhile, Hamm Roe was mad his employer was gone, and he was out of his job, not to mention the opportunity to find her riches. Queenie disappeared without a trace and so did her minions except Karine. Karine waited to see what his plans involved. Karine let him into Queenie's apartment for two nights while Queenie was in the hospital. Hamm figured out where her security cameras were on his first visit and put heavy tape over them while in the apartment. Karine checked to make sure no one saw Hamm while she hung outside the apartment.

Karine didn't know he found the secret elevator. He couldn't figure out anything other than it led to the apartment downstairs which was an empty apartment. There must be a secret room with the antiquities. He planned to come back, but now there was a blasted For Sale sign.

He knew the items were gone. Hamm didn't know what to do other than get another job at an auction house. He took Karine with him to his apartment thinking she might be valuable in the future to help retrieve the objects. He always used women. Hamm would be tracking Queenie.

17   Annual Party in Miami

JESS AND DEREK brought their family group private photographer to David Dunker's fortress room. He had installed special laser lights which would set off all kinds of electronic alarms and doors to protect his valuable finds. He allowed them to hold the objects with special gloves and take accurate measurements. They also weighed the objects and set up the photo shoot.

"The finished photo shots were stunning."

She stared at the close-up's which showed the exquisite eagle carvings beautifully. She truly was happy the items were in safe hands.

David was pleased he could share his love of the objects. He loved the top part of the scepter also. He thought it was amazingly beautiful and the exquisitely carved diamond ring a true work of art. Louisa's drawings of the gold antiquities were an inspiration to search and find all of them.

He knew the Wrights had planned to donate anything they found to their Los Angeles museum like they did with their sunken treasure. Jess also gave him a brief description of that journey and Louisa Renaliere's history information about the dolphin run. He also hoped the police would find the murderer or murderers. He was glad that he hadn't shared his special locked room with Queenie.

The Wrights' motorboat was loaded with their crew and close crony families. There were huge quantities of food and liquor on board when they motored out of Miami Beach traveling to Fort Lauderdale. This year, War Julio was with his wife at the hospital in Rio de Janeiro awaiting the arrival of their child.

Everyone onboard put on their feather masks. The group pictures were taken while the boat moved slowly away from the dock. Derek would send pictures to War Julio on his cell phone. They installed special sun shades on the motorboat so that people could mingle between decks. The motorboat moved slowly through the ocean on its party route.

After the box lunches were eaten, they set up the tiny helicopter games upon reaching Fort Lauderdale. The group had a prior party one year with the taco food theme and they voted for it again. The Mexican taco bars were created for the evening. There were hot batter-fried fish, pulled beef, and ground pork. The corn taco baskets were small, so they could try all three meats.

The chef made special macaroni and cheese-fried squares for the children. The Miami brothers kept eating them. The only thing was they added to the treat. It was heaven in a hot cheese cube slathered with sliced jalapenos on top. The boys kept looking at each other and laughing while singing "hot cha, cha, cha." Derek tried one and had to run to get his cold beer to douse the fire.

Mounds of various tomatoes, lettuce, and jicama were available to make a salad. There also were small soft taco rolls with various cheeses and refried beans inside. The ladies on the boat selected the larger fried baskets for their salad. All the assorted trimmings were in the center of the motorboat with veggies and fruits.

The chef gourmet-made sauces were put in medium-sized squeeze bottles. The men threw the bottles to each other and doused everything. The chef set up a special set of sauces with a sign "Ladies Only." He put a little more honey and mango in their blend. They set up the wind fans to a generator to keep any bugs away and keep people cool on deck while the boat was anchored.

For dessert, there were hand-dipped chocolate bars with an assortment of toppings or frozen butterscotch-dipped bananas on a stick. Every kind of tequila drink and flavored juice or soda for the children was sitting in coolers of ice. Massive quantities of crushed ice cones were eaten by everyone as they watched Derek manipulate his drones over the water.

Before they headed back, they rigged a large outdoor screen and showed photos of the eagle antiquities much to everyone's amazement. On the return trip, they played a movie about eagles for the children in the lower lounge and a coffee espresso bar for the adults was topside. Several of the men grabbed their guitars and strummed softly.

Reaching the outskirts of the Miami Beach port, they slowed the engines and threw out the edible lei's in the water. They all toasted Dean Crain, their friend who had passed away. The children loved to throw their lei out into the ocean. Usually it landed two feet from the boat. The captain worried about the motors a tad.

"Goodbye everyone" said Jess and Derek when they docked.

The motorboat would start their journey back to Los Angeles with the crew and the Wright family.

"Don't forget to send in your vote for next year's annual party dinner and location."

Their extended family exited the boat and received their eagle gifts. The ladies received their gold scepter pin and scepter shaped cologne and the men their eagle wing money clip. The children received a popcorn object in the shape of an eagle wing, a special balloon, t-shirt, and eagle storybook. Skid helped Jess create the book and write the story. They designed the bags to hold the gifts. There were gifts for all their friends.

In the evening, Derek opened the old scotch bottle and went to the bow of the boat.

"It was another grand party you arranged. I feel great. We've safeguarded our family and had a great time. I'm still reeling from the jalapenos. I think they grow them hotter here."

Jess laughed. She saw her husband make the dash for beer and later ginger ale. "Yes, the party did work. It was time for us to say our own goodbye."

Derek held Jess tight. She was glad this past party was calm. Not one bullet was fired. Derek was relieved. He and Jess went below to their own private party. Both worked together as an amazing team. Jess turned out the lights and turned on the soft music and came back into his arms.

She wore a special, short midriff, new t-shirt design with an eagle eye. Derek smiled because she hadn't shown him this design.

She asked, "Do you like?

Derek replied, "I like. Yes, my eagle angel, always."

Derek traced the design on the t-shirt pressing the known pleasure centers of his sexy, beautiful wife. "Honey?"

"What sweet husband?"

"I believe you should design some other amazing pieces like maybe lingerie."

"I'm already on it."

"Of course, you are."

He slowly removed her top, kissing her soft skin, barely touching her. He held her arms stretched out like the eagles. His fingers found her fingers. Fingertips touching fingertips. He could hear her heart beat. Their hands held for a moment having received their message of direction. Then he picked her body slightly up. The female was following, leading, following him.

The two of them flew like the eagles in the video, each dancing, soaring close, wings touching in the air. The sky held no boundaries. The air lifted them above the beyond. Their air was pure and exhilarating. There was no one else in their domain of passion and desire. Raised high enough to almost touch the stars, he followed her again to do the familiar dance. The larger eagle was drawn to her, enjoying the ritual. The eagles owned the sky. Every slow fall was capture and release.

The dance complete, they disappeared until early morning. It was a perfect end to their party.

18   Queenie's Revenge

HAMM ROE SEARCHED for Queenie via the computer search databases. He checked with all the collectors in the Miami area and found David Dunker. He dragged Karine along to visit him. David was surprised to meet Karine because she looked like Queenie. They explained that she had been chosen to protect Queenie. They explained the reason for their visit. They were worried about her and were trying to find her. David thought they should stay away from the woman until the police talked with Queenie. But Derek asked David to keep his information under wraps.

Hamm explained, "I work at one of the local auction houses and would like to get the commission on the sale of the two items I saw her advertise in the past. It would help pay the baby expenses for our child."

Karine looked at Hamm because she wasn't pregnant. She decided to let the story go. She saw the look of disappointment on David's face. Karine recognized the look David gave her. It was one of friendly curiosity and desire. She would remember David Dunker.

Hamm wondered about Queenie. What did she see in the old man? He didn't appear to be her type.

That may have been why the attraction failed and she moved onto some younger man. What younger man could she find? He absolutely must be a rich man for the Queen.

David was rubbing his leg which hurt whenever thunderclouds moved in the area. Hamm saw the movement and David volunteered, "I broke it playing polo with my friend in Alabama."

Hamm noticed a picture on the bookcase of a handsome young man in a polo outfit on a beautiful horse.

Hamm knew that was more like her real boyfriend style.

David explained that he didn't know where the young woman went.

Hamm left David's home thinking about the rich friend, Scott Barrow. Karine thought they left without any further information as did David.

XXXXX

Elizabeth found a caretaker for the tiger and stayed a few weeks to make sure her beloved Felidae would be all right.

She stared and stared at the African designer woman's business card. Strange things happened right after she met the woman. She wondered if she was the person who cut her brake line on the white sports car, the super wrecked sports car. It was time to check with the woman's employer in Miami.

Looking at herself in the mirror, the face was still partially swollen from the plastic surgery. Her cheeks were raised, and her lips made fuller. The deep scar almost gone. She put more of the heavy makeup on and powder to be sure. The new look and black shiny hair would do. She would have it dyed every three weeks at the roots to disguise the blond tresses of the former Queenie.

The plane landed back in Miami and she picked up a rental car and drove to the designer store.

A young man approached the beautiful dark-haired woman. She told him about this wonderful designer lady whom she met, and they became such good friends. She was in town and dropped by to see if her beautiful African friend wanted to do lunch at their favorite restaurant. She showed him the business card the woman gave her at the mall.

He told her the woman went back to Dakar, Senegal, Africa, to her negative edge pool, but he would be glad to help her if she needed anything.

Elizabeth thanked him, "I know the address but can't remember the street name. Can you help me with the name?" She kept clicking her fingers trying to look forgetful.

The young man disappeared and came back. "The name was Seaside Drive."

"Of course, where went my mind? The name goes with her pool. She told me that it was exquisite. They have brilliant parties there with their friends. I'm so glad she asked me to be her friend. I like parties, don't you?"

The young man looked eager and shook his head. She thanked him again profusely and drove to the airport getting tickets to Dakar.

On the plane, she drank a glass of champagne to chase her headache away and think about the facts.

"The address is a known one. It was Santan Chesin's old residence before he changed his name. It is the residence in Africa where Sphinx went to party and make deals. You did tell me about the wonderful pool and expensive parties."

She could visualize the place in her mind.

"It makes perfect sense. You did help me kill the man in London with the poisoned rum because he was your most immediate enemy at the time. Santan would have ratted on you. Then you did amazingly escape from the Congo, burned your house down, and bought Santan's house. You are living in total disguise. Well, I have found you. You're not so clever."

The Sphinx or Tiger was very smart in business and always covered himself very well. No one would get Santan Chesin's connection to the man, except maybe a tired judge. She owned voice tapes that would show the connection. The Sphinx or Tiger would remain undercover until he killed her. She didn't want to die. She was determined to find out who the woman was with the business card.

Therefore, she would meet her contact first to get the blowing package.

She watched the house one day and knew this residence held Tiger Black and his family.

"Tiger was the feral Sphinx."

125

The angry rage started when she understood the designer woman she met in Miami was his wife.

"You told me you would never, ever marry. You wouldn't marry me, but you did marry this other woman. No, I'm not jealous, just disappointed. One more mess that I stepped into with you."

She called the emergency phone number the young man at the designer store in Miami gave her. The number was an African area code. She dialed the number on her disposable phone. The device was already implanted on the husband's car in the garage.

Her Sphinx answered, "Hello, Tiger here."

She held the phone and was unable to move. She watched the phone slip from her hand. She shook herself. Five minutes later a car drove out of the gate.

She checked the license plate, "The car with the device was the Sphinx's."

She followed the vehicle on the windy coastal road toward town at a safe distance. The person who gave her the blowing package told her it would detonate in six hours. The time was about twelve minutes away and suddenly, the car blew. She hadn't expected the device to blow so soon and almost slipped off the road. Perhaps the man wasn't that good with a timing clock. She stared at the wreckage.

"The device seemed more powerful than what I paid."

She was skeptical about those two facts, the early release and fire power. Elizabeth knew she must kill the Sphinx or the now Tiger-person because he tried to kill her three times.

"The situation involved murder or be the one who is dead like a piece of meat in a cold metal drawer." She also couldn't have him kill any more people around her.

"You are the insane, hostile, arrogant criminal. It is not me. You were the one who put me into a cage first."

Elizabeth was glad everything was over. With relief, she finally turned her car around and drove to another large city private airport. She flew back to Alabama.

19   Elizabeth's Movement

IT WAS TIME to find her beloved tiger his new home. A zoo lost one of their elder male tigers and were looking for another one. Elizabeth went to talk to the zoo owner. She brought all the documents on her tiger plus current veterinary records. She showed him pictures of her beloved boy. She could no longer keep him because her soon-to-be-husband was allergic. She really needed to give up her tiger, because she felt it could lead people to her. Then her name change, and new look would have been for naught.

The zoo people came out to see her tiger. She offered them the cat with a one-million-dollar donation if her name remained anonymous. The papers were drawn up and she hugged her beloved cat goodbye. She tried to visit him one time, but the cat could smell her and became agitated.

Elizabeth had a tattoo put on the top of her foot where a shoe strap would go. The tattoo read the word, *Felidae1*. She was being nostalgic, and she wanted to remember something that loved her unconditionally.

She leased a small coffee shop in Scott's town, close to the edge of town where he lived. There was a small room above, where she could live. Her warehouse was put up for sale. There was a small bank nearby, and she opened her account plus three large lockboxes. She placed the objects in black velvet bags and took them to her bank. Each object was in its own box to allow plenty of room. Buying a long gold chain, she put the three keys on it. The keys disappeared somewhere below her large round breasts.

Her red car was driven close to Scott Barrow's private, magnificent, and heavily secured polo farm. The black wrought iron gates contained six security cameras. There was a pool and pool house close by with another smaller private access gate. She noted the pool gate showed one camera and a punch code access panel. She thought that camera could easily be disabled with the proper tools. Elizabeth looked around at the beautiful countryside.

She breathed in the smell of the fresh earth, large trees, wildflowers, and pretty streams. Green hay swayed in the breeze and she thought it was food for the horses. She heard the horses whinny to someone in the distance.

"The horses represent money." She needed money.

Loosening her battery cable, she waited. Scott drove his large Suv-type vehicle down the road and the huge gates opened. He pulled over to help the young woman. Stepping out of his vehicle, he said, "It looks like you have car trouble. I'm an expert with expensive cars and horses. Is it all right if I check things out?"

Elizabeth almost purred. She loved men who were expert.

"I'm Elizabeth Banks and here are my keys if you think you can start my pretty machine. I would appreciate it because I need to open my coffee shop. I made a wrong turn and will accept any directions to town."

He tried to start the car and popped the hood. He tightened the cables and the car started.

"I am unsure how your cables became so loose. Your car dealership should have checked everything. The car is obviously new because of your lack of permanent plates. There is a guidance system in this new, siren-red car."

Elizabeth laughed, "I like siren-red. I'm not sure that is the car color name. You've made the name up. Wonderful! It is now my favorite color. Oh, my car dealership knew that I was in a hurry to leave Miami. I'm not used to the voice commands. Besides the woman in the little box doesn't listen to me, so I gave up."

Now Scott grinned. Elizabeth Banks was a Miami girl. Scott once dated a crazy rich girl from South Beach. He noticed her tan and thought, "Definitely Miami."

She told him the name of her leased coffee shop and wished he would stop by her shop. She would give him a free roll and hot or cold coffee as thanks. Or she could buy him dinner if he didn't drink the beverage.

Scott stopped and looked at her. Elizabeth was young and dark-haired beautiful in her soft red silk dress and expensive heels. Her dress revealed wonderful curves. He was currently in off-mode with his girlfriend. Scott became interested, having completely forgotten why he was driving into town.

He thought, she might be a fun interlude. He was ready for a change. His girlfriend's tactics to try to get him to propose were wearing a little thin. Flush with money, he could afford to take her partying. "You look like you like to play. I can show you a version of my kind of high society and fun. Do you know how to ride?"

Elizabeth took riding lessons in Africa. It was one of those times when she had been in tune to the rich ways of the horse crowd.

She said, "Yes. I love the creatures and all that amazing muscle." Elizabeth looked at Scott's muscles.

Scott smiled and knew this was going to work. She was the amazing creature. He could show her muscles, amazing muscles. She loved horses and could ride, too. A beautiful woman was standing in front of him. He felt feelings moving him forward. Scott wasn't crazy yet.

"I very much like the beverage and will see you soon."

Elizabeth waved, got into her pretty expensive car, and drove the direction he pointed. Scott did drop by one day at her coffee shop for the dark brew, and the two of them started dating.

One day in the barn, she saw him wrapping the horse's feet in white tape for a local in-state polo match. It was something he loved to do. He told her the tape protected the animal's feet from the ball, mallet, and other stresses during the chukkers or the six periods of play. Besides there was always the horse and player's thousand or so pound weight that also entered the field. The tape was a support device.

He took her with him to the game. She loved putting the divots of grass back on the field during halftime. She went with him on his delivery of polo horses all over the world for three months and then he proposed.

"Marry me. Please marry me so we can be together. I want you. You're finer than my prize competition polo horse."

"That is the first time anyone compared me to a horse, but I understand the love of an incredibly talented creature. Yes, I want to marry you. I was sure the first day we met that we're going to be a couple."

Scott twirled her around the room and kissed her.

"This is crazy to feel this way."

"Yes, it was crazy."

His friends were shocked, but delighted. They all wondered about the new girl, excited to meet her. They previously wrote Scott off as a permanent polo playboy. Scott had wanted to be a playboy until he met Elizabeth. They were pleased that he found his dream girl.

20   Alabama Police

THE BOOK ABOUT gold antiquities was postponed by Jess and Derek until they received further information regarding the rest of the objects. Jess and their friend, Skid, were working three more eagle children's books. Their children were also sharing in the stories. They went to the wildlife habitat places to talk with the caretakers of injured birds and their possible re-release into the wild.

Derek found out Queenie Pyra's last known appearance was at a Miami hospital from a bad car accident. He read the police report on the totaled car. The brakes failed due to a small straight puncture in the line probably from a sharp knife which caused a small leak. The car recently was serviced by a temporary worker who quit after two weeks. No known record of the person was found.

Derek thought, "The accident was another hit. A missing worker at the car dealership was another huge red flag of deception. It was beginning to look like she was possibly the victim."

The doctor didn't have any information other than her injuries which were a severe concussion due to her head. Swelling occurred which was now considered minor because she had all her cognitive abilities. Her arm was broken, and she received a deep cut to her face. The doctor said she never checked out, but her insurance paid everything. He did give her a card for a plastic surgeon. A woman would want to fix the deep scar. Derek called him, but Queenie made no contact with the plastic surgeon doctor.

Jess and Derek thought she ran because she knew three attempts were made upon her life. They thought Queenie knew her attempted killer. They also were sure she would change her appearance. With the underground's help, she could find someone who would help her. Queenie had survived a long time.

A new identification card was an easy thing to obtain. Jess did it once to ditch Derek before they were married. That was a terrible spot he didn't want to remember. She became Mary and blew up her own cottage when a poison killer got too close. It was a time when Derek failed to protect Jess.

"You were smart and so was Queenie. Her survival is amazing. But you didn't murder people unless it was self-defense. We believe Queenie possibly killed three people: Santan Chesin and the two brothers. We can't prove it one way or the other. Every time the police get close to her for questioning, she disappears. This makes her look suspicious. There are unknowns with this woman."

Jess mentioned to Derek, "Queenie will take her animal with her." She didn't want to comment just yet on the woman's survival. Jess applauded Queenie. The woman made it this far.

"I think so, too, because our friend, Jim Michaels sent me an article his wife saw. A small zoo in Alabama did receive a donation of a male tiger and an anonymous donation of an unknown amount of money. People are always donating animals to zoos, but usually not with a donation. It is worth checking out," mentioned Derek.

He saw his wife's quiet mood. Something was up with her. Derek would have to wait until Jess disclosed what was bothering her. He knew it was connected to his case.

Derek contacted the Alabama authorities. They went to the authorities who explained the donation amount was a million dollars from a woman and the police checked the address. It was a warehouse in their state. The woman already sold this place in their state and funds were wired to a now closed off-shore account. The funds were untraceable.

The police weren't sure who owned the warehouse, because the person didn't have any background. They contacted the lawyer who handled the transaction, and someone broke in and stole his files. He didn't use computers nor have any security cameras at his business. The company, persons, and money were unknown to the police and that was all they could enter in their databases.

Per the police, Queenie wasn't in Miami or Alabama or anywhere. Derek ran his hands through his brown hair.

"The woman vanished."

This case was like seeing some birds sitting on an electrical wire. There were more birds involved that were hiding in the trees. Some of the birds would arrive and get pushed off or electrocuted when they lost their balance. Derek hoped she survived. He might have to await the arrival of the biggest bad-ass bird first.

21 Elizabeth and Scott's Wedding

IT TOOK ANOTHER three months to plan their large wedding. Scott insisted, "I want to give you the grandest affair possible because I'm enraptured with you. This wedding is our start."

Elizabeth was elated. She made it. It seemed a dream.

The invitation list was impressive with his list of friends, polo buddies, clients, old world money people, and dignitaries. She selected some of her coffee ladies for bridesmaids because she didn't have very many friends from London. She lost track of them. The bridesmaids wore pale green dresses very light in tone. The color of their dresses was almost white. They carried white roses.

The huge garden was set up for the wedding. There were large opulent topiaries brought in to make the aisle she would walk down and the narrow white carpet was installed for the day. The pool area would be the bar. Clearing the garden of chairs, a dance floor was created with buffet tables of food set around the edges. The cake cutting would be on a specially designed white marble table under their rose arbor. Red rose bouquets adorned every walkway into and out of their yard. Even the polo stalls were adorned with flowers. The polo horses whinnied, thinking they won their ribbons. It was show time.

She flew to New York earlier to select her white satin designer gown and incredible honeymoon wardrobe. Elizabeth went to all the couture shops. She found special white satin heels for her wedding with a wide band to cover her tattoo. Her flowers would be a massive bouquet of red roses.

Scott bought her a brilliant five-carat ring in platinum with plain bands which she insisted. The men wore white tuxedoes with the same pale green-colored ties. He put a huge amount of money into her account for her.

Scott was generous in every way and experienced in bed. She began to think, "Maybe I won't need to do you in, but know I should be prepared to run. Your past girlfriend keeps hanging around. Your old girlfriend is like a despondent puppy until you walk in the room. She brings doom with her. It was hard to feel special."

Elizabeth hated that girl and thought she should just go away. She kindly told her that fact and the old girlfriend complained to Scott.

Treading lightly around the girl was something she never did. Elizabeth would have to put on her actress face for some time. Then little things happened to the old girlfriend. She developed a strange rash and wasn't around for a week. Then her hair dresser put the wrong solution in her hair and she had to get it cut short.

Elizabeth thought the mousey short hair matched the lanky long body. She believed the old girlfriend was doing those things to get Scott's attention because he would visit his friend to make sure everything was all right. The tension the girlfriend caused between them was not good. Elizabeth looked in her mirror and wondered how she could make this marriage work. She needed to take control of the situation.

Elizabeth knew David Dunker was coming to the wedding. She would have to avoid him as much as possible. He was a major person from her past who could potentially recognize her.

The wedding day arrived, and the weather was a perfectly bright day. There were so many guests that the entire place was a mob scene. They knew Scott, but not the bride. They wanted to meet her and swarmed around her like bees to honey. Scott kept having a hard time getting close to his wife. He would be ready to leave the party. He smiled and waved to his wife. Elizabeth smiled back.

The champagne and great chef-prepared food disappeared fast. The cake was four tiers consisting of chocolate with fudge, applesauce with caramel, white with raspberry delight, and orange with lemon meringue covered in white fondant. Handmade white roses engulfed the cake. The cake was an instant hit.

139

and everyone loved the story that they couldn't decide the best flavor.

She saw David approach toward the end of the evening and she told Scott, "I must change. We should be leaving to drive to the airport shortly."

"Anything you want is fine with me. I'm ready to exit the crowd."

Scott was glad this whole affair would be done. He knew he needed to leave. He saw the old girlfriend in the distance and knew to keep her away from Elizabeth. He didn't want any thorns marring his honeymoon night with the new wife. He asked David to handle the old girlfriend.

The teary-eyed old girlfriend approached, and David intercepted her.

The honeymoon plans were that the Barrow couple would take a late flight to visit New York City and then travel to Germany. So, Elizabeth went to her room to put her red two-piece linen suit on. Their bags were packed waiting for the butler to remove them to the car.

Scott made his apologies to his guests and went after his new wife. She was more important.

They flew to New York City enjoying the sites, riding ferries, and eating hot dogs in the park. He took her to the very best restaurants and ate lunch in the Upper East Side. They found food trucks, noodle bars, and New York-style pizza with lots of cheese. She located the boutiques along Fifth Avenue and Madison.

Shopping continued at elegant flagship mega brand shops and jewelry stores. He bought her a screen print t-shirt that said, "Elizabeth Loves Me." She bought him a shirt, "Polo Jock." Scott didn't want to let her go.

They went to Broadway plays, stayed up late talking. Both watched the morning sunrise unfold from their penthouse suite. It was the honeymoon suite, the very best for his bride. She told Scott they should buy a penthouse there and then they would have a base to stay. Whenever they delivered his polo horses, the stopover would be great fun. Elizabeth showed him a real estate flyer she was sent by a realtor. The pictures were stunning as was the price.

"The penthouse can be our pied-a-terre. I would love our own temporary place."

"Let me think about the real estate property. I love you except the wedding and everything were expensive. I need to recover. I can, and we will someday buy a place. I promise you."

She almost made the mistake of telling him that she owned money in her three gold antiquities. She did pull the wedding off. No one recognized her or knew her past. She spoke to herself, "I can't mess this up, not yet, anyway."

Receiving several verbal invitations to future parties at their wedding, she felt accepted into Scott's world. Her life with Scott was easy and she began to feel normal.

"Now I can work on my other plans." Elizabeth had never had anything work for her in the past. She thought of her marriage to Scott as temporary. There was nothing real or golden in her life. She thought about her past. It was deplorable, and Scott would never forgive her.

Elizabeth knew she must always be prepared to run. It was part of that insecurity thing and lack of trust. She knew Scott loved her now. He may not love her if he found out about her horrible prior life.

There would be a photograph in the paper and it would be a picture that she could approve from the ones taken at the wedding. She didn't realize there was a magazine photographer friend who would put their picture with Scott's approval in the Polo Magazine. It was an earlier photo of the two of them with their horses.

That picture and a story about them would be a problem. Scott preplanned the article and thought she would be pleasantly surprised. The magazine would release its print a day after their marriage.

"I thought it was a good idea to advertise our new life and expand the business. I'm proud of my new beautiful, smart wife." He was wrong about the magazine article.

She blew up at him about the Polo Magazine article and was mad for a few days. Then she said, "I forgive you if we can develop some new friends instead of old ones."

Scott knew which old friend she was talking about that brought disturbance in their life. "I want to make you happy. I can move forward with new friends."

He would give up the old girlfriend. It was somehow important to his new wife. He would roll with the flow.

The old girlfriend wasn't invited to their parties anymore and was safe for now from Elizabeth.

22   Tiger Hunting the Murderer

TIGER BURIED HIS gorgeous wife in London. The dead bodyguard was sent back to his parents in Liberia. He sold his home in Dakar and moved their children within two miles of her parent's home in London. They babysat them when his nanny couldn't, so the arrangement worked. The children were in a private school. The school was good about not releasing the children without approval.

He created a new will, because his heart was still giving him problems. He got a job as one of the passenger cart delivery persons taking people to their airplane gate. Tiger thought that he might see Queenie, or whatever her name changed to, walk through this airport someday. It was large and busy but mostly, it was the main artery to other destinations in Europe.

"You will never go to Africa again because you think I'm dead. I am not dead, but my wife and bodyguard are no longer on this earth."

The horse Polo Magazine was left at the airport in Tiger's special cart. He decided to take the magazine home to show his children the pretty horses in the pages. One day he was supposed to pick up this newly married couple to take them to their next flight when an elderly woman carrying her luggage tripped and fell in front of him. She needed his help in retrieving her cane.

He called the office, "Send another cart to pick up the newlyweds because I'm going to help an elderly woman to her gate. She has fallen and was having difficulty."

The old woman was outside his cart and he would take her to her flight. While she was digging in her purse for her ticket, he looked toward the other gate.

Tiger saw the woman and she looked familiar in the way she walked and moved her hands. She was young with long dark hair. She was beautiful. The woman reached in her purse for her gold compact and looked at herself while touching her hair. Tiger had seen that gesture many times when he was with Queenie in his vehicle.

He knew the young woman was Queenie. "No doubt about it. You look very good as does your handsome, unaware husband. The husband has no clue who you are because I can tell. You look rich, part of the world's first-class elite. You have real class, girl, always going after the money. Money buys the impressive life versus a primitive one. You did learn well things that I taught you. Those are things I paid for. You still owe me."

Tiger couldn't stand the stud husband. He would change that happy look. The revenge fire was burning hotter.

The honeymooner cart took off. He knew the other driver was a wonderful conversationalist with his passengers.

The elderly woman suddenly found her ticket and waved it in his face. He delivered the old woman to her gate and went on break. He talked with his work buddy who also took his break.

Tiger asked, "Did the newlyweds make it to their designated gate? I did see the pretty woman. I wondered where they were flying to on the next leg of their trip. I'm just curious because it's fun to monitor how the rich live. Usually, the rich fly out of New York."

"I drove them to the gates for Germany. The husband was delivering his polo babies to a client."

Tiger repeated the important question, "And where were they from exactly?"

The buddy said, "I can't remember the hometown name. The man mentioned a fort, but I believe the original gate was in Chattanooga, Alabama. The wife didn't talk at all and was very quiet and reserved." Buddy showed Tiger the large tip the polo man gave him.

Tiger went home and found the Polo Magazine. He was upset. He found and read the article about the newly-married couple. He talked to his nanny and his dead wife's parents. Tiger told them that he needed to take time off in about two weeks for a much-needed break. He wanted to go back to America where he spent some time with his wife. They were good with the fact that he wanted to do that. He called in work and took time off three weeks from now believing the young couple would be done with their business in Germany.

He found the fort name in the magazine. He made his reservations for Alabama.

Tiger also contacted a person to see if they wanted a job. They did.

23   Hamm in Alabama

HAMM FOLLOWED DAVID Dunker to Alabama to his friend, Scott's wedding. He couldn't get close to the house because of all the protection of the dignitaries. Karine came with him and she didn't mind because she caught glimpses of David when they ate at some of the nearby restaurants. He didn't see her.

She liked him when they first met and would have liked to talk to David more. Hamm and Karine stayed at a cheap motel which was close to a nice coffee shop.

The married couple immediately left for their honeymoon.

Hamm and Karine read articles about Scott Barrow, a renowned and rich polo horse breeder. There weren't many articles on the upcoming bride other than she owned the local coffee shop.

Hamm had trimmed his beard and his friend wore a wig just in case it was Queenie. They didn't want to freak her out because they knew she changed her name and appearance. Also, they weren't sure she would welcome them because of her new life.

Seeing the newspaper photo and article regarding the wedding, they weren't sure it was her. They went to the coffee shop and talked with her employees casually like a tourist might have done. They were told the married Elizabeth woman was from Miami.

The couple wouldn't be back for approximately two weeks because they went to New York for their honeymoon and then on to Germany to talk to a client.

The two of them decided to wait until the honeymooners returned. They wanted to at least see this Elizabeth Barrow in person before they left.

The couple did return, and they tracked Elizabeth's movements. A zoom camera took pictures of her. One day they heard her voice in the back room of the coffee shop and were sure it was Queenie.

They also met Scott's former girlfriend who was disheartened about the whole affair. The old girlfriend missed Scott who didn't seem to want to be around her anymore. She didn't like Elizabeth at all but didn't know much about her. The old girlfriend knew that was what bothered her the most. That made her wonder if Scott knew anything about his wife.

The old girlfriend went to the house and would talk to him about that very thing. First, her friend at the bank might divulge information if Elizabeth owned any strange accounts. The friend told her about the three lockboxes. Then, the old girlfriend drove at a high rate of speed to Scott's house for a serious chat with him. She didn't believe she was meddling in someone's affairs. She told Scott that he should hire someone to follow Elizabeth and check out her background.

Scott told the old girlfriend, "Stop involving yourself in my personal affairs. I'm sure there is a perfectly good reason for my wife renting the three lockboxes. I trust her. I would trust her with my life."

Scott confronted Elizabeth about the lockboxes at the bank when she came home. She wondered how he knew but then he saw her necklace of keys and hadn't asked about them before this time. Sitting down with him on their new living room couch, she explained.

"A friend did pass on and there were two objects which I obtained, and later, I bought the third one directly from an auction clerk's brother. There are three very old, gold art pieces that are wrapped in black velvet pouches, and I did place them each inside my bank lockboxes."

She let the information sink in.

"I thought about selling them through an auction house, but never found time to do it. One time I did send a photo and my expectations on price to an auction house, but then my mind knew the time wasn't right for selling my objects. Now that I do own a third eagle piece, all the items are probably more valuable. At this point, I don't have any idea their worth."

Scott knew nothing about antiques.

"I met you and our life became a whirlwind."

"Our life is an amazing whirlwind and fun riding horses." Scott kissed her.

"I am glad that this antique business between us is over with. Your gold pieces are important to you. You don't need to worry about selling them, because I make enough money. You can always talk to me if you want more money."

"I appreciate that, but I will be glad to show the objects to you."

"I never was into antiques and don't really care to view your eagle objects. If they were horses, that might have been another story. Maybe I can view them next year when we aren't so busy."

24   Elizabeth's Overthrow Plan

THE POLO HORSE babies were fun, and she liked to play with them when the mother was eating. There were fresh baskets of carrots for the horses every week. She fed the mothers the hard, fresh crunchy nutritious carrots, and smiled. That's what raw carrots were made for.

She learned quickly about Scott's business. He introduced her to his clients and taught her about breeding horses. Once they were married, he showed her his fortune and business books. The money he made from his business was more than his inheritance.

"I have gained sufficient knowledge of everything. It was time to steal some money. My plan should work."

Every morning when they were in town, they went for a ride on the regular horses to a small lake on the property and took their clothes off. Scott would make love to her on the cold grass. They would enter the lake and have more sex.

"You are my fantasy come true. Sometimes you receive a massage from me when you are spectacular." Scott enjoyed her massages and performed every time to please them both.

A wood baton was made that she carried inside her saddle to move tree branches out of the way. She had a second one made with a lead weight in it. She practiced in the morning moving the weight into a pattern of exercises to strengthen her arms. Elizabeth looked like a circling tiger after its prey in her mirror.

She thought about the special baton. "A few hits and you will be out for enough time. I can then disappear, leaving the authorities to believe someone forced me to transfer the money while they kidnapped me."

Elizabeth found out that a woman and a bodyguard died in the car bomb in Africa. There was a mix-up of the cars.

"If the Tiger is alive, then I'm in grave danger. It was too dangerous to stay."

Elizabeth looked at the pile of tape she had accumulated on Scott's desk. It was huge. She must have found the other carton of tape in his desk drawer. She couldn't remember finding the other tape. She knew that she was losing it. There was no amount of tape that would create a large enough safety net that she required. It would take a boat-load of tape to cover just the room. Elizabeth felt threatened. No, she felt lost and didn't know where to turn. Her life was in massive turmoil. There were no smiles in this room filled with tape. She needed to leave. Run was resounding everywhere in her mind.

The Tiger person she had known would harm Scott. She needed money to leave and would take her gold antiquities. Selling them now was out of the question. When she could, Elizabeth would figure out a way to give Scott back the money she stole.

Elizabeth knew that she must leave. There was peril happening. She couldn't breathe. Moving was hard and the phone rang. It was the house phone and she must answer it. Elizabeth must function. She didn't want to pick up the noisy instrument. She gulped a breath of fresh air and tackled the phone.

Scott's old girlfriend called the house to see if Scott talked to her about her bank items. Elizabeth shuddered. This woman was too much and was constantly in her and Scott's life. She felt her throat constricting. Then, her courage returned with a vengeance. How dare this woman intervene in her life? It was crossing the line. Elizabeth let her have it. She unleashed her anger at this stupid, alien person. If she was leaving, then she could let whatever fall.

Elizabeth told her, "My husband always talks to me. He loves me absolutely, totally, beyond your comprehension," and she hung up.

What did this person matter in her life? She was having her own issues. How dare the other woman barge in right now? She couldn't handle it. It was minor, like a nasty bug in the night.

"Let the bug light take care of her. Poof, electricity at its finest hour. No, make that a snap-it in half-a-second. Gone, gone, for good."

Elizabeth thought there ought to be a book about how to convincingly kill all your enemies. The sale of that item should run in the millions. Elizabeth felt that she was flaking out, but there was the girlfriend on the phone to deal with. She looked at the house phone and wondered why it was there. They should drop the service. No one used this phone other than the bad-ass girlfriend. Maybe she should call to disconnect the service. It was a thought to consider.

Elizabeth now knew, "What a nosy bitch and she talked to my husband about my lockboxes at the small bank. The girlfriend, obviously, had connections at the bank. I wish that I could take care of that little forever-nagging problem of an old girlfriend. Killing her would be too good a solution."

Elizabeth walked toward the door. She saw the pool house. She was getting a migraine.

"Maybe I could introduce her to one of those rich boat boys in Miami who would drop the old girlfriend overboard in the Bahamas."

She knew that woman made her more frustrated every day.

Elizabeth threw the pile of decimated tape away in the large garbage bin outside their residence so Scott wouldn't find it. She felt relieved to hide her problem with tape. She knew it was obsessive. There was no reason to cut the tape. It made no sense to her. But, somehow peeling the tape off helped.

She didn't understand it; but believed afterwards, she became calm. Maybe that was the key, she didn't need to understand things. She had to accept those facts as truth. There were stresses in her life that created the tape mess.

Calm was what she would reach for in the future. Maybe seeing a psychologist would help, but not now. There was plenty of time to check out her maniacal tape problem. She walked back toward Scott and their magnificent home. The cell phone in her pocket rang. She saw that it was her people from work.

The lady supervisor from her coffee shop called and told her there was a younger couple that asked questions about her from Miami. They were at the coffee shop now if she wanted to meet them. Elizabeth was due for her hair appointment in an hour and decided to leave a few minutes early to check out the people at her shop. Then she would make one more stop to get her three objects out of her bank lockboxes.

Elizabeth was clueless what awaited her down the road. Revenge spilled onto her life like a raging flood, sucking everything into its horrific wake. Her enemy tried to pull her world down. The blinding pain would almost make her wish that she had died. But there was more than one enemy and that would push her. She would choose life and fight back.

25   Jungle Man

THE JUNGLE MAN dragged the fallen female target over the ground through the trees to the field of high hay. He had forgotten to use the solution on the tip of the spear to knock the woman out. The man knew he was slipping on the job. He pulled out the razor-sharp spear. He had, however, remembered to sharpen it this morning and clean the blade. That's what took time. He raised it high to his gods before coming in for the final blow. The jungle man was paid highly for this kill. He was told her name was Elizabeth or Queenie.

He laughed because it didn't matter what her name was. To him, she was already dead.

Elizabeth came to and saw the man with her blurred vision caused by the wound. She was disoriented and wondered if she was at the circus. Her mind raced around and round on some merry-go-round, out of control. She saw a beautiful tiger on her merry-go-round. She thought it was plastic until the tiger moved. It was standing in tall grass. Where did the grass come from? The grass didn't look real. It looked like hay.

She tried to lift her hand and thought the tiger moved closer. The animal was in stealth mode, approaching silently. She liked the tiger for some unknown reason. Why was the tiger so secretive? His huge paws silently lifted from the earthen ground. Did tigers learn to do that? And if so, why? Was there danger near? Too many questions rolled through her dulled mind. Her heart was racing faster than her mind. She could hear it beat with each step of the tiger.

She looked back at the man standing over her. The mud and dried grass caked on her wound, slowing the blood flow. The man's image cleared, and she thought he must belong to the caravan of odd creatures at the carnival, like the person who held snakes or the three-legged woman. Billboard pictures flew past of the circus signs when she was a child. She couldn't recall a jungle man frame. The man looked foreign to her. She hurt and didn't know why?

"Where am I?"

The jungle man vision cleared. She saw her new reality. It wasn't a dream or a past image. This was real. The jungle man existed. She was in danger. No, she was in imminent failure on the living scale. She wanted to live. The metal on the spear gleamed in the sunlight. He raised the spear higher, and then she remembered her attackers. She knew he was going to kill her.

She barely whispered, "Felidae."

The jungle man looked at the wounded woman's eyes. He wished she hadn't spoken.

"Who was Felidae?"

The young woman's eyes cleared to mirror glass reflecting his stark image. Then, the jungle man couldn't believe what he saw. He rubbed his eyes to remove any sweat. In her eyes, he saw a ferocious golden tiger with bared, very sharp saber teeth. He must have a fever, because the saber-toothed tiger had been extinct since the ice age. The evil man shook his head and realized that it was just one tiger. He could handle an aged tiger.

The tiger's ancestors suddenly stood behind the beautiful male tiger. The animals were standing ready. The tigers roared loudly, magnifying their voices together in one terrifying sound. The tiger, protector of the forest, was shielding the downed woman.

"This vision is crazy. The woman must be a witch or something worse."

He looked around. Something was watching him. He could feel the thing was close. Then he realized. She was in the tiger's protected forest. He kicked at the hay. The woman was the Goddess who tamed and rode the tiger. He heard of such a thing a long time ago. The tiger and the Goddess would fight a dragon with their combined ferociousness. They would fight anything that came to harm them. He was reminded of the story. If he killed her, they would ride immortal together.

"Superstition or true?"

The birds in the trees stopped chirping and the silence became eerie. Where did the birds go? They were hiding. They were out of danger. He didn't want to look at her. He knew what he saw might be true. The downed woman was the something that meant worse. It wasn't worse for her. The situation had been reversed.

"I'm a mere jungle man."

The creatures in her eyes looked more ferocious as they crouched.

He remembered trying to kill a tiger once as a young warrior and failed. But he was older now, except there were also too many. He could remember the thing staring at him when he was young. His spear had fallen short. His spear should have hit the tiger. It always bothered him that the tiger got away.

As a small child, he learned from his father about the golden tiger and its reign. Anyone that hurt the golden tiger was doomed. If he killed the protected woman in the tiger's forest, he and his family would perish. The jungle man heard his father's warning drums. He didn't want to see the vision anymore and avoided her eyes. He thought the tiger wore a small gold crown. He couldn't be sure it was part of the animal's fur.

His father's stories could have been filled with hysterical voodoo. Madness was always part of his father's stories. The jungle man couldn't believe he heard his father's drums. The vision he saw now was beyond the earth in a realm of the outer worlds. The woman and her tigers were real. The jungle man had enough.

Fearing for his life, he lowered his spear and quickly backed away from the imaginative animal world of the ancients. He backed away because he was told that he must never run from the wild creatures. The jungle man heard a rustling in the grass. The thing was there. He knew it. Fear coiled around him like a demented eagle or fierce dragon which was filled with fire, spraying the countryside and anything in its path. The thing in the grass would kill him. He must leave immediately. Suddenly, remembering the keys were part of this deal, he looked for the keys. They were around her neck. He laid the spear down to show the tiger that he meant no harm anymore to the woman. The gold chain was yanked from her neck and he quickly retrieved two keys.

The grass moved closer.

"This whole scene is wrong." The jungle man slid his spear toward him and stepped away. He looked back at the woman one more time searching the grasses. There was a glow from the sun in one spot. It was a reflection that blinded his eyes. He rubbed them. The tow truck engine diverted his attention. The woman was not worth his time nor the creature thing in the grass, but her car was important to get out of sight. The road was empty, but someone could come along any minute. His female comrade in crime with the gun was waiting for him. She called to him, bringing him back from insanity. The red sports car meant more money. He wanted money. It was always about women and money.

After leaving her in the guardian forest, Elizabeth drifted in and out of consciousness for ten minutes. She awoke and knew that she still lived. She saw the same ancient vision of tigers, heard the silence, and then strange drums. There were noises on the road and then more silence. Or almost silence. The wind seemed to separate the sheaves of long grass for some reason.

The third key lay by the side of her arm.

Her red sports car was loaded on the tow truck with purse and car keys removed. A white plastic cover was placed over the vehicle and tied down. The jungle man drove the tow truck to a chop house and received his money. He was glad to escape the tiger and its ancestry. The jungle man knew she would live and he was safe from the reign of the tiger. He didn't care about the man that hired him because he was a fly in his world. The jungle man would lie to the Sphinx. He had done it before.

The jungle man went to the rendezvous point to meet with the dark-haired girl. The dark-haired girl stole Elizabeth's identification card, money, and two keys. She headed to the bank. She retrieved two black velvet bags from two large lockboxes and put them into a brown shopping bag instead of the large purse.

The shopping bag was left with a man waiting at a table across from the coffee shop. The dark girl picked up a smaller bag that was laying on the table. The girl and jungle man disappeared. Tiger Black went to the airport and flew back to London.

XXXXXX

Hamm and Karine knew something was wrong because Elizabeth didn't make her hair appointment. They drove slowly back toward the horse estate. Hamm stopped the vehicle because he saw blood in the gravel.

He told Karine to stay in the car. He followed the trail and saw Elizabeth on the ground with blood on her shirt lying in the tall hay. He saw the third key by her arm and picked it up. It was the bank key.

Elizabeth saw Hamm Roe and tried to speak. She needed his help. Hamm gave her a baleful glance. He maliciously spoke, "The two brothers did hold the bottom part of the scepter, but then you somehow managed to buy it before I could murder them. You caused me a lot of time and money. I'm going to take what is mine."

His decision made, Hamm didn't look at her anymore either nor help her but left the wounded woman to die. He didn't see the vision because he hadn't touched or tried to wound her.

Hamm went back to the rental car. He told her Elizabeth was dead. Karine wanted to call the police immediately. He told her they should wait a bit after they left the area, so they didn't get into trouble. They drove back to the motel room. He told Karine to pack and he would get gas.

He drove to the bank instead and opened an account. Then he changed the deposit number on his card to Elizabeth's key number. He always carried a special ink solution with him. He went back into the bank and a different guard inserted the magic key and then his key to open the lockbox. The removed item was put under his dark shirt.

Hamm hid the items in his large travel backpack, refueled the rental vehicle, and picked up sandwiches, chips, water, and soda. They were leaving the area. Halfway to the airport, Karine made him stop and ask the gas station person if he could use their phone. It was a small one with no cameras. Pretending to call the police, he talked into the buzzing phone. They flew back to Miami.

Karine broke up with Hamm and found a job at the mall where David liked to buy his expensive shoes. She didn't like the fact that Hamm lied. She also didn't like his crazy obsession with finding these eagle objects.

Plus, she began to become afraid, because he told her that he saw Elizabeth dead. Then Elizabeth's body disappeared from the field per the newspapers. She wasn't sure what he saw that day. She knew he hadn't called the police and lied about that.

Karine thought there was something seriously wrong with Hamm. There was no empathy about Queenie or Elizabeth's disappearance. The whole episode with Hamm was unreal and very off. There were more lies in his story. She was sure of it. Her mind told her what she must do next, "Run was the message on her brain".

Run, she did.

26   Elizabeth Missing

SCOTT WASN'T DISTRAUGHT until eight o'clock in the evening. Sometimes his wife stopped back at her coffee shop to order supplies and do her books. He called the shop and her cell. There was no answer. He called one of the girls from the shop at her home. She hadn't seen Elizabeth all day. Her hairdresser also called the shop because she missed her hair appointment. Scott was now worried and called one of his high school friends who was a local cop.

His friend, Ben, drove out to pick him up and they drove around town looking for her vehicle. On the way to Scott's estate, the headlight caught the blood. They stopped and with flashlights looked at the heavy tire tracks in the gravel. Then they followed the trail of blood through the trees to the bloodied spot of flattened hay. Scott found the gold broken chain and Ben told him not to touch anything. He called for additional backup. Before the rest of the police arrived, a fine mist started to fall.

Elizabeth figured it was her wooden baton exercises that strengthened her arms. The strength helped her remove the knit slacks and apply them like a tourniquet to stanch the blood. She awakened from her unconscious state in time. Felidae had rubbed her hair in her dream. He waited until Hamm left before approaching her. He was the rustle of the grasses she heard. The rustle scared the jungle man off. She was sure of it.

She rolled over, got to her knees, and stumbled back out of the woods the same way she was dragged in. She saw the truck tracks. Those tracks fueled her anger. She would live. She walked a short distance on the road and made it to their pool house. The pool camera was disabled by her earlier. She also called the security company that day in the morning to let them know there was a problem and she contacted the repair people to fix the chewed wire from a rodent. They would be there when she was long gone.

Drinking some orange juice first, she popped two pain pills in her mouth and swallowed. Elizabeth knew she must find super energy to get through this ordeal. She hard-wired her brain to not think of the pain. She told herself she could do this. She needed to just pretend she was running in a marathon.

"Breathe, breathe, girl. You will make it. You can't run, but you can walk and ride."

The pills were taking the extreme pain to a softer razor edge. Her tiger saved her. She needed to honor him by surviving.

"Felidae, I love you."

Washing in the pool house shower with cool water, she found the antiseptic and sewed the front part of the wound. She took tape and tried to tape the wound in the back closed as best she could. Then she put more antiseptic on. Taking super large bands of cotton sterile gauze, she placed them over the wounds. The antiseptic helped stick to the gauze. Then she wrapped additional stretchy, rolled bandage around her body. Stretchy bandages added more pressure around her body to compress the wound. She went to the closet and put on a zip stretch top, pants, and dark shoes. Elizabeth found her dark cap and sunglasses and bankroll of money with new identification card. She found her other sets of penicillin and pain killer pills. The scissors, extra gauze, bandages, and antiseptic were put in the bag with another set of clothes and the medicine. She wrapped all the towels, old clothes, and garbage in a roll and fastened a bungie around the roll. Elizabeth would put those in a dumpster far away.

Checking the room and shower one last time, she grabbed several bottles of cold water out of the refrigerator. She picked up her money and keys and left to get the motor bike hidden in an old shed on the edge of the property. It was a small distance from the pool house, but far enough away from the house. She put her rain slicker on because a fine mist descended. The mist would dilute and wash away the crime scene. Elizabeth put on the wig and helmet. Her motor bike started immediately, and she took off heading west, sitting very straight in the bike seat so as not to break the tape on her back. There was an old dirt road that connected to the highway. She alternated her hands steering. Her youth, strength, and determination pushed herself and the bike down the long road.

"I can lead my killer as far away from you as possible. It is all my fault. I don't deserve you or your beautiful polo lifestyle. Trouble will always find me and hurt everything I touch. I'm the problem."

The beating she received from her first boyfriend long ago pushed all the negative images of herself forward into her mind.

"I am making the right decision. You will be safe." Scott must remain safe. He was the one that was good. He didn't deserve this mess.

"I've never ever been good. What did I do that was good?"

Elizabeth saw in her mind the scary jungle man ready to kill her. Then she saw her sweet tiger who loved her in her mind. *"The golden tiger is the one thing that was good. The tiger is my obsession now."*

Scott shouldn't pay for her bad decisions and past. She needed to leave. Elizabeth felt guilty, because she planned to leave him anyway. He just didn't know it. Once he knew her plans and her past, he wouldn't want her ever. She could feel his disgust towards her. Her lying to him was major. She was being proactive.

"I shouldn't have come here. Ow, I'm in pain."

The pills were barely working. The bad man only wanted her. She would lead him away. She knew how to hide. He would give up finding her here. Her mind kept circling from the shock and pain. The lights from the merry-go-round went out. She blinked and could barely see the tarred road. She knew it was now dark. She finally turned on the motorbike lights.

"You will be smart, Scott, and eventually marry your silly old girlfriend."

Elizabeth convinced herself leaving was the only choice.

She revved the engine to a higher speed. She needed to rest. Elizabeth drove the last fifty miles thinking about her beloved tiger boy. "The tiger is like me, unwanted until I did find him." It was great timing that she found her creature.

"You're part of a beautiful, fearless heritage. You are an animal I will protect."

Elizabeth didn't understand she was reacting to great duress and was close to a major breakdown. Her judgment was impaired by the pain and confusion that happened. She always ran. It was her only reaction to difficult situations. It was her way to solve an abnormal situation. Her coping mechanism meant escape as fast as you can. She never waited for police or explanations. It was easier not to give any. Her decision to leave changed everything. She would realize later she was running from love, the human kind. Scott wouldn't have been afraid to help her. She was the one being dysfunctional.

The leased old gas station garage was seventy-five miles away in a small out-of-the-way town. In the breakroom, she previously stocked the tiny refrigerator with three weeks of food. There was a soft leather couch, low table for magazines and books with a standing lamp nearby. She replaced the furniture and most everything with new, comfortable accommodations. When she left, the owner would be surprised. A new notebook computer with Wi-Fi, and a new cell phone sat on the table with the new microwave. The computer would keep her up-to-date plus she loaded some movies to watch. Everything in the room was repainted and new carpet installed to make it more habitable.

Elizabeth stored the bike in the garage stall, shutting the door with her remote. She was glad she installed one. She limped to the inside door of the garage. It would be her haven for a little while. The blood-soaked bandage needed changing. First, she heated some sandwiches from the freezer in the microwave. They tasted like sawdust, and she picked up her bottle of gin. The gin couldn't hurt. Antiseptic went through her brain. What berry made gin? She forgot. She was pleased with herself because her brain was firing a little.

"Of course, juniper berries."

The food meant energy. She was tired. Grabbing the soft warm blanket and wrapping it gently around her damaged body because her teeth were chattering, she knew she was going to miss Scott's healthy, gourmet-conscious chef. The rain slicker was still on her body. She slept a few hours.

The nightmare of a jungle man brought her into a wide-awake state. Her heart was pounding with fear. She calmed down when she surveyed her surroundings. The boogey man was gone. She was alone. She was safe for the moment.

She got up from the couch in massive pain. The pain pills wore off. Her rain slicker hid her jacket with the dried blood. It began oozing again when she moved the jacket. Removing her clothes, she finally stepped in the small bathroom looking at the ashen-faced woman in the mirror.

The entire bathroom was replaced with newer tile, fixtures, and a hot water tank by the owner because his insurance company paid for it when a former tenant destroyed things. Elizabeth leaned on the cool tiles. She knew there was a fever, because she was hot and cold. The pills would fix the problem, but now the shower awaited her.

She turned on the cool-warm shower water. She waited for the water to soften the blood, bleed a little, and stop. Then she carefully dried herself and put new antiseptic on the wounds. She considered the reflection of herself in the mirror. The steam still lingered around the edges. Elizabeth didn't recognize the woman in the glass. She felt distorted, half there and half not. She was the fog on the edges. Slowing the realization hit her. She was only a ghost of herself, changing so many times to fit some other way of life. Elizabeth took the scissors and cut piles of tape, one strip at a time. There was white tape on the mirror and the sink. She kept cutting and cutting until she reached the end of the roll. She stared at the empty roll, not comprehending. She didn't know what she was doing.

Elizabeth slipped down to the floor weeping for her past life. There was only emptiness. There was devastation. It was the tape. She was crying over tape. Finally, she got up. Using the mirror as a guide, she found the bandage material and slapped several pieces of tape over the gauze. She wrapped herself in fresh stretchy bandage. She cut off all her feelings at the damage. There were plastic surgeons in her future if she made it. She had to make it. Securely tucking the last piece in, she was exhausted.

She left the bathroom blitz of tape. She was glad there were many more rolls of the stuff. She would clean it up in the morning. The tape hadn't been a waste after all. The tape was significant. It was her way of protecting herself.

Elizabeth laughed. Her feelings were swinging left and right. Currently, they were way right. She wanted to swing again and dance in a room with chandeliers or walk on a beautiful beach. What a funny thought? She would play ball again with her tiger boy. He loved the balls just like the polo horses did at their match.

She remembered the ping pong balls she tried at the first warehouse. She bought a package of ten balls. The tiger crushed all of them and brought them back to her one by one. There were ten crushed ping pong balls at her feet. The animal looked proud.

Elizabeth looked in the bathroom mirror.

"Hold on, girl. Be proud. You are going to look and be great again."

The image looked back at her. It was the too pale girl with large staring eyes. Her hair was a knotted tangle. She was a person looking like a junkie after an all-night dose of meth with heavy marijuana thrown in. She wondered if marijuana helped.

"How did I get here? No marijuana required because the brain was ricocheting enough. Think, Elizabeth. You have a bucket list. Find the magic. You should take one ping pong ball at a time. It doesn't matter that they are crushed. You can do it. Learn the lesson. Forget the tape. Go wash your hair. No, maybe tomorrow. Tomorrow will be fine to begin." It took three more days before she cared enough to wash her hair or comb it.

Elizabeth took more headache pills. Time was what she needed. That was the secret to survival. She went back to the warm blanket and couch collapsing until morning. She dreamed of polo horses running in a match. She was sitting in the stands yelling for them to win. Winning was on the list of wants. She repeated the process for the next fifteen days. She put the tape away after two strokes with the scissors. Elizabeth was in control again.

"Or rather feebly in control was more like it."

The pain subsided. Finally, she decided it was safe to leave the garage. Elizabeth felt closer to her normal state of mind. Her rental car was parked three weeks ago, and was close to the ramp. The windows in the garage were painted with a white washable substance which hid the car from site. She encountered no problem riding the motor bike up the small ramp and laying the bike into the large car's trunk. She left the garage.

Staying at small motels until she reached Los Angeles, finally she stopped running. The rental car was turned in at the airport. She was good at improvising and disappearing like a chameleon.

Watching the Alabama news once, they listed her as *Missing*. The police found strange tire tracks on the road and it looked like a body was dragged to a field. Her gold chain was found broken in the spot in the field. The police collected some blood samples and they belonged to Elizabeth Barrow because they matched her blood taken before she married. Foul play was suspected in her disappearance and her vehicle was also missing.

Scott, her husband told the news man, "I'm vowing to you and the media that I will find my wife and bring anyone who harms my beloved to justice."

Somewhere on the road, Elizabeth changed her hair to a redhead and cut it with the scissors in a short straight bob with bangs. The wig was thrown away. She bought low intensity eyeglasses at the drugstore and used them upon checking into a motel. She bought dark baggie, flowered hairdresser tops so no one would notice her figure or bother her. Boring was her new look.

Once in Los Angeles, she found an apartment and stocked it with food and supplies. Then she took time to check her wounds and make tentative plans. The scratches on her face and back healed as did the front scar on her chest. The back scar was bumpy. She would have to find a plastic surgeon.

She bought exercise knit outfits, running shoes, and a new beige hat to blend in with the other joggers on the beautiful sand beach. Walking and jogging on the beach everyday helped her become stronger. Her body became fit, toned, and tanned.

"I love being close to the water again and I'm feeling warmed by the gorgeous sunshine. It reminds me of the freedom I did feel when I lived in Miami."

The everyday fresh air took away the ashen face and bolstered her spirit. Elizabeth Banks Barrow was a casualty for sure. She couldn't think about Scott anymore. Erasure of the past was required. She would use her new identity.

"I can't remember what my new name is?"

She took out the card again, it read, "Ara Landt". She repeated her name over and over. It wasn't sticking in her brain. Maybe she received a small concussion when she fell. There were still headaches. She tried to recall when was the last time she ate any food. She told Ara to try, because she was out of the chaos and alive. "Eat some food, girl. No, eat some nutritious food, like a good girl, Ara."

She knew who her enemies were. Ara also knew the gold antiquities were stolen and by whom. She should have sold them when there was an opportunity. It was money gone.

Ara would need to be ready for her next stage entrance, but she would take a month or two off first to get well and find a doctor. She was too tired to be angry about her lost prior world. Ara felt alone and missed her tiger and polo babies. "I know my tiger saved me."

She also missed Scott a little and thought he loved her. She thought maybe she loved him, too, and cried a final time. Emptiness surrounded the walls of her apartment. The soft blanket did nothing to soothe. It reminded her of the animals that loved her unconditionally. They waited for her touch. Ara shook her head. Her life was in a mess, a very complicated disaster zone. Ara wanted to stay in her equestrian way of living. She could try to be good, but felt it was too perilous for both. Her mortal enemy was on the loose. There was no use thinking about it. She knew the Sphinx would not stop his revenge mission.

"I don't know what to do with boundless human love where Scott is concerned. I don't know what to do with either man."

It was such a foreign idea to her brain. She didn't believe she could be an average person, living the life others lived. The police wouldn't understand. They would be skeptical of her story. Only foreseeing trouble, she must remain hidden. Hiding was crucial to her survival from the evil man.

"Speaking of brain, I'm also having more nightmares." The jungle man reappeared in her mind and was as scary looking as before. His spear had more bones.

Ara shivered. "Just so it wasn't my bones."

She hadn't made any friends, not trusting anyone and fearing someone would recognize her. She needed to eventually see a regular doctor. Her stash of pain pills was gone.

Ara would start drinking more water and juice to see if that helped fortify her body. She needed to take better care of herself and eat healthy salads. She stopped looking in the mirror so much, because she didn't want to see herself. Her mind and body had been stripped bare of emotion. She was raw from over exposure. Time would happen and make her stronger. The sun would wash the bad away. The warmth would free her true soul. She would live.

Reaching this beautiful beach at sunrise, she ran and remembered other sunrises with Scott. Then she forced her brain somewhere else. It was an effort to focus and notice her environment. She saw the seagulls, the sand, and a wave, anything to forget sweet sorrow for her past life. Ara needed to mourn her past. She mourned and found renewal. A beginning day opened, and beauty surrounded her. The past would always exist, but she knew how to push it behind her. The light was waiting. Ara held her arms open to grab all the incoming light. She was ready. The early morning light enveloped her.

The warm and sunny days were the quintessential Southern California experience. She visited all the tourist sites and took the ferry to Catalina Island from Dana Point. She treated herself to an expensive restaurant meal at a large hotel overlooking Hollywood Hills.

She thrived again enjoying the open-air ocean front view and homes as she jogged past. The lush tropical plants, flowers, and trees were adding to the pleasurable place. She went to concerts in Laguna and walked on sawdust while watching glassblowers make a very large drinking glass. Ara was adapting to her surroundings.

One day she laughed at some children trying to surf close to shore. The children looked beautiful, free, and were having fun. She was surprised she could laugh. It had been so long. The nothingness feeling had disappeared. The fog had cleared in her brain. She was a whole young woman again. How did she know this fact? It was because Ara missed fun. Fun times were what she required now, but first she needed to fix the body and buy pink nail polish, shoes, and new clothes. A little makeup couldn't hurt.

"Yes, a new person is moving forward again. No more hesitation in my step to slow me down. I'm ready."

27   Jack Jones the Doctor

HE WATCHED HER walk and sometimes run down the beach every day early in the morning and was fascinated by her. She was a redhead with a slim, nice curvy figure. Her hair touched her shoulders and swayed with her movement. He could tell she was young. She wore a beige hat and tight knit pants and top. He felt something he hadn't felt in a long time. Jack didn't recognize the emotion until the fifth time he saw her on the beach. He wanted her.

One morning she wasn't there. He wondered where she went and if she would come back. He became anxious because the second day, there was no beautiful girl running.

The third day, he saw her. She bought a new hat. He went to his high-powered telescope. It had become a dust collector because he never used it. The telescope was a gift a long time ago from his first wife. She liked to look at the young men on the beach. He saw her head turn.

It read "Catalina Island." That's where she went. Then he moved the lens to see her face. The young woman was pretty.

"Very nice. Who is this person and where do you live? Why are you running?"

179

Jack put the telescope away in a closet in the spare bedroom. He wondered if he could sell it online to get rid of the snoopy thing. It contained bad memories like the couch he dumped off at the charity place with a rental truck one day. His neighbor helped him load it. It was one of those times that he couldn't stand to look at the despicable couch another minute.

He was a lucrative plastic surgeon and drove to his office in downtown Los Angeles. He was older and was divorced. His two children were grown and lived on the east coast, so he rarely saw them.

His girlfriend moved on when he told her, "I refuse to get married again."

Jack just didn't want to marry anyone just yet. He needed some space.

He laughed, because, "Why am I looking at the woman outside my window? So much for space."

Jack used to run the beach when he was younger and not so busy. He remembered the salty smell of the ocean, the birds spiraling, and the surf pounding the earth. It was exhilarating to be down there feeling that morning light and rush.

He knew the woman felt the rush. Jack wanted to join her. Maybe he needed to take the time and walk the beach. Jack would have to think about that one. He could sit out on his deck and see if she saw him.

The girl looked lonely somehow. He wasn't sure if he met her, what he would say to her. It had been a long time since he needed to flirt with a woman. He saw women patients all the time, but their conversations were about what business they could afford. He could afford to quit his business if he wanted. His ex-wife had her own money. Their divorce was amicable. He rarely saw her. She ran in different circles than he did. Jack went to work in his expensive sports car.

Ara saw the sports car move out of the driveway from the beach house and head toward Los Angeles. She missed her sports car too, and was envious. She stopped to look at the houses in this area of the beach town. They were probably in the ten to fifteen-million-dollar range. Ara thought, "Nice area."

Moving in the direction she parked her motor bike, she hurried up the steps.

"Dr. Jones, your patient, Ara Landt is ready in the next room," said his nurse assistant.

Dr. Jones read her chart as to why she was at his business office. She had two scars that she would like to disappear. He smiled because he was good at making things disappear. She carried no insurance that would cover, and she would pay cash. She currently was not employed, but produced an adequate funds letter from her bank. He walked into the room. There were no mirrors in this room. He was glad she was standing and staring at the ocean and couldn't see his expression. The girl was, "My dreamy morning beach girl. I can't believe it."

He took her outstretched warm hand and said, "Hello, nice to meet, let me check your name again."

"It's Ara Landt," said the young woman.

"How can I help you?" He never forgot names, but somehow stumbled with hers. He felt like an idiot.

181

Motioning her to step up onto the doctor exam table, she sat on the padded leather table with white paper. She explained there were two scars from a spear fishing accident that she wanted fixed.

"Where did the accident occur, and was there a police report number?"

She made a move to step off the table. He stopped her and said, "It is a standard question. I'm required to ask. Please sit down."

Jack didn't want her to leave. He didn't know why he said it, but he told her, "It will be all right."

She relaxed and let him see her two scars. That spear must have hurt. This woman was familiar with abnormal pain. He also noticed an older long scar from a prior plastic surgery. The scar which almost covered the length on her face repaired nicely. Jack thought he shouldn't probably ask that surgeon's name.

He bet there were some broken, healed bones that would show up on x-rays. He asked her about prior surgeries and implants. She explained she had some in her cheeks. He was surprised. He explained his process, procedure, and costs. She wanted to proceed as soon as possible. His nurse assistant took her to x-ray, and she made her next appointment.

At the end of the day, he looked at her x-rays.

He drove home and pulled out an old bottle of whiskey and opened it. He thought about the girl named Ara. Jack saw the perfection that must have existed in her body originally. Someone or something was unkind to her. She had hired a good plastic surgeon in the past to change and repair her. He knew she was a runner, probably from the police as well as someone who damaged her.

"Who would want to hurt such a beautiful woman?"

Jack needed to understand, "Why?"

The blade narrowly missed vital organs and there were old and new broken bones. Jack felt the woman needed someone strong. He was strong and wasn't doing anything important. His life was getting too dull.

Jack knew he was moving toward deep water. Bored with his life and ready for change, he felt exhilarated. His ex-wife would tell him that he was a fool. His wife always knew what was in his mind and heart. Jack knew what he needed.

"Screw my ex-wife. You found pool boy whom you allowed to sleep on that stupid couch in my house."

Jack made his decision. He wanted a different life. He waited long enough. He was going to check the pretty woman out. She could live in his hemisphere. The woman who ran past his beach touched him. His old life was easily thrown away. He felt better already.

28   Ara and Date Night

IT TOOK OVER two months because the back scar needed to be recut, and the badly healed skin removed. Once that problem resolved itself, then they worked on any scar removal. It was her last appointment with him and he told her she was done as his patient.

She agreed. Her back looked better. The doctor had magic fingers. It was why his business was exceptional. He was more than exceptional.

"Would you like to go for a drive sometime down the coast and eat dinner? I have a favorite place that I like to eat on occasion. It is a wonderful steak and seafood restaurant. The place also has amazing salads if she was vegetarian."

Ara liked the man and felt warm inside whenever she saw him.

"I would love to feel the ocean breeze with you and eat something different and any kind of food geared toward heavenly gourmet. Steak sounds so much better. I dream of a thick juicy steak at night. The thicker the better is my favorite meal. I am tired of seafood currently because it is on all the cheaper restaurant menus. Also, I'm giving up on stale bread with jalapeno bologna. Even peanut butter is sounding good, but I intensely do not like that stuff."

"There is not one jar of peanut butter in my house. I love juicy steak. What is wrong with the jalapeno bologna? I prefer my jalapeno bologna in lettuce wraps. I can make you some next time. We can feed the stale bread to the birds."

The man hadn't mentioned carrots.

She was glad. "I do like the green stuff called lettuce and I could bring the jarred red peppers if you can provide the wine," said Ara.

"I will buy a whole case of wine just to eat jarred red peppers with lettuce and bologna. It's always better to eat a meal with someone across the table. I know exactly where to find wine in the vineyards of heavenly grape country. Don't you know all about California? Fields and fields of the grape stuff. Then there are the peppers, tomatoes, and glorious artichoke fields. Total pure heavenly country exists waiting for us to find."

She knew he was fun. The dinner with him would be enjoyable conversation. She missed talking with men.

He gave her his address because he shouldn't leave his nice car in her unfriendly neighborhood. She found the home easily and sat in his driveway for ten minutes on the motor bike.

"I have run by this house every morning. Did you see me? I wonder?"

Jack was on his phone with a patient and noticed her drive into his paved area on his security system on the computer screen. He wondered why she didn't get off. He told his client he must leave. He raced

185

downstairs, skipping the elevator, and came out to her bike. She already turned the wheel to leave.

Jack said, "Welcome to my humble abode. I did find the perfect vineyard for the case of wine. I can show you the first of many gourmet treasures."

Ara laughed and put the kickstand down while removing her helmet. She swung her leg over and put the keys in her pocket. Ara placed part of her hair in a soft braid to keep it out of the way on the ride over.

He gave her a hug, touched her hair braid lovingly, and led her into his amazing digs.

They drove down the beautiful Highway 1 coast in California in his expensive sports car and ate lobster and steak with another glass of wine. She told him lobster wasn't considered seafood in her world. It was considered the ultimate supreme of delectable and outclassed every food group. There should be an extra slot for lobster on the food chart. Jack hadn't thought about lobster quite that way. It worked for him that she was pleased with dinner. She was showing him the world she lived in. He was having a good time.

He asked about her tattoo. He noticed it in the examination room the first day. He knew it was the tiger species. He liked tigers, but wasn't sure around them. They were very large creatures with big teeth. She must love them. She told him about her wonderful tiger, Felidae.

"Have you ever thought about transferring your tiger to one of the Los Angeles zoos? I do know many people, which I can ask, about how do we accomplish the transfer. Then you can visit your tiger boy when you want and perhaps even touch him like you used to do in an internal cage. Of course, you might have to sign a legal waiver or something that you won't sue for the zoo's protection."

"I haven't thought of that. It is a wonderful idea."

She told him that she should probably find a job soon.

"Let me know if you need any help there."

"I just need some friends now. Thanks."

He invited her back into his wonderful digs.

"Maybe next time," said Ara. She wasn't ready for a relationship. She would need to think about the situation.

Jack was disappointed because he wanted her to stay. He knew not to push women. "I will see you soon."

Ara thought that was a crazy way to tell her he wanted to see her again. He should have asked her outright for another date. She knew she would have to make the next move to see him. He was a gentleman. Jack was cautious since his divorce. He told her briefly and quickly about the ex-wife. It was the quickly part that gave her the clue that the ex-wife hurt him.

He walked her to the bike and kissed her a long goodnight kiss. Ara smiled, and Jack waved her off. It was a week before she called him back.

The next date, they stayed at Jack's place and talked while he cooked pork chops and made a tossed salad. The baked apples with cinnamon and dumplings on top were his special dessert.

He took her into his bedroom and opened the patio door to let the night air and surf sound enter the room. Jack felt unsure how to proceed. He touched her hair again, caressing her cheek as he approached her.

Jack suddenly remembered how things worked and gently took her into his arms. He slowly kissed her soft lips and knew the desire built immensely.

She saw the burning fire in his eyes and gave in to her conflicted feelings. The need had been too long. This incredible man treated her like she was the most exquisite thing he knew on the face of the earth. She wanted him also.

Ara wrapped her arms around him.

He knew how to do this. Then he made love to her the only way he possibly could. It was with his whole heart. It was the beginning for the two of them.

Ara felt that love hit her like an incoming wave. It totally blew her away. It was entrance into an unknown land. For the first time in her life, she felt loved besides the love from her tiger, Felidae. She felt a glimmer of the high wave with Scott.

Jack welcomed and enveloped her into his life.

When his receptionist left, he gave the job to Ara. He convinced her to move in with him because then things would be easier for them to travel. He gave her a credit card and told her to have a good time. The two of them planned trips to exotic places. Jack took her dancing at expensive nightclubs. They went horseback riding.

He started jogging with her on the beach. Friends and lovers combined to form an amazing team.

They went everywhere, but she wouldn't fly through London or go to Africa.

Ara blossomed and so did Jack. She began to feel safe again. His home and office contained the latest technical innovations. One day he took her to a wonderful sports car dealership and told her to pick one. She selected a gold sports car this time because it matched the tiger's eyes.

Ara let her hair grow long and put it back to blonde. Jack went a little crazy. He loved her new look. It was very close to her original way of looking. She was trying to get back to herself, the person she knew and liked before everything went south. She wanted to please him.

Jack was happy and wanted their life together to continue. He couldn't imagine life without her. It wasn't too long before Jack proposed.

29   Ara and Jack's Proposal

"I REALLY WANT to marry you, but it's complicated. Why don't we live together instead?"

"I want to live with you as a married couple and can't understand your reluctance. I imagine your past life was an unhappy one. I did see your battle wounds, but I can help you with finding a therapist. I want you to get through any blockage to a relationship with me. You are very important to me. I love you and want to share my world. That is what marriage is all about. It is being good to each other. It is the best way to live. You are good for me and vice versa. We both need each other. My love for you is huge, larger than the ocean sand that we run on in the early morning."

Ara said, "I want you also. Things between us are good, exceptionally good. Yes, it is more than the ocean sand. Love is new for me, but I feel it with you. But speaking of good, there might lay the problem. What if I'm one of the bad people in the world?"

Jack knew there could be problems. He hadn't wanted them but wasn't afraid. "How bad?"

"Everything in my past is exactly that, a broken-down, bad ass mess. I have done some bad things to get away, but I can't seem to escape. Evil people keep following me. My life is one horrible experience after another. The paths that I have chosen seem to always lead me into high danger. The police will never believe my story. It's way too scary to even think about the events. You are the only thing good besides Felidae that I can relate to."

He said, "Then we'll find lawyers and judges who can help us."

Ara knew it was time to tell Jack. She hadn't wanted to talk about her former husband. It was a tightrope she hadn't counted on taking. Her emotions had been buried since the last time she fell off.

"I'm still legally married to someone who thinks that I am *Missing.*"

Jack was stunned. This knowledge wasn't even remotely on the radar screen or in any of her written application for plastic surgery. Knowledge that there was another man made him not flinch an inch, even though he wanted to. He reasoned that he had picked Ara out of all the women that crossed his life.

"What kind of missing?"

Jack didn't care that she was still married. He reasoned that was an easy fix.

She said, "The situation was more like a kidnapping scenario. Then there existed the other thing or maybe the other thing was much more."

Jack didn't like the word kidnapping, but he encouraged her to tell him everything. He was there to listen.

Ara told her story to him.

"There is an African man who tried to kill me in the past. He was a former lover and drug trafficker. I stole money from the man. I did mean to steal his money because I needed it to live when I chose to escape our life. It was quite a bit of money. The problem is that I stole two valuable gold antiquities which the man received in a drug deal. I stole the objects because I know they are valuable. Unfortunately, the African wanted those two objects and stole them back from me when I lived in Alabama."

Jack said, "We can just pay him the money back. I have lots of money."

Ara told him, "I thought the drug trafficker tried to kill me by cutting my brakes on my sports car when I lived in Miami. Later, I did try to kill him, but somehow the bomb killed his wife and a bodyguard instead. They were, mistakenly, in the African man's car. They shouldn't have been there. The schedule with the drug trafficker man never changed, but that day, it did change. That's where the error came into the problem. I also know about his past drug deals which is why he still wants me to die."

Jack got up and grabbed the old whiskey bottle and poured themselves both a drink.

She told him there was a little more to her story.

He wanted to reply and changed his mind.

"This same African gave me poisoned rum to give to his enemy, a diamond smuggler in London. I did bring the bottle into the residence. I was trying to protect myself because the diamond smuggler's bodyguard told me that I was to be dumped in the river. The diamond smuggler drank the poisoned bottle because he enjoyed his rum. The poison did the job correctly, and he did die. Then there is one more gold antiquity that I bought, probably stolen, that two brothers somehow obtained. The African did hire a jungle man with a sharp spear to kill me when I was married to Scott Barrow from Alabama. I did not die, but fled the scene. Hence, that is when I was listed as missing. My animal caretaker stole the bank lockbox key and retrieved the third antiquity from me before I exited the area which was a hayfield."

Jack shook his head. He had gotten the story, but was struggling with it.

"The animal caretaker left you in the hayfield to die after the African hired a spearman to kill you. Your spearfishing scars were from a hired hit. That's when you lost the three gold antiquities or rather when your bank boxes were robbed."

"Yes, that is exactly right."

She kept in her possession the diamond and drug conversations on tapes of the two men with their clients. The diamond smuggler was dead. The former drug trafficker and animal caretaker were alive. She explained those facts to Jack.

"If they knew that I'm still alive, they will try to kill me and anyone close to me."

Jack sat there shaking his head. It was difficult to comprehend.

Ara said, "I have stayed too long. You don't need to get submerged into my awful mess and possible trap. I must leave."

Jack got up and told her, "Please stay."

He held her and kissed her. He told her that he loved her. He knew a wonderful ex-detective who had other great, smart friends. It was time to stop running and join the near-normal world. He wanted her to stay and try. He still wanted to marry her. She deserved sunshine in her life.

From what she told him, "Most everything was exploitation and self-defense. Your abilities in trying to handle staying alive were a might strange but you are still moving your world to elude the bad people. Your lack of judgment and inexperience made you fall deeper into their underworld."

Ara nodded. Jack was using logic in understanding her story.

"What you want are people with big guns and heavy artillery to bring these culprits down. You need a combined group of intelligent masterminds to set their trap to catch the two of them and any of their criminal friends."

Convincing her to go to bed, they would talk tomorrow. It was the weekend and they could take it slow and be together. They made sweet, amazing love before falling asleep. Jack awoke, and she was gone from the bedroom and the house. Her purchased sports car was in the locked garage. He worried that she left everything and ran again.

He looked out the window onto the beach and she was jogging. Ara turned toward the house. "Good girl."

She believed he could help her. He hoped he could. Their future together depended on that fact. He wanted to be her protector. She was everything. Jack didn't want to go back to a dull life. His network of friends would come in handy. He briefly thought about leaving the country.

30 Jack's Friend Jim

JACK JONES KNEW Jim Michaels for a long time. He helped Jack with quite a few bad characters in the past. Ara would stay behind at a hotel room. First, he would meet and talk with Jim at a quiet outside coffee shop. If he felt things were safe, Jack would contact her after the meeting. Or if the police needed more time, he would let her know with a balloon delivery to show he needed one more day. If no balloons by six in the evening on that day, she was free to leave. If she left, he wanted her to make one phone call to him directly, so he would know she was safe. No messages could be left. Jack already talked with his lawyer about their legal rights and international law. He explained those to Ara.

Jack and Jim met. They picked up their coffee at the counter and selected a table away from others.

"I have something very important to discuss. It is a proposition. I don't quite know where to begin."

Jim said, "Whatever it is can't be that bad."

"I wish it was simple. The situation isn't."

Jack looked at his friend and began, "I'm familiar with a person who knew Santan Chesin, aka Mann Nisee, aka Charles Mann whose last residence was London. It is my understanding that this bad dude is dead. This person also knows the other bad ass person whom she knew while in Africa by the names Boyd Reeker, aka Sphinx Reeker, and aka Tiger Black. In my person's accounts are some tapes of the two men during some conversations in illegal transactions with their clients."

"This person also knows Hamm Roe who possibly is some other person. He told her that he killed two brothers from Walnut Creek, California, when he left her for dead. This person is my friend. She also was known by the police as Elizabeth Banks Barrow from Alabama and Queenie Pyra from Miami."

"Geez, Jack, what is going on?"

Jim had been in the loop with Derek and Jess on this whole terrible mess. Jim asked him if he also knew her tiger's name.

Jack nodded he did, "It's Felidae."

"Man, you are into this deep. Have you seriously thought about your relationship with this woman?"

Jack said, "I want to be there all the way. It wouldn't matter how deep, because I'm too far gone. I love Ara. That is her name when we met."

Now it was Jim's turn to nod. He knew the spot and had been there. Jim said, "Go ahead, I will listen."

Jack went on to explain, "She wants to work with the police on a plan to catch the two very-much-alive, major criminals so they won't kill her."

Jim could have twenty-four hours to get back to him. Jack would be waiting at his home. If she didn't hear from Jack, Ara would disappear.

Jim asked, "How do you know the tapes are real?"

Jack opened his briefcase and handed the envelopes with the tapes to him and the drug trafficker's contact list of names that Ara had written down.

"She believes the police will want to catch the bad guys here. She hopes they do because the Tiger person always escapes justice somehow in Africa. She will also volunteer as a decoy in any plan to bring them down."

Jack didn't want that to happen if they could avoid it.

"I don't want anything to happen to her because we are in love and want to marry. I miss being married, and Ara is the only one I want to do that scenario with again."

Jim nodded again. He knew their divorce sat hard on Jack's ego. Jack hadn't a clue his wife was running around outside the vows of marriage. He reached out to his friend and patted his shoulder.

"I understand and will contact the very best, my friend, Derek Wright. He will know how to handle the situation that you and your friend are in. He hates the bad guys and will want to catch them."

"I know the Wrights. They are good people. I have been to parties on their motorboat when Dean Crain was alive. Their friendship is something Ara needs to know can exist."

Jack left the coffee shop relieved to share his knowledge. He didn't like bad guys, either. He hoped they caught the pricks.

31   Derek and the Legal System

JIM LEFT HIS friend at the coffee shop and went to Derek's office. He called him on the phone and Derek immediately called in his superiors to the meeting.

They listened to the tapes with the police and everyone in the room smiled. There were names of people on Santan Chesin's tapes. Tiger Black's tapes were amazingly clear. It was like being in the same room with the voices. The police liked the written list of names Ara gave them. They knew the tapes were real but not always permissible in court.

The police had no warrants out for Queenie Pyra or Elizabeth Banks Barrow. The Miami police wanted to talk to Queenie about the car accident. The Alabama police would also want to know what happened. The police figured the woman felt her life was in danger and was tired of running.

The police saw the pile of knowledge she obtained. The huge network of criminals mentioned would place her in a high-risk category. They were surprised she stayed alive this long. The police wondered if she was also running from the law and were worried what might pop up. They decided they would need to talk further with her. They didn't want to offer her any guarantees.

They put a tap on Jack's phones but believed they probably bought disposable ones for talking to each other. The tapes were secured, and a meeting was arranged to meet the woman, her lawyer, and Jack Jones. They were sure her lawyer would prompt her in what not to divulge. They were surprised at the additional information she revealed.

Derek went home to talk with Jess about the plan they talked about a year ago, regarding the lower part of the scepter. He wondered if David would allow them to use his top of the scepter and ring also as a ploy to pull in the thieves and murderers.

Both thieves and murderers were crazy-obsessed with the gold antiquities and killed because of them. Also, Jess and Derek knew the person who gave the police the valuable evidence tapes was Queenie and Elizabeth. Derek thought the tapes weren't enough and there needed to be a plan.

Derek told Jess, "On one of the tapes, Santan told his girlfriend about a hit woman who agreed to take me out in Los Angeles for an expensive fee."

Jess said. "I'm glad the hit person never found its mark." She remembered vividly the car chase scene with the strange woman who thought the person in their sports car was Derek. It was her.

Then Derek told her Ara's story.

"She has faced major evil since her teens. Ara tried to adapt, but their machinations enveloped her plus others, which caused much suffering. Her knowledge of their world is extensive. Ara understood that her information meant power. That's why she disappeared."

"Those people betrayed her. A hit by a jungle man? Unbelievable," mentioned Jess.

"It was amazing. How does someone walk out of a field from a spear wound and live? That's a small miracle. Stew Avery is now called Hamm Roe, by the way. He left her there in the field. There's your second monster. She does own a tiger after all, and the animal was at her Miami warehouse. Her beautiful cat, Felidae, resides now in a zoo in Alabama."

Derek thought Jess would wrap her brain around his comment about the tiger. She often took their children to all type of places to view birds and animals.

"Felidae is a nice name. I would love to see the tiger sometime. What does Queenie or Elizabeth look like now? Correction, what does Ara look like?"

Derek showed her a picture he had his secretary take of Ara for their files.

"The woman is still very young. It seemed incredible she found Los Angeles and stumbled into nice Jack Jones. Jack brought her to you. Jim knew we would help them both. That is perfect fate. It was time for Ara to betray the bad people, way past time."

Jess contemplated further and said, "Do you wonder about their being in love? They have the same glow."

Derek hadn't even considered that part of the equation. It now made sense. The way Jack treated her should have been a clue. Jim did not tell Derek very much of his friend's conversation at the coffee shop.

Derek thought they were friends. "I'm working too hard lately to not have noticed. Good catch, honey. The woman did offer herself as a decoy to catch the criminals."

Jess looked at Derek and raised her eyebrows.

"It is definitely love, and I'm worried what her husband, Scott, will think of this complication."

More amazing was that Jack trusted their good friend, Jim, enough to bring things into the open. The woman and Jack could have remained hidden. They knew Jack had the means and funds to disappear. Jack and his first wife were at one of Dean's parties. She wasn't surprised her sweet husband missed the love angle. He was working too hard.

Jack made sure he wasn't followed and hooked up with Ara in the hotel. He called the lawyer and the meeting was early tomorrow at nine. He cancelled his appointments for the entire week as did the lawyer for the afternoon discussions with the police. Jack held her while they watched a movie. Then they went to bed and made love.

They didn't know what tomorrow would bring. Jack started to get worried. He felt everything was going to get worse. He hoped they chose the correct path.

Running suddenly sounded safer. Jack knew places they could hide, having traveled extensively with his first wife. He was going a little crazy. Jack talked to himself and relaxed. He would pull in all his reserves and stay calm.

Ara was safe, at least for now. It was good to unload all the bad experiences she kept hidden. Now she could focus her energies toward helping the police. She was glad Jack was beside her. She would handle her life better this time. Her freedom now held greater significance.

32   Police Interview

ARA TOLD THEM how she met Charles Mann, the diamond smuggler at age eighteen. She knew his other names. She easily broke into his files and safe. She explained how Charlie was her lover and she feared for her life because he told her his business. He also told his bodyguard to dump her in the river because Charlie didn't want her anymore. She couldn't blame him. It was a time in her life when she became introverted and depressed around him. He was not an easy person to live with.

She told about meeting the Sphinx, or Mr. Reeker, who wanted the diamond smuggler, Mr. Chesin, dead. Sphinx gave her the poisoned rum, and she mentioned how she brought the bottle into the London house. She explained how Charlie was the type of person who favored rum over any other liquor. He chose to drink the rum and was popping pills. She was afraid of Charlie and was glad he died.

She talked about the Sphinx and going with him to live in Africa. Ara talked about his lies and her inability to leave because she, again, knew too much. He was also her lover and was told by the Sphinx that he owned her. She was his prisoner. He said she was his property. That's when she rebelled and developed a plan to try to dispose of him.

Her lawyer stepped in and reminded the police so that it would also be recorded, "My client has given you the list of Sphinx's contacts and dated evidence tapes of illegal dealings on both men."

At age nineteen and a half, she told about stealing the Sphinx's two precious antiquities which were a gold crown and clasp with an eagle design. She stole his money in accounts that she found from the great Sphinx's locked desk and room. Those riches came from his illegal business activities. She paid her people to drop him in a crate in the Congo River.

She explained how he escaped and found her in Miami at age twenty and hired a hit man to strangle her and use poisonous snake venom to kill her, only he killed two of her guards who looked like her. Ara said she thought Sphinx cut her brake line. This was the reason she went to Dakar to try to kill the now, Tiger Black. When the explosive went off early, she believed her final job worked.

She married Scott Barrow at age twenty-one in Alabama after paying one of the brothers from Walnut Creek, California, for the lower part of a gold scepter with the same unusual eagle wing design. She put the three antiquities in separate bank boxes and carried the keys on a gold chain around her neck.

After her marriage, she found out the car bomb she planted in Africa didn't kill him. She had no clue who was in the vehicle. She looked at Jack who frowned.

She corrected her statement to the possibility there were two people in the car when it blew. Angry Tiger Black, the former Sphinx, sent a jungle man to kill her with a spear and left her to die in a field. The jungle man took two of the bank keys. She was sure that the crazy-dressed man, and his girlfriend stole her items out of the bank. Then her animal caretaker, Hamm, was there in the field and took the third key.

While Hamm was leaning over her, he told her he murdered two brothers to get the bottom scepter and would take what was his. She managed to put a tourniquet of her slacks around the wound to stop the bleeding. She walked to her pool house to sew the front of her chest and bandage the back. There was always medicine in the house, antibiotics and bandages.

Elizabeth fled for her life at age twenty-two on a motor bike to an old garage. After two or so weeks, she escaped to Los Angeles to continue hiding and get well. Time was of no consequence. It could have been longer that she stayed at the garage. It was confusing. She went to a plastic surgeon once she received her new identification card as Ara Landt. There remained the scars. She went to a plastic surgeon to fix her problem. She and Jack became good friends. He encouraged her to stop running and entreat the police's help.

She was still afraid both men would kill her, that is Hamm and Tiger, or possibly harm others near her. The Tiger probably has two of the antiquities. He obtained them originally in lieu of payment in a drug deal. She was sure Hamm stole the other antiquity from her. She did not trust the police before because Tiger was too powerful and Hamm too slippery.

Ara was tired of her life being embroiled in heinous crimes. She wanted it to stop and would help the police. She was almost twenty-four now, still young enough to have a life. She needed to have a normal life and looked at Jack.

There was silence in the room and the man turned the tape recorder off.

Jack got up and stood behind her touching her shoulders. She reached up to take his hand. He heard her story three times now and she always seemed to disappear. She hadn't told them about the first bad boyfriend. She told Jack and the lawyer she couldn't.

Ara didn't need to tell them, because they already knew.

Derek showed her some drawings of crowns, clasps, rings, and full scepters that Jess put together. She selected three of the objects which were the exact ones from Louisa Renaliere's drawings. Derek smiled.

Ara smiled. *"The golden obsession was about the antiquities."* They were the treasure which branched out like a tree and led to everyone. She knew the mess became bigger when she took them.

"Was there a smaller crown in the collection?"

Derek said, "We don't believe there was a smaller one. Why, is there something that you have seen or discussed with an investor?"

"No, it seems odd that there wouldn't be a smaller one," said Ara.

Derek didn't want to even think of another crown and certainly wouldn't tell Jess now.

Arrangements were made to put Ara in a safe house under protective custody. The police would work on their plan to apprehend the bad guys. Jack would not see Ara for a while for her protection. Derek would be their interface. He would bring them together once the final plan was ready.

33   David's Top Scepter and Ring

DEREK FLEW TO Miami to meet with David Dunker. When he arrived, he was surprised to see one of Queenie's guards there. She obviously was his new girlfriend.

Derek approached her. Having introduced himself, he asked about her former career.

"My name is Karine Kline. You did guess correctly that I was one of Queenie's guards while she lived in her apartment building in Miami."

Karine responded, "Welcome to our home. Can I bring you some coffee?"

"I am fine for now. I drank too much on the flight." Derek picked up on the words: our home.

David and Derek went to the study and closed the door.

"The two of us met and enjoyed each other's company. We have plans to marry. That is why she said our home."

Derek congratulated him.

David explained further that Karine became a security guard at the mall close by. They ran into each other one day and he invited her out. They both fell in love and had been living together ever since.

"I plan on selling my antiquities so the two of us can travel the world."

David chatted with Derek further that Karine wasn't that crazy about his old stuff. It was all right to let everything go. His mother passed away and the luster of collecting was gone. He would rather be wherever Karine was.

In confidence, Derek told him the police plan to catch two killers. Derek wanted to personally purchase the top scepter and ring today from David for the plan to lure them into the arena.

David Dunker proposed a change to the plan. He offered the rest of his antiquities that he owned be also used as a lure to privately-invited investors to a different first sale. They might try three different sale dates. This would allow the last two days of the show for an opportune time to catch the criminals. That way he could also unload some of his items to the best collectors.

Derek thought it was a wonderful idea.

The first sale would be with only the private investors to purchase and reduce the inventory, plus it would be a good advertising ploy for the next sale. The cops could do another set-up to catch the bad guys on a second and third day.

Derek made a call to his superiors who approved and would work on things for the next day for a transport of David's valuable treasures. That way David could also get a higher price due to the Los Angeles location. They would use Derek's auction friend to handle the sales and agreed-to-commission amount. A team of police and heavy security would pack the items up and deliver them to a private airfield in Los Angeles and a truck would take them to one of Derek's secured warehouses.

David would have the listed items with full descriptions and his lowest auction price. The list would be signed off by Derek at pickup and delivery.

Jess would work with the photographer, police, and eventually auction clerk to create the catalogue. They would tell the auction clerk the first sale were to a select group of investors.

Derek wrote him a check for the two valuable gold items and David printed his description documentation and receipt. Derek brought special velvet pouches and a special locked long briefcase. They went into his antiquities room and placed the two items inside. Derek was surprised by the room and the number of objects inside. David explained there used to be an old private bomb shelter on the site. He saved part of the thick walls to build his room. It was a perfect place to store the ancient items. Derek agreed and would return the next day with the police packing team.

Derek hesitated, but then told him the names of the two murderers.

David couldn't believe it, "How is that possible? I talked with the man named Hamm and it's hard to believe. Karine dated Hamm when she worked for Queenie. We must tell her."

"I cannot divulge any more information, but she needs to know of his problems with the police. You might want to start your cruise early and be gone until the shooting is completely over."

"We will certainly do that very thing. I want my new wife out of danger from that creep."

Karine was invited back into the room. Derek asked, "Do you know where Hamm Roe is living?"

"I haven't talked to him since we broke up. Why?"

She gave Derek their former address and he gave the information to the Miami police to check it out.

She was alarmed when Derek explained. The police suspected him of the murders in Walnut Creek, California, of two brothers. She started to cry. David came and comforted her. Karine had something to tell Derek and her potential husband about the polo wife missing in Alabama. Derek got out his special cell phone and she agreed to the voice video.

"Flying to Alabama, we thought we should see a woman who lived on a polo horse estate called Elizabeth Barrow. We thought that she might be our past employer. We wanted to make sure she was all right. She left for her honeymoon, except Hamm insisted on staying longer for some reason. He said he had to talk with her about some antiquities."

They waited at her coffee shop which they knew she visited. They watched her routine a few days before her wedding.

Derek knew the African man, Tiger Black, and his killers also watched Elizabeth's routine. The

African man had recognized the woman as Queenie at the London airport.

Karine talked. "Elizabeth didn't make her hair appointment one day, so we drove slowly back to her polo estate home. I stayed in the car and Hamm disappeared through the trees when we saw blood on the gravel road."

She wrung her hands and explained that he came back and told her Elizabeth was dead. He wanted to leave the area immediately which they did. She packed, while he disappeared to get gas. He was gone over an hour.

She told Derek the time of their flight and which airline.

"Halfway to the airport, we did stop. Hamm told me he left anonymous information for the police on their phone at the second gas-and-go place to report Elizabeth's location and accident."

When the story came out, she knew he lied to her. He hadn't called the police to report Elizabeth's accident or location in the hayfield. That's when she became afraid and left Hamm.

Derek and David knew she was lucky to be alive. Hamm could have killed her, too. Derek explained to Karine that Elizabeth didn't have an accident. It was a premeditated killer's attempt on termination of Elizabeth's life.

David told Karine about their expedited plans to board their cruise early.

Derek left the Dunker home and sent the voice video to his superiors to distribute. The information corroborated Ara's part of her story for the police that Hamm left her to die. Derek knew the rest of her story was also true.

They saw the images from the bank video. The woman and later appearing man had gone into the vaults. They wore wide hats and their faces were barely visible. The woman carried a large handbag going into the bank. A handbag and paper bag were in her hands coming out. There was a lump under the man's shirt when he came out. The thieves stole the gold antiquities out of Elizabeth's bank lockboxes.

34   Antiquities at the Warehouse

THE ANTIQUITIES ARRIVED at Derek's warehouse in Los Angeles. The workers and police left. Derek's security people were in place outside. They set up tables with black cloth tablecloths per Jess's request for the photography session the next day. Their Miami group photographer and wife were coming tomorrow for the photo shoot. Jess met Derek there and he opened the long briefcase.

Jess looked in the long case again. "Two of the beautiful gold antiquities are now ours to share with others who love art. Louisa would have loved seeing her family's heirlooms."

She thanked him, "You are my very sweet husband."

Derek was pleased, "You are my brilliant wife. It is a good day. Have your wonderful eagle lingerie samples arrived yet?"

"Not yet. They should arrive later this month."

"I hate that word later. How about we try things without the lingerie?"

Derek was teasing her. She grabbed him and said, "More, more, and more."

He picked her up and carried her off to the extra bedroom at the warehouse with the bunk beds. They took a much-needed love break. It was time for the break because their bodies were ramped up from finding the antiquities.

Derek kissed her sweetly and moved her body to fit his own strong one. "I love you. You are better than all the gold in our warehouse."

"Just the warehouse?"

Derek knew if he wanted more, he should sweeten the pot. "How about the sky, the earth, everything."

"I love you. I will take everything."

Derek knew this part with his wife was the best. He could give her dreams and then some. He was good at those things. Everything of her wants were on his list.

With confidence, he wrapped her in another caress and then another. Their love filled the room. There was no need for rockets or stars because the neon color of their love was hitting all wavelengths in the spectrum. The diamonds and gold in the other room were dim in comparison and were soon forgotten for the moment. It was all about their tremendous gift at finding and feeling love. Their eyes and bodies entwined in a treasured embrace that brought them to a sweet spot. No paint could match the color of their love. It was a white cloud from a jet stream crossing the sky. The day disappeared, and their blue sphere changed to a Northern-lit, Alaskan sky. Lightening added to the brightness. Thunder didn't dare enter the room. Sound gently disappeared to leave two lovers in a secret place. Softness filled empty space, while the cool rain fell, dissipating the heat. Magic happened.

After some time, they went back to the items in the warehouse. With white gloves, slowly, they took out the top scepter, placing it on the tablecloth, and admired its beauty again. The gold shone. Then they looked at the smaller object, a gold ring painted with diamonds. She grabbed a gray velvet cloth and placed the ring half on the black and gray backgrounds. The photograph would be perfection to show the ring's fire.

Jess brought the fake, newly-designed bottom scepter out of a different box. They laid them together on the table. The bottom screwed on and then stopped, not quite closing. They would need to take the two pieces to their friend's shop who had created the fake bottom. Derek thought it was a thread problem. The objects needed to fit tightly. He would do that project the next day and bring them back to Jess for the afternoon photo session.

The Miami photographer was bringing the gems from Florida to temporarily place in the top scepter. The Miami people had a sultan friend who had a ruby close in size and emeralds that would work for the eagle eyes. The small diamonds were from a friend's diamond shop. There was a special clear plastic stand that would rotate around in the show, holding the whole scepter secure.

They unpacked the items and carefully checked them off the list. Jess went to their copier and placed the description with price next to each object. David had printed a beautiful write-up page for each item for her. The originals would be kept secure with the rest of the auction documents.

Jess picked up the box of plastic holders to place the description and price page. They decided to wait until the next day to do the work.

"It's time to head home." Derek looked at his wife, catching her vibrations.

"Yes, I'm tired from too much excitement." She took off her white gloves and glanced at Derek. He was happy. He threw his gloves in the trash. He held his arm out to Jess and they exited the building. He drove a very tired wife home. He guided her into their bedroom and covered her with the warm fur blanket. She was out and fast asleep. He was still charged up and went into his private library and sat for a long time before going to bed. He looked back on past events and worried. Was there anything that he forgot? If he was a lesser man, he wouldn't have cared. However, there was a part of him that would always keep searching. He couldn't turn the search light off. Tomorrow was another day.

He scanned the new day's horizon while making coffee, and he hoped there was nothing to worry about. The horizon was aglow with peach, mauve, and golden fire. It was a good sign. He hummed an old opera song while flipping homemade pancakes on a small burner at the bar. The sausages were cooked and waiting warm in the microwave. He turned off the burner on the pancakes and assembled the items on a tray to take to the master bedroom.

Derek knew how to greet his wife and welcome her to the next day in style. There was no chance involved; things for breakfast were assuredly very black and white. Jess loved pancakes with blueberries,

219

real maple syrup, and country sausages. It was one of her faults, blueberries, sticky syrup, meat on occasion, and him. There was no deviation. Derek looked heavenward. He was blessed. "Thank god for a perfect breakfast."

The next day, they arrived early. They specially-labeled white boxes to put the objects in for transport to the sale with the bar coding. Each box could be scanned in upon reaching the correct room destination. Their two items would be in a separate room with some lesser items.

The fake scepter bottom was corrected to fit the top, the gems placed in the eagle head, and photographs taken. All the rest of the items were photographed, and everything repacked in their boxes. They chose the photos for the brochure but would correct the jeweled scepter photo later. The photographer and his wife flew back to Miami. The gems remained in Derek's safe.

Jess picked up the children, Sami and Justin. They drove back to the motorboat because they were going to take it out for the weekend. Derek must first attend a meeting. He would join with them later.

Jess felt pleased that the brochure was almost ready, but would review it with Derek's timelines before printing or e-mailing the investors and auction company.

35   Derek's Meeting with Ara

A FEW DAYS later, the lawyer called Derek's office and informed them that he couldn't make the afternoon meeting.

Derek received a text from Jess that she was on the motorboat. He smiled remembering his time with her.

Derek turned to Ara and Jack. He told them that Karine, her former bodyguard confirmed the story about Hamm leaving Elizabeth for dead in the field. She was a witness who was there on the road. She verified the location of the field, trees, and the miles they drove from town plus time of day. Karine signed a police statement regarding the video and those facts.

Jack got up from his chair perplexed how someone could do that. It was an unconscionable thing to do. He would never have left a hurt person to die.

Derek went on to tell them the sale items were inventoried, catalogue numbered, and photographed for the final auction catalog. He told them about the scepter as the draw with some gem stones they would use from Florida. If they didn't receive information that the African was heading into their country, they would have to bring Ara into the equation with a photo in the newspaper about her attendance as an experienced investor from Los Angeles.

She had already been fitted for a bullet proof vest under her dress and microphone equipment. Jess's red satin platform heels and flared dress fit her perfectly. The heels held a special knife blade in them. Ara smiled. She liked the outfit.

Or Derek proposed an alternative. They could use a backup person named Tami to stand in. Jack voted for the stand in. Ara did not want to be close to the Sphinx unless it was necessary. She agreed to their plan to use Tami Cortez. It would work better.

Derek asked her one last time if she wanted to talk to her husband, Scott Barrow, before they proceeded with the auction sale and throw-down. The police checked him out and he was clean. Ara moved out of her chair to Jack and held onto him for a moment. Jack caressed her.

Derek knew Jess was correct about Ara and Jack being in love.

She walked back to Derek and told him that she did not want to contact Scott. She thought he would just get in the way of things and would bring his team of lawyers into every corner of the investigation, hampering their plans to catch the real criminals. Scott could wait on the sidelines in a safer zone, like his polo estate. Capture of the two criminals should take high priority.

The police were also withholding the information she had given them for fear any arrest would trigger caution in the criminals' attendance at the sale. Once all the logistics were revealed, Derek would share with them, so they knew the placement of the cameras, protection teams, tailing devices, and sharpshooters. There would be blockades set in place if there were any problems. They created a group of scenarios.

Jack asked Derek, "What if your scenarios don't work?"

"Did you know another scenario?"

Jack looked at Ara, "You need to tell him about your nightmare."

Derek sat down next to Ara like he did with his wife Jess.

He picked up her cool hands. He remembered Jess's cold hands in Tomales Bay when she stepped on a dead body. Ara was afraid like his wife had been. Derek needed Ara to trust him. He didn't want her to bolt like Jess did long ago.

"I know all about women with dreams. Old Louisa, a very dear friend, plus my wife and daughter, are masters in seeing something that was right there in front of everyone. I don't understand their vision or intuition, whatever it is called. Those astounding women in my life have very important things to say. I do always listen to them. I did not in my earlier career. I learned that the women I know were correct every time."

She felt a change in Derek's voice when he talked about the women in his life. It was a different man from the cold, aloof investigator. She felt his warmth and love for those women.

Derek could catch her bad guys. This was his turf. She trusted those feelings called tenderness and goodness. Derek would be her friend and Jack's friend. She would tell the vision her tiger showed her.

Ara told Derek her nightmare. "Tiger Black, the Sphinx, will send his henchmen to wreak havoc upon the sale, distraction personified. The henchmen will steal the objects for him if he decides to steal them. Their weapons will be silent, either smoke, gas, poison, or knives. Everything happens quickly, and they will disappear with the eagle antiquities because that is one of his crazier of obsessions."

"Tiger always moves fast. Tiger already knows where I am and is waiting to get me. I'm his other fanatical obsession. I always thought he couldn't kill me personally because he hired people to perform the job for him. Except in my nightmare, the two of us are alone in a room. I don't know this place or the room. He brought his gun up, pulled the trigger, and fired at me. Next, I awaken."

Derek ordered extra security and called Tami Cortez to bring her red dress and shoes and fly to Los Angeles as fast as she could. They needed a decoy. "Do you have a light blondish, red-haired wig and if so, bring it. They can trim it to match Ara's current hairdo." She needed to appear the same, as Queenie and Elizabeth, yet look different like she was hiding who she was in the past.

He called his superiors and code three was put in place. He called Jess and his crew to be ready, code three. He called the Miami group because some of their team were in Los Angeles. They were to arrive for extra security on the motorboat and bring large guns.

Derek contacted the San Francisco people to send their three best knife, gas, and poison boys to a specific warehouse meeting. The San Francisco leader told him a whole crew of men were moving his way. They were taking a wonderful vacation because he heard it was code three.

Derek verified the code. Code 3 in their protected group meant no hold on anything, high emergency. Derek thanked him and would keep him in the loop. He called his warehouses and Jim.

The pizza people arrived, and Derek let them in. The people changed outfits with Ara and Jack. The two left together in the pizza vehicle for a special pickup location. The detectives ate the pizza with the delivery team and waited for the all clear. Then, they too, could disappear.

Once Ara and Jack were picked up, they were taken to the Wrights' motorboat. It motored out into the ocean and setting sun.

Derek drove to his home and posted extra security on his home. Another Chinese food delivery truck arrived at his home and he was driven by that vehicle to their warehouse with the antique book library and bunk bed room, where he planned to stay the night.

He let Jess know, "I'm safe and the two people need to stay out of sight of any boat within a certain perimeter of our motorboat. The captain will know what to do."

"I'm familiar with the drill and will let our guests know. Our guests are interesting."

"I believe they are interesting, too, but Jess, honey, all they need is a safe place. The motorboat was my first thought."

"Yes, it was a good thought. A moving ship was hard to track."

Derek wondered about his decision, because he knew his wife. Jess would try to help. Then he remembered Jess learned to help from Dean Crain, their friend. And Derek was doing the same thing by placing them on the armored motorboat.

Derek would meet the next day with his other teams at the designated warehouse. He gave the safe house people the text to leave their location because the package was secure.

36   Hiding Ara and Jack

THE MOTORBOAT ALWAYS headed straight out westward into the ocean and turned towards its destination when they could no longer see land and no boats showed as a danger on the radar screens. There was a storm headed around Catalina Island, so they motored north toward Monterey, California.

She texted their shortened language to Derek that they were going to "My", the first and last letter. Derek responded, "K", for all right. Once underway, the children joined their mother's company under the upper, outside deck canopy. The children, Justin and Sami, were twelve and a half and nine years old, respectively.

Jack told them, "Their eighty-five-foot motorboat is an amazing yacht. I remember the yacht when Dean was alive. He had super parties when he owned it. My wife and I liked the group and good food."

Ara looked at him distressed. He didn't like to talk about his ex-wife.

Jess knew Jack was previously on the boat with his first wife. She didn't know what Ara knew about the first wife, but needed to steer the conversation elsewhere.

227

Jess told them the story of their friend, Dean Crain.

"He had originally been a good fence in the underworld of stolen goods, but the police caught him only once and he did a short stint in prison. Once he was out, on a whim, he went to Las Vegas and won a load of money playing poker. He kept gambling and kept winning. He bought a sailboat which a bad con artist blew up because the psycho thought I was on board the sailboat. They nicknamed the creep, the Salamander. Dean purchased the larger motorboat and helped Derek catch the killers. Dean and I were good friends before I met Derek. I lost my father and Dean lost his daughter. Our common loss helped us to bond. Along the way, I met Derek again, fell in love, and we married. Dean gifted the motorboat to us by putting the motorboat in our names when he passed away."

Ara caught the word, again.

Jess explained, "Derek and I went on two dates and I dropped him because he was an investigator who worked closely with the police. I planned on stealing the diamond necklace that was stolen from my mother. Derek secretly tailed me and followed me to Napa, California. The jewelry store in Napa that I was going to rob had already been robbed. People were murdered. Derek met me on the road and we hooked up after the robbery. He was in Napa to help with the police. But our permanent relationship didn't happen right away. Dean helped us later find each other. Then we truly fell in love."

Ara visibly relaxed. She figured Jess was this perfect person. She realized Jess and Derek knew her world very well. Jess loved her husband and family. Derek loved Jess. He tailed her. She could see him doing just that thing, tailing a woman he seriously loved, thought Ara. She smiled. Jess was the major love she had glimpsed in Derek's eyes.

Sami asked her mother if they could show Ara and Jack their dance routine they were practicing for the next annual party. They needed to perform in front of people. This would be a small audience. Sami liked Ara.

Jess looked at Justin. He nodded it would be all right.

Ara overheard Sami. "We would like very much for our guests to watch our calypso dance."

Jess told Sami they could perform. She smiled at Justin. He danced beautifully, like his father.

Sami went to the music console and hit button six. Justin took Sami's hand, and they performed the dance perfectly. Jess was pleased. She had been working with them to tighten their steps together. Justin was relaxed when he led his sister. Justin wanted to impress pretty Maggie, Skid's daughter, so he learned the steps well.

Ara watched Jess's face and saw the twinkle in her eye. Jess was tapping her feet and nodding. She bet Derek also knew the intricate dance steps. She would love to see that dance. Ara laughed. She saw the picture of what it must be like to live the Wrights' life. She wondered if Jack would like to have a child. Ara looked at Jack. He smiled back at her and squeezed her hand.

She told the children about her tiger, Felidae. Upon Jack's nudging her to tell the story, she felt it would be fine to tell them. Sami looked at her foot tattoo fascinated by the word. Jack knew they would like the first story.

Ara began talking, "it is called *Felidae, The Golden One.*

"There was a young girl who wanted to own a tiger. She read a book about the Felidae, which is the scientific classification or family name for a special cat. The cat is the largest of its species. The cat is the orange, white, and black-striped tiger. A Panthera Tigris is the cat's subfamily name. She liked the name, Felidae, because she also read about the animal's strong ancestors in their forest. The golden cat's forest was ruled by a beautiful woman whose name, of course, was Goddess. Who doesn't know about goddesses? All little girls know about them and other princesses or queens.

Their goddess liked to use her magic arrows and brought the cats meat. She would show them the best hunting grounds in the forest, but first they had to cross the river. The cats never swam before and never crossed the river. They would have to trust her. They looked at the river. She encouraged them to wet their feet a little bit on the sandbar. They drank the water. They liked to drink. The river flowed very fast. The cats looked at the woman one more time. She nodded that it would be all right. They all leaped into the deep water, their bodies strong, and they floated along. The cats were happy to reach the other side. The woman was smart. They could swim. They licked their large paws after their meal and rested. The animal's tails were flicking their contentment. They rolled in the tall grass. This was their new forest.

She taught them tricks, and they would lay down at her feet. She sometimes rode the largest and strongest tiger. They liked her, because she shared things. The cats got together and softly growled with each other, but they made their decision. They voted to give the goddess special powers. It was a very special gift from the golden-eyed, charismatic creatures. Her first power was strength. Next, they gave her the power of speed, so she could run fast. The third power was something she already had. It was love. She used her powers well because the tigers offered her so much more besides their love. What can be more important than love?

What was the important thing? Protection for her always. The words the Felidae family used were. protect the goddess at all cost, protect forever. How long was forever? It is a long time. A baby tiger boy was born. The tiger was caught and put in a circus for a while with his mother. He saw a young girl. The young girl waved to him and blew a kiss. He caught her kiss and smelled it. He would remember her. When he was older, he met the woman who was the little girl. He was thrilled, because she looked like the goddess. Could she be the one?

The young woman purchased the retired circus tiger boy and played with him. She gave him his own play area with plants and rocks. There was even water in a small pool. It was like his forest. The tiger boy became friends with her. He decided she was the one he would be with forever. He could do that, because he saved his wish. If you are taken by someone, you were granted one wish. The tiger had been taken by the circus people. The young woman

231

gave him the name. She called him, Felidae. She loved her amazing tiger boy. He learned all her difficult tricks with ease, performing everything correctly. Alas, she must take him to the zoo to live. She can't care for her beloved anymore. It was a sad day. She found a great zoo for him. It looked like the forest, too. He can play there. The tiger will be happy. Then the worst thing happened.

What happened? She couldn't run. The young woman had fallen in a strange forest. She was in imminent danger. Felidae, her cat at the zoo heard her whispering with her last breath, calling his name, *Felidae*. The tiger brought his ancestors with him. They swam the river to find her. The tigers knew how. In a vision, the family of tigers scared the strangely-dressed bad person away. The golden tiger helped her to safety. He would always be there for her because he loved her. The young woman, a person could clearly see, had become his real Goddess. His wish was granted. He was her great magical tiger, the golden one."

Jess knew Ara's story ended as Sami looked interested, mesmerized, weepy, and then happy. She loved that Ara included their word, *magical*. She knew Ara saw visions, too.

She turned to the storyteller, "Ara, you should write a children's book. I know this publisher and now my eagle books are sold at many of the world's zoos, plus they sell stuffed toys under our trademark name. You could do tiger toys and put a nametag on him to match your story book."

Jess told Jack her literary agent and name of publisher. He also knew her editor. Jess told Ara her trick in writing the story was to verbally tell it. Then write it. She knew a good friend who drew pictures and took great photographs for her books. She would be glad to share the information and help in any way.

Jess retrieved her tape recorder and Ara told her story about training the tiger to wait, walk with her, stop, jump, and to play with beach balls. The children were fascinated. They went down below, and Jess showed her how to use the book publisher software on her computer, and Ara typed a story into the system from the taped story on the recorder.

Jess told her that it flowed well. Jess called her friend. He would work some tiger drawings. She sent him a disclosure document and then a copy of the rough draft. Ara and Jack were excited. Everyone turned in for the evening.

XXXXXX

In the morning, the boat was anchored in Monterey, California. The crew wrote down Ara and Jack's sizes and took the watercraft into the pier. The crew would buy tourist clothes, swimsuits, hats, sandals, etc. Ara and Jack would remain out of site until they changed. The chef had prepared scrambled eggs, hash browns, sausage, Boston lettuce rolled in brie cheese with smoked red peppers, and toast in buffet trays for everyone. Coffee and juice were on the side with small cartons of milk. Caramel sweet rolls were on tiny silver trays, and balls of soft butter were in teacups. Dressed in the new clothes, large hats, and sunglasses, they looked like tourists on their boat for vacation. No one paid them any attention.

They stayed in Monterey a few days and then went to San Jose until Derek let them know to return to Los Angeles.

The drawing pictures for the book were received and placed within Ara's book. They sent the draft to the literary agent. He let Ara know via e-mail, "It is an instant hit among his other staff. Does she have a picture for the front cover?"

She did, "But I can't access it right away." She told Jess the bank account location where the documents and storage device were stored in the vault. She signed a permission slip for Derek to retrieve them. He did just that, scanned the photo file, and sent the documents to her.

She selected her favorite picture of her beloved tiger boy for the first book cover and inserted the photo into the cover on the computer. The second draft copy of Ara's tiger children's book was sent to the editor. Ara and Jack were pleased. The children told her the book would be a hit.

Ara hugged them and told them, "I hope so. I couldn't have done it without your help." Ara thanked Jess.

Jack told Jess, "You're amazing. It is nice to have friends."

Jess laughed and hugged them both. Jess was glad positive things were happening to Ara. Ara needed their group's love and family protection. Jess would let the group know about the wonderful tiger book and new friend, Ara.

"I will be happy to have you as friends on our motorboat any time."

It was a good day when Derek sent them to the motorboat. Jess would let her husband know once again their decision was correct.

Jess made a surprise plan for the next time she saw her husband. She checked her cupboard for a special bottle of old expensive scotch she had custom made with her eagle mini t-shirt design with lots of glitter around the label. She even requested they put glitter on the inexpensive highball glasses. She told the chef she needed fresh oysters with garlic balls that she could microwave quickly. The chef would put them in their room refrigerator for the Wrights' scheduled last vacation. It was the weekend before they took the motorboat out of the water. She gave the chef the date.

When they went on vacation, it was going to be a supreme night.

Her design of the eagle lingerie was complete, and she received the package of samples in her size. She knew Derek would want her to model every one of them in private.

Jess started singing the opera song Derek knew. Jess knew how to soar and do sexy. "Oh, yeah, more, more, more. Cloud nine, crazy more."

Being around Jack and Ara reminded her of important things like taking time to live in the moment.

37   Poker with Green Stream

HAMM ROE WASN'T ever good at judging people's true character or so thought his father. Hamm was embarrassed that his father had been a butler, a mere servant. His father warned him about evil people.

Hamm liked to engage with unsavory people who always seemed to have money. He liked money even more than women. Then he remembered that stupid Santan Chesin who disagreed with him regarding a diving expedition. Santan was a bad experience and the drunk failed miserably trying to kill him. It was his loss, not Hamm's. Nothing was ever Hamm's fault.

Hamm encountered a group of people in Los Angeles who called themselves Green Stream and started hanging out with them. Their leader was named Randy Moore who owned several restaurants in the area.

Later, he met the original loyal members of Green Stream. They kept talking about a guy named Minnow who was their leader, not Randy. They didn't like Randy or his wife. They could hardly wait for Minnow Surf and his girlfriend, Amy, to get out of jail.

This second group asked him if he wanted to make some money on the side. Of course, he wanted to make money. They said it would be small jobs. An example was provided. It could be delivery or movement of already stolen goods. It would be easy because all the hard stuff had been done. Sometimes it would be delivery from the shop to a client or the other way around.

They liked Hamm very much because he was doing a good job for them. Consequently, they would let him in on a secret poker game. Hamm was invited to the swanky home of the leader, Randy and Sandra Moore, for the poker party. He didn't know much about poker, but thought he could learn. They were playing with poker chips, so he thought everything was cool.

It was all right until the next sports car pick-up and drop-off. The woman from London canceled the job. Stew already counted on that money happening. He splurged and bought himself some new clothes and rented a better apartment. He wanted to start dating again and would need nicer things.

Then his life became worse. He was in trouble with the Green Stream people. Nobody told him the poker chips represented money. He felt conned by the group. He didn't know if Randy was in on the scam but figured out real soon that it was the Minnow Surf guy's clan. Hamm made the mistake of telling the Green Stream people that they cheated him. He didn't know how warped and evil the second group truly were.

The evil dudes informed him in a private meeting in the busy, noisy restaurant kitchen their philosophy about poker. Hamm willingly entered the stolen sports car game. He was now extremely connected to their family. He was like their poor relation. They tried to help him and now he was stepping out of line. There was a sign over the bar about the price of the chips.

Hamm interrupted that there was no sign at the bar in the home when he was there.

Now the bad dudes had asked Marcie to drape her shawl over the sign. They invited Hamm to the next party. Hamm didn't play poker when he read the sign. It was right where the clan said it existed. The darned sign was over the bar.

"No, no, no. How did I miss it?"

He owed an exorbitant amount of money and felt ill. The bad dudes arranged another meeting.

In the meeting, the leader with the strange gold ring sat down. The leader saw Hamm stare at the ring. He said it belonged to Minnow and he was keeping it safe for him while he was in jail. Hamm didn't look at the ring anymore. He knew Minnow was in jail for armed robbery.

"Who robs banks? Bad people do."

Hamm wished at that moment he listened to his father's advice.

The leader waited for total silence before speaking. Hamm owed them a fair amount of money. Because it wasn't considered a lot of money in their world, they would give him the family package of three months. Or they could possibly extend it to four, because Marcie sort of remembered putting her shawl near the sign.

The leader looked at his group and they nodded. The leader smiled because the majority selected what he thought was fair. They could be fair. Four months was the time granted to Hamm to repay their money.

Hamm moved to leave, and the guns came out. He sat down feeling like he was in some very bad movie about gangsters. He remembered old black and white shows his father watched on the VCR machine. The VCR machine was long gone. He wished he was long gone. There was no act of deliverance from this bad decision. He wondered how bad it was.

The leader informed him there would be no cushier delivery job with their sports car group. It was an exclusive group and incredibly profitable chop-shop for their rich clients. Hamm was no longer a member there, because he had been cancelled. It wasn't total erasure, because he was poor relation.

Hamm started to feel lucky. He wasn't erased permanently.

The leader continued, however, there was still the money consideration. If no proof of funds or valuable assets in four months, there was a resolution.

Their group would accept an asset as payment. So, if that would be easier, then so be it. The group leader spoke, "The resolution solution to resolve the end, if there is a very end to the end, was perfectly simple."

It made the leader smile to know he understood perfection. He needed Hamm to understand.

"The terms were ensanguined dry."

The leader rose, and the gang left the meeting.

Hamm was perplexed by the last conversation until he looked up the meaning of the weird word. He became more ill. It was a word an undertaker might use. If a person wrapped the word into psycho definition and stretched it out a little further to the absolute, very end to the end, it hit the realm of dry, very dry of your blood.

The words meant, "Bled out."

Hamm became afraid. He didn't want to hit the end of the very end of anything.

"Who thinks or talks that way? Criminals."

Hamm was in deep, very much over his head. Santan's method of resolution in the Atlantic was looking better. He could have swum to shore in a yellow raft. He knew rafts usually carried shark repellent. It was standard equipment in most countries.

"No blood. Where does that lead a person? Deader than dead, the end."

He drifted off. He was on the yellow raft at night and saw a red light coming toward him. There was a boat driving at him full speed. It was full of the Green Stream people. He would have to give them the right of way. He reached for the flair gun and it was missing. He was shit-out-of-luck as the boat wave tipped him over. Shuddering awake, he realized that he needed money fast. There would be no help from the police, so he couldn't report the scam. Besides, he felt like an idiot. He didn't want to be found floating in brackish water and used as some lab specimen by newbie forensics people.

"The major Green Stream clan do want to kill me. Their plan is to scare the crap out of me first. Well, they succeeded."

His vacation and possible life in Mexico was given up long ago. He had more pressing issues. Suddenly, his friend in the auction house called him about a potential sale of gold antiquities.

"I'm going to surprise the poker clan and get the money. It will be easy to accomplish the capture of those funds. Heh, they aren't so bright after all. This news is an ace up my sleeve. Screw your sign over the bar."

38   Antiquities Sale - Day 1 and 2

THE FIRST DAY sale of David's antiquities was for his well-known collectors and was a private sale. The eagle items would not be on display at all. This sale was to potentially sell David's items and to possibly flush out Hamm or Tiger's first team. The police were ready. The sprinkler system would be turned off. There wouldn't be a distraction created to scare people en-masse out of the building.

They hired a crew with gas masks, bulletproof vests and special neck, helmet gear, and boots. They even had some new laser goggles to reduce glare. Sharpshooters were in place even in the basement. There were drones and helicopters standing by and the bomb squad if needed. Police barricades were ready, and the Miami and San Francisco guys knew the perimeters of everything.

The first day there were no problems. There were only two visible guards watching people and the investors. The first day sale items were removed from the exhibit and mailed to the collectors. Derek thought David would be pleased with the check and the number of funds from the sale.

The other objects were rearranged in the rooms. The bottom fake part of the scepter was in a more private room with some lesser items. The scepter contained a tracking device. The second day sale was an advertised sale and they placed two visible policemen outside to keep traffic moving. Tami was installed in the scepter room as the possible decoy.

The second day of the sale, a man came with what appeared to be a pregnant lady. The man walked strange as if he broke his leg. The woman pushed a baby carriage which security made her leave by the door. She told security her child was with another woman outside. There was a woman outside with a child. Consequently, they thought things were fine. A delivery van just pulled up.

The man and woman pulled out their guns in the early morning when the crowd was light. The people in the room moved to the side. A security guard magically appeared at the door blocking any new people from entering the exhibit. The man pointed the gun at the security guard who stopped and held one of the doors open for the thieves.

The man didn't even notice Tami. They knew the criminals were not the Sphinx or his group. The man took the scepter and ring. The woman hid them. They concealed their guns and walked to the awaiting delivery van. The security guard closed the exhibit door to wait for the all clear.

Derek radioed that the package was moving and described the van to the police. He gave the all clear to his people when the second part of the chase had been passed to the next team.

The lesser items were put back into the main exhibit. The door to the room was closed with a sign that the scepter and ring would arrive for tomorrow's sale. About twenty people inside the room were part of the San Francisco team. The public, who made it inside during the incident, were ushered by the police to a different room and told not to reveal what occurred. So, no one inside the sale would report any strange gun incident to the press. The rest of the public were allowed back into the exhibit.

The police tracked the van's progress to an empty warehouse parking lot where three robbers stepped out. The woman gave the package to one of the men who jumped in a rental car and took off toward the airport. The other two men jumped into a beater car and left the scene. The woman got back in the van and left.

Separate undercover groups tailed the three vehicles and nabbed the criminals when they stopped. The fake scepter and ring were brought back to the exhibit. Hamm Roe was taken into police custody with the others in crime.

Hamm would be sent to the closest penitentiary, the same one that Minnow Surf currently resided.

Derek texted Jess, "First package secure." He also let David Dunker know. Day One and Two went exactly to their plans.

Jess informed Ara and Jack that Hamm Roe was in custody.

Jess brought out the expensive scotch and asked the chef to make wonderful appetizers. She also told Ara that she could be an author if she wanted and handed her the contract she printed off. The literary agent made the courtesy call to Jess. She was sent the note because Ara was on the Wrights' motorboat.

Jess told her to read the e-mail from the agent with the original price, and additional term pages. Ara and Jack were ecstatic about her first published book and the pre-amount. They wanted to hand out stuffed little tigers free for the first five thousand books to push sales.

39 Antiquities Sale - Day 3

THE POLICE RELEASED the tapes and list of criminals to the police in Africa and London with Ara's signed confession. They agreed to give the Los Angeles police twenty-four hours to catch their criminals before they rounded up the ones in their countries.

Derek sent Jess a text message, "San Do now, pp fly Cur and WJul to RO. Wait." Derek learned Jess's writing codes, having read many of her notes on their books.

Jess informed the captain to head to San Diego, their favorite port and location for a pickup package. Some of the Miami group would take them to their chartered flight. Ara and Jack were to fly to Curacao, and then War Julio would bring them to Rio de Janeiro via helicopter. They were to await there until they received the word things were safe.

The real bottom scepter was found in Hamm Roe's apartment in a black velvet pouch with a sewn tag inside that read, *Felidae3*. Ara left her signature on each one of her bags. The pouch was in a large travel backpack.

Jess showed Derek how to open the secret compartment on the bottom scepter and he used her jewelry tool.

In his department's screening room, he opened the secret compartment of the recovered bottom scepter. Inside were the small diamonds, two emeralds, and large ruby. He sent Jess two pictures of the items.

She loved it. The Renaliere jewels were kept, and the real top and real scepter bottom were put together with the tracking device in the lower section. The whole authentic scepter with original jewels was taken to the sale and professionally photographed again for Jess.

Everyone was in place exactly like they were before, only the Miami and San Francisco boys interspersed throughout the rooms and outside as did the police. Some heavy-set men entered the room and went directly to the scepter room.

Derek told his teams, "Be ready, we believe things may be going down shortly."

The men dispersed the gas and smoke into the one room and the police gas-masked men entered the room while the bad guys with their masks were trying to leave.

The people at the main exhibit door were halted and the Miami group led the people inside quickly out of the main exhibit room to safety. Several shots were fired by the police bringing three of the bad guys down. A fourth person tried to escape through the door and was quickly tackled down by both the police and Derek's group.

The African man a distance away lowered his binoculars and left the scene. He thought the scepter was a fake set-up to catch him. He would have to lay low for some time to find Queenie or Elizabeth again. He drove the taxi cab back to his point of contact blending in with the crowded street of cars. He dodged into an apartment over the bakery he worked, hiding inside the perimeter of the police barricades.

In a week, he read the story in the paper about a team of thugs who were captured at an antiquities sale. The thugs were from Africa. Included in the article was his name as the leader who was wanted by the police. They believed he had been involved in the stolen goods and other criminal activities such as an illegal drug trade. The police had obtained a list of many other unsavory characters due to an anonymous tip. This source had also given them names in London. The source possibly was connected to the leader.

He read the article a little further. The thieves tried to steal an authentic, two-part, golden eagle scepter with real gemstones worth eight million dollars and a diamond ring worth seven-hundred-thousand-dollars. The ring was safe and secure as was the scepter. The objects once belonged to royalty several centuries ago, owned by the Renaliere family. The pure gold scepter was part of a collection that included a crown, eagle clasp, and diamond ring. The only items missing were a gold crown and gold clasp. The police believed those objects were also stolen.

Tiger knew that he was screwed.

"The gold items that I wanted to purchase for my collection were at the sale after all. I, erroneously, did think they were fakes. The scepter looked as good as the one in the 1806 painting of Napoleon by Francois

Gerard, only the top of that scepter showed a full eagle."

Tiger signed, because he knew they were real.

"That profound fact amazes me. It was bad luck to miss seeing the treasures in person. Unfortunately, there was no way to disguise my height. If she was at the sale, I would have been recognized."

He stared out his crummy apartment room's window. He hated waiting. The smell of fresh bakery bread permeating the smoggy air had no effect. He wasn't hungry for food. It was a lot of surveillance and paid services for nothing. He wasted his time trying to find her.

"I can't go home to England to my past life or see my children permanently. All my contacts will think I'm the anonymous source or the person who was careless with the list of my client's names. Someone on the list will surely put a hit out on me. The police know who I am. I'm the suspicious person who did try to kill Elizabeth in Alabama. I can't sell my priceless antiquities because everyone knows they are stolen."

Flying back to London with a stolen wallet for identification, he placed his two antiquities in a safe in the grandparent's home. He believed they were hidden. Only his son knew where the key was, and he promised to tell no one. He left his children in the grandparents' care and told them he was going to enlist for a year in a good-works program in Africa to save the environment. They believed him.

Tiger knew Queenie played him, because now he was the person running. He was the person cut off from everything. He still had his money and antiquities. Tiger knew how to survive. His hatred for her bloomed into a higher hell-fire. Feelings of love slid off the scale.

40   Room in Ara's Dream

WAR JULIO TOLD Jack that things were now clear. Jack needed to return to America and provide a normal front. He knew they were correct, and Ara would be fine and in good hands. He kissed her goodbye in Rio de Janeiro and went back to Los Angeles. The two of them had already made plans to meet again.

She was writing two more tiger children's books, and she would be busy. Jack Jones went back to his plastic surgery business and would occasionally fly to South America for vacation, traveling to many of its coastal cities. To cover his real activity, which was seeing Ara, he told people that he wanted to write a travel book because he was bored.

Derek also worried that Senegal may not clear Ara for the bombing. She provided them the name of her contact on the explosives. The person's name was not on her other list. She had held onto that name as a possible bargaining chip. He wasn't sure it was enough. Two people died in the car bomb.

Derek hoped their next plan would catch the real Tiger-Sphinx-Man which was the name the police silently called the criminal. They were thinking of using the Curacao location for that capture plan. The draw would be the tiger book author, Ara Landt. Ara was growing her hair out again and would put it back to blonde when the plan was ready. She would look exactly like Queenie used to.

Ara did not want to see Scott Barrow when the Alabama police told him that she was still alive. She thought if she did, it would put him in more danger. She wrote him a private note apologizing for her deception and wished him well. The police did not know her whereabouts.

Her lawyer in Los Angeles would be contacting Scott's attorney shortly. She filed divorce papers stating irreconcilable differences. She was not required to appear in court because she had signed special papers. Ara also met with the judge in private chambers before the third antiquity sale to witness her divorce decision. Derek had flown her down to the meeting on his motorboat helicopter.

Jack was working to bring Ara's tiger to a zoo in Los Angeles. She was excited when he told her that they had found a zoo which made space for him. The zoo would contact the Alabama zoo to see if they would relinquish the tiger. Jack would let War Julio know the Alabama zoo's decision to relay to Ara.

If the Alabama zoo wouldn't cooperate, they would try another anonymous donation to try to get them to budge. If that didn't work, they would offer them a year's worth of the children's tiger books to sell in their zoo shop.

Jess had given them the name of a gold jeweler who would make beautiful tiger and diamond wedding rings for them. As soon as their lawyer gave them the word on Ara's divorce finalization, they would have a private, secret ceremony in Rio.

Jess and Derek were pleased for them. They knew how hard everything had been for Ara and Jack.

Ara talked to Jess about how she never knew love other than her tiger. Jess was getting their group of people together to chip in money into a wedding fund for the couple named: Bring a golden obsession called Felidae home. His home would be the Los Angeles zoo. The group also wanted to invite them to their next annual party.

Jess already talked with Derek and she chose their theme for the party.

One day, War Julio was showing Ara and Jack pictures on his computer of his family, children, and how his office looked before. He just completed the extra security, clear bulletproof glass in front of his desk. He had split the room in two. The glass moved sideways into two pieces before it joined as one. Then another wall activated to totally close off the viewing.

The entire area was painted from a pale yellow to ocean blue. He kept his Indian painting and had moved it to the inside part of the office. The outside part was blue and contained a large painting of dolphins, which was a gift from Derek and Jess.

The ceiling mirror was made smaller and an upgraded security camera and computers were installed. Ara and Jack only saw the outer part where there were comfortable chairs, table and lamp, an Italian rug and a small refrigerator with a clear door that held water, soda, and beer. The small table held bags of nuts. There was a door that led to a smaller room of more dolphin paintings. The room was like a mini-gallery to keep people entertained. Then another door went to a small bathroom.

Ara saw a picture on the computer. She asked War Julio, "Stop, it is the room, the room in my nightmare. The painting is the same only I saw just part of it, because the Tiger Sphinx was blocking the painting while pointing the gun at me."

War Julio took a key out of his pocket and pushed the small button. All the walls moved out of the way to reveal the desk and large oil painting of war horses running toward the viewer with their war paint, bows and arrows raised.

Jack said, "Scary."

War Julio laughed as that was Dean Crain's reaction a long time ago. War Julio would have to tell them the story, but he needed to let Derek know what Ara told him, so they could decide if there should be a change in the location for the plan.

Ara's nightmare happened in his office in Rio. She couldn't explain her vision to War Julio or Derek. Derek talked with her on the phone and told her not to worry about anything. Ara began to relax.

41   Rio Book Set Up and Scott

JIM MICHAELS WAS best man and his wife, Mary Beth, helped Ara get dressed at War Julio's horse estate in Rio de Janeiro. Jess was bridesmaid and wore a black strapless dress carrying a green palm. Ara's flowers were orange tiger lilies with flowing green palms. Her dress was a white plain design made of organdy material in a scoop front and backless dress. Her heels were tiger fur and Jack gave her diamond earrings. War Julio and Derek were the others attending the small beach ceremony.

A walkway and platform had been made down to the beach. The Bird Sanctuary was closed for the day and traffic was minimal. They would have a small catered affair on War Julio's estate away from prying eyes. Their family photographer was there. The Wright's children joined them at the reception. They had agreed to keep their wedding secret until the Tiger Sphinx was caught. Afterwards, they spent three nights onboard War Julio's air boat in a cove, specially guarded.

The next day everyone was together to discuss the children's tiger book signings. The three books were packaged together or could be purchased separately. They hoped the book signing would be the draw to pull the Tiger Sphinx to Rio.

The books were released under the name Ara Jones. She knew they would marry and she wanted her new name on the three-book package. A large picture of the young, beautiful blonde woman was on the outside back cover. The books were released online and printed in several languages.

The zoo in Rio was the location for the book signing in the building for the larger cats. The large cats were in their outside areas during the day. The empty inside cages were immaculately cleaned for the three-day book signing and locked shut. The large open area was where Ara would be located.

There was extra zoo security because the tigers were outside on the back part of the enclosure and they didn't want anyone to mess with them. Only twenty-five people at a time were allowed into the inside space with Ara and her guards. Consequently, the line for the books and a visit with the author was long.

After the signing, she would be taken to War Julio's estate in his huge vehicle with tinted bulletproof glass. She would be dropped off and the vehicle would pull away once she was inside. She would enter through his front office door which looked like a normal house estate door. The hope was that someone would follow her into the house. There were three days of book signings.

The first day there was nothing. The second day, she was followed. Everyone stood in their concealed places in case this person was a fluke. He was a white person. Ara entered the outer office and Derek told her to enter the gallery and lock the door.

Derek recognized the man as did Jack who insisted upon being in the undercover room. Derek told his people and the police to relax for now, it was her ex-husband, Scott Barrow. They hadn't counted on that occurrence. They were surprised he was there.

Scott entered the room. He called out, "Elizabeth."

Ara heard him and opened the door.

Jack moved to go to her. Derek touched his arm, "You must let her explain to him or it will always be something between you."

Jack sat down because he was not sure if he meant Ara and Scott or Ara and him.

Ara went to Scott, tenderly put her arms around him, and gave him a quick kiss on the lips much to everyone's amazement. Scott stood there looking at her and holding her gently. He wasn't sure who she had been or was now. It felt good to hold her even with her blonde hair.

Ara took his hand and led him over to a chair. She brought them both bottles of water. She smiled and took his hand again. It was good to see him. No one had tried to hurt Scott after she left.

"I'm glad you came to see me. You must have seen my children's tiger books, and know that I will be here in Rio for the book signing. My lawyer told me that you did ask about my name."

She hesitated. Ara wasn't supposed to explain her name. She continued, "It was a long way for you to travel, but then you do travel everywhere with the polo horses. How are they?"

Ara knew she was babbling.

Jack was surprised, because Ara hadn't told him those facts. Her lawyer was his friend.

Scott looked at her, "Why, Elizabeth? Why did you run? I have plenty of money and resources to protect you. The horses are as good as ever."

"Good."

He shook his head. She didn't answer him. He told her, "I don't understand the divorce. I thought our marriage was working great until you were missing. We didn't have much time together. What differences? There's nothing I wouldn't reconcile."

Ara's eyes became misty and she stood up, so the cameras couldn't see her face. "Our marriage was working, but you have no idea the massive evil person who's tracking me and would murder everything in my path, just to get to me. That was the huge problem."

Scott said, "I don't care. I love you. You are worth dying for."

Jack moved from his chair and started pacing the room.

Ara came over to Scott and told him, "I can't let that happen. The evil one has killed my friends and it hurts too much. You must understand. Every time he kills someone, he kills me inside. He killed the vision of me over and over. The evil one knows all about you and where you live. I won't let him destroy your world."

"Was the evil person still at large?"

Ara told him, "Yes."

"Then I will wait. I want to wait for you. I can wait with you. Afterwards we can buy the beautiful pied-a-terre in New York City that you wanted."

Jack stopped pacing and watched Ara closely.

Derek let out a long breath. He wished Jess were here. She would know what to do.

Ara took hold of his hands, "It isn't about the penthouse. You need someone who truly loves you. What about that nice girlfriend of yours?"

Scott smiled, "My old girlfriend has been amazing and supportive."

Ara told him that she was glad. She sat back down. Then there was a long silence between the two of them. The men in the other room looked at each other.

Scott finally asked, "Will you call me when everything is over, and the criminal has been caught?"

Ara nodded. She couldn't speak.

Scott got up to leave and told her he was driving to the airport. He held Ara again. She walked him outside where he kissed her the way he used to. She came back in and went to the bathroom and locked the door.

Derek notified a car to follow Scott Barrow and make sure he made it to the airport. His contact was to watch Scott get on his plane back to Alabama and out of harm's way.

Jack went down and waited twenty minutes, and then he knocked on the bathroom door. She let him into the bathroom where there were no cameras. After another hour, the team went to the horse estate with a quiet Ara and Jack to wait until the next day, which was the final book signing.

42   Red Herring

ARA WAS GLAD it was the last day and there was a steady stream of people to keep her mind off herself. There were still enough free small stuffed tigers for the rest of the day. She was tired from her meeting with Scott and hadn't slept most of the night. She rubbed the name tag on the toy to bring her luck. She looked at the fuzzy thing and remembered when she first saw the baby tiger. She blew the creature a kiss.

Jess ordered extra stuffed tigers because the zoo workers had children and would receive a free book for any child under ten years old. Jess told her the zoo people were her best marketers.

The book tour ended, and a tired Ara was driven back to the door of War Julio's estate. Ara brought one of the toys home. She entered the outer room and sat down. The large vehicle drove away.

A large black rental car drove down to the Bird Sanctuary and sat a few minutes watching the estate. It drove back to the front of the estate and a tall African man stepped out.

Derek told Ara to position herself. The wall of glass and outer wall closed. She sat down by the desk and put the toy on top. If it was the wrong person, she was to explain that she was War Julio's new secretary and she would get him for the person.

The black man sauntered into the office. Ara couldn't believe it was him.

"Hello, Sphinx."

He laughed. "You are now called Ara. I was surprised when I read your book. How do you pronounce it? Is it a Ra-like name from the Egyptian deity? He was their Sun God. Perhaps you picked this name to honor me?"

Ara looked at him filled with apprehension. She didn't know where the conversation was going. She knew that he called himself Tiger, but she refused to say that name for him.

"You were fond of your name once, Queenie. So was I. It was fitting. Now my new name is Tiger. Isn't that ironic. I selected the name in memory of you, my beloved girl. Don't you like my new name?"

Ara didn't speak and waited for him to take the lead in their conversation.

Tiger Sphinx had always liked the way she said his old name. He wanted to hear her say his new name, but knew she wouldn't. He liked the fact she was uncomfortable. He looked her up and down. She was as young and beautiful as when she belonged to him. He smiled at her like he always did in the past. The Tiger Sphinx used to desire her. He still wanted her.

Jack got up from his chair in the upper room. He didn't like the man.

Tiger Sphinx moved closer to her, smelling her beautiful perfume. It was expensive. It was the same perfume he bought her in Africa. That fact made him happy. She hadn't changed that much. She still liked rich.

"I did see you married the polo boy. I saw him when you passed through London."

Ara frowned because she didn't know she came that close to him. "Yes, I did marry."

"Don't you remember what I told you? You belong to me," said Tiger Sphinx.

"You must stop your madness."

"No, I don't think that I will. I can let you go, but I've decided not to. I do have my precious antiquities back. It isn't enough. You still don't understand, I control everything."

Ara felt anger at the man who called Scott a boy, but remained distant and held her ground in defiance.

A second truck approached, and a delivery boy opened the door and moved the Tiger Sphinx out of his way, bumping him to the right side of the room.

Derek looked at War Julio who shook his head. They already had the bad-ass bird in the room. Were there more coming to the party? If so, they would be busy. War Julio didn't know what could be in the package and did an open hand gesture with a shrug. Derek said into his microphone, "Catch delivery boy, unknown package arrival. Suspect in house is still the main target."

Ara looked at the package on the desk and returned her gaze to the man who had moved.

Tiger Sphinx came a little closer and saw the stuffed toy. He picked the item up and squeezed the soft fur. The toy looked much like the jungle cat with markings. The toy emitted a small sound. He had a faraway look in his eyes. The horse lessons weren't enough. He thought he knew women but somehow failed. She reached for the toy and he put it in his pocket. His eyes looked at her.

Ara knew what night he was remembering. She remembered. She saw the clear tape in its holder and began taking small pieces of tape off. She stuck them to the paper pad in front of her. One by one, she cut the tape. She hesitated and looked at the man across from her. She wondered how much tape was on the roll.

"If I bought you a tiger back then, would you have stayed?"

Ara mustn't say no to him. She chose to keep their conversation on a level plane. She learned in the past to ask his permission. She said, "I would have loved to own a tiger if you approved." She reached again for the tape.

The Tiger Sphinx stopped. He saw her nervously handling the tape machine. He noticed the pile of tape. The tape was in the shape of a bird. He wasn't going to let her fly away. He stared at her. The man caught her mood of flight. He trained her well or she was trying to distract him. He laughed louder. "My second wife didn't adapt to my world like my intelligent Queenie girl."

She worriedly looked at him. Ara willed herself to stop and forget the tape. He always knew what she was thinking. She must park her thoughts at the back of her mind and stay present even though her insides were turning to jelly. The anger was dissipating. She wanted her Felidae toy back. It was the one she kissed earlier for luck. Ara started to feel ill. This was not working well. More tape was put on the pad. There was almost an inch of the stuff. A person couldn't see through the tape anymore. She remembered her knife wound and the pain standing alone in the tiny garage in Alabama. The man in front of her did that to her. The tiger fish in front of her had hurt her. He damaged her. The tape was to hide from him. It was to cover up the bad. The bird meant escape. She acknowledged the logic of her problems with this man. She was trying to rid herself of his control. Ara looked at the stuffed toy and wished the man in front of her was dead.

"I'm not afraid of the hocus pocus transference that you did to my hired man. It doesn't work on me."

Ara caught her breath.

The Tiger Sphinx said, "When you were in Africa, I knew it was you on the phone. Why didn't you talk to me? Huge effort was made by you to find out where I lived. It was old Santan's house or should I say, Charlie's? I bought the house because I could. Why didn't you come to the front door and face me? You owed me a visit. I changed my world because of what you did to me. And you failed to kill me in the Congo. I'm still alive." His voice grew louder and angrier. His eyes bulged and looked, somehow, off.

Ara stood up from the desk chair. She couldn't do anymore tape. She must get away from the man.

"I really wanted to talk with you that day." His sarcasm filled the air.

Ara felt the trap door closing her world. She couldn't breathe. The tape was too thick. The bird couldn't get through the bars of the cage. She wondered if should give Derek the signal, but the police needed more information. Her true freedom was at stake.

Jack saw her distress and raced to the door where War Julio intercepted him. Ara hadn't given them the signal. Jack reluctantly moved to the side, because he promised Ara he would behave no matter the conversation. She told him everything could get very difficult. She assured him that she knew how to handle the man. Jack was worried. He hadn't seen Ara this way. She was acting strange. He saw the pile of tape. It wasn't like her.

Ara cleared her throat. She wanted a drink of water, but didn't dare move to the cooler. "I was afraid, because I did place a bomb on your car. The bomb was obtained through one of your African contacts."

The Tiger Sphinx liked her distress and grinned mischievously.

"I did make my wife and her bodyguard get out of her car that day and step into mine. My explosives contact is an old loyal friend. The friend told me about the bomb on my car. The contact gave me the remote device to detonate the package. You wouldn't know when I hit the button. I had hoped you were a little closer to my car. But you kept a safe distance. I know the time allowed on the device. My wife must die for her sin because she tried to kill my *beloved* Queenie girl without my permission. The bodyguard must die for banging my wife. It was just that simple."

Derek smiled, "Bingo, we've got him on two murders and attempted murder."

Jack was having a hard time with the way this man was calling his wife beloved. He missed the fact that the man confessed to recently killing two people besides attempts on his wife.

Ara knew there were no morals or love inside the big man. It hadn't been there ever. The only thing he cared about was money and obviously, his treasured items. Tiger tossed the toy onto the desk and she jumped. The air conditioner clicked on and a slight breeze swirled the room. Suddenly, she felt freezing. She smelled death or something strange mingling with his cologne. Ara acknowledged that she was very afraid.

Derek and War Julio looked at each other. Both thought the same thing, "This murderer must be put down. The pursuit of this woman was relentless and would never stop."

"The other man failed. You deceived him with your imaginary images in Alabama. We shall see who wins."

The Tiger Sphinx made his decision and reached for his gun. The black barrel appeared.

She froze; it was her nightmare. Felidae warned her. She thought of her beloved real tiger. She looked at the toy lying limp on the desk. Soon, she would be broken. Time stood still for her.

In that one second, War Julio looked at Derek who nodded. War Julio pressed the start key button.

The Tiger Sphinx was sweating as he aimed. The glass wall began its closure. The raised gun fired. His arm was like a piece of lightning when it lifted. He struck, fast, swift, and deadly.

Jack quickly exited the upper room, flying down the stairs.

Ara saw her tigers in their forest in her mind. She reached outward to them. Shots fired were an explosion, one hit her, and brought Ara down. She floated into unconsciousness. Her blood littered the clean white porcelain floor. The walls were sprayed with her blood.

Tiger Sphinx exited the house before anyone could reach him. He dodged police bullets outside to reach the rental car. The man drove crazily toward his man who would help him escape. There was one last turn in the road and he could disappear. His eyes were bulging more from heightened excitement.

"It was so easy to kill. She is now my senseless and useless, Queenie." He laughed cruelly. He fingered the warm gun and could smell the smoke expelled from the fired bullets. Tiger Sphinx inhaled the smell. He felt good. Suddenly, he developed a coughing fit. Feeling slightly dizzy, he rubbed his lower lip. He looked in his dashboard mirror. His image was covered in sweat and his lip was slightly numb.

Soon there would be no more vile words exiting his mouth. The steady drip of the calciseptine in his bloodstream caused the muscles to relax. A snake skin became dislodged from its hidden place in the windshield visor and floated past his eyes out the open window as the car reached the turn.

The package was the red herring. Snake woman was there as the delivery boy and touched him. Tiger Sphinx tried to turn the wheel. His hands were frozen in a permanent grip. He suddenly realized too late what was wrong.

Slurring his words, he mumbled, "Tox, tox...in."

It was something he had not counted on. He tried to speak and began screaming inside his brain.
"No, no, I can't die. There's my money. I will give you mine or the gold. You like gold! I have information. We can make a trade and collaborate. That's the ticket. I know who killed your first lover in prison. You want to know, don't you? Wait, just wait a minute. Come back; I need the antidote."

No amount of money in the world could help him recover. It was his unlucky day. The Snake woman owned her own fortune. She didn't need any of the Tiger Sphinx's money at all. She also knew who killed her first lover. There would be no exchange of information. The man betrayed her whereabouts on a favorite private island to the police. The action taken by the African man was unforgivable in her mind. He sealed his own fate. The man failed to remember her higher skills and power. She tracked and disposed of her enemies efficiently.

Tiger Sphinx looked at his outside rearview mirror and saw red lipstick in tiny letters. The letters spelled out one word: No.

He couldn't believe it. Next came cold, mind-numbing paralysis for the man. The rental car jettisoned over the cliff. The net of death enveloped his mad heart and lungs. His final seconds were suffocation. Tiger's lips turned a purple-black, close in color to dioxazine purple and mars black from an oil painter's pallet. His body fell forward into the steering wheel when the heart stopped.

The color of his body changed to a beginning moon-glow color around the edges. Or some British people would call the color, wretched cemetery-stone. His foot slipped off the gas earlier. The car hit a large boulder, bounced, and inched erratically forward. Heading down an embankment, the Tiger Sphinx was dead before the car rolled to the water's edge and was stopped by a piece of wood. There was no roll or flip of the vehicle into the ocean.

The once powerful man in the heavy car was stopped by a shot of Dendroapsis polylepis, the black mamba snake venom. His game was over; the jaws of a reptile and its more fanatical keeper got the best of him. She won.

43   No Rush, A New Day

JACK REACHED ARA and took his shirt off to staunch the flow of blood on her head.

Her last thought was that the tiger fish finally won. Then Jack held her, and she felt him there in her unconscious state. His warmth spilled into the room, warming her body with his love. Ara held on.

The police followed the rental vehicle and ran down the hill. Swarming the Tiger Sphinx's vehicle, they peered in the open window. It was clear the driver was dead. They waited for the ambulance which accelerated down the road, lights, and siren blaring.

War Julio fired up his helicopter and they put Ara in the new large helicopter he recently purchased. They flew her immediately to the hospital and into surgery.

Derek sat with Jack until War Julio and his wife could relieve him. War Julio's wife liked the young woman and man that were their guests. She worried about Ara and said her prayers.

Derek left the hospital and sat in one of the police vehicles at the hospital waiting for his rental car. He asked himself why he hesitated. He should have had his team rush in. But the Tiger Sphinx moved fast. It was like he was hopped up on something or worst, almost inhuman, pure evil in the final moments. Ara had been afraid of him and rightfully so. The Tiger

271

Sphinx was one scary piece of malevolence which super decayed in those last seconds in the room. The man was the worst Derek encountered for some time. Jess was right in the beginning with her word, fierce. The Tiger Sphinx was fierce in the room. He shuddered.

Derek drove to the police department. The coroner came on the phone line. He thought the Tiger Sphinx did not die from the car accident. He thought the victim was poisoned by some strong form of poison so that he would die quickly. The coroner would have to run more tests. The package the delivery boy left behind didn't show any lethal substance.

"Try checking the poison against the African Black Mamba. The snake skin and toxin were found at a prior case, but not this one." The coroner thanked him.

Derek asked the police, "Did they catch the delivery boy or a possibly disguised woman?"

They hadn't and were still looking. Derek knew the Snake woman was gone. Her ability to vanish was remarkable. It was almost as if she evaporated into the air. He knew she used many high-tech gadgets and people to cloak herself. They could find no trace.

The kill was payback for divulging her name. She used her favorite gray-colored Mamba. Her experiments were successful every time. The Snake woman believed the Tiger Sphinx was the anonymous person or the person who divulged a list of hit peoples' names to the police. She knew many people on that list were arrested and all were connected to him. Her wrathful condemnation toward the man came to a satisfied conclusion which was his death. She felt righteous in eliminating the Tiger man. The Snake woman was her own judge and jury. She disguised herself and did the kill.

Derek liked the evil con artist killing another one. He wished it would happen more often. Ara taught Derek the importance of turning them against each other.

The coroner told him the man also showed signs of a bad heart and wouldn't have lasted much longer. Derek let his superiors know what transpired, and a copy of the tape was sent to them and the police in Los Angeles.

The video tape would exonerate Ara of the two murders in Africa, so she could return to Los Angeles. They would be satisfied with her prior valuable information and this tape.

Tiger Sphinx's family would be asked about two gold antiquities, and the son would give the safe key to the authorities and show them where the safe was hidden.

The doctor thought Ara would be fine. They were keeping her unconscious until the swelling stopped. She would need some minor repair. The doctors felt good that she would have function as good as before the shooting. The bullet had miraculously not hit major brain systems. She was young, and her body was strong. Ara would stay in the hospital two weeks.

XXXXXX

The analysis of the bullets trajectory would show the bullet nicked the thinner edge of the protective glass which deflected it slightly away from her. The bullet almost missed. Derek looked again at the video and slowed everything down. It was as if something held Ara a second before the bullet deflected. Without that pause, the bullet would have hit her head on.

Derek sat in his car looking at the photo taken of the envelope the delivery person left. The return address label read: *Nothingness, PO Box No. 1, Can Stop, ME*. There was a red rubberstamped message that was smeared a little bit. He zoomed his phone to increase the image. He read the words, *No Rush, A New Day*. It was a message directed at him or the police. Derek swallowed, because he thought the notes were directed at him. The message was to stop pursuing her. It showed her over-confidence at not getting caught.

He smiled, because now he knew Snake woman's estimated height and build. Her stature would be difficult to hide in the future. He saw there were actor's skin, makeup, wig, and special clothes to disguise her figure. It was hard to tell her nationality, but he would guess she was from South or East Asia. She used the word "nothingness instead of nothing". This key element was important information. Jess made Derek take an Asian philosophy course a while back. She wanted him to expand his knowledge. It was a good class, because he remembered some important stuff about the concept of nothingness. He also had a copy of the tape from War Julio's office to view repeatedly.

There was a certain way Snake woman turned and walked.

"Know thy enemy and you will be strong," said Derek to himself.

Perhaps the Snake woman wanted him to have these hints about her character. He would turn everything that he had over to their police profiler. The study they kept on her would grow. She would be known better than ever. It was difficult to live anywhere currently without nosy neighbors to remind a person of the community rules. They reported strange, reclusive people, or those outside the boundaries of rules, to a homeowner association. Most neighborhoods wanted a person to conform.

Snake woman was reclusive and obeyed no rules. Nothing was leashed, especially her poison or control. She believed the earth and sea belonged to her. Unfriendly neighbors might be the thing to trip her up. Or he could look for dead people near each other in nice neighborhoods. She cleared the land quietly when she met the unfriendly or was unhappy. He would use all the advantages that he could get.

"There is time. Yeah, no rush at all. Your schemes will wait. Catching one bad guy at a time works for me!"

He whistled an older jazz song about time. It was a song that his old girlfriend from Rio constantly played. The words of the song resonated in his brain, helping him figure out the message further. The song was, however, a rush.

He wouldn't tell Jess about the envelope or his ideas, nor the old girlfriend. The old girlfriend was a sore point between them. It hadn't occurred to him that maybe Jess could be better at interpreting the Snake woman's message until much later. *No rush* meant she was working a new game.

Oblivious, Derek was back to his normal self. He didn't let evil hold him down for very long. He was confident that the tide or a power beyond the criminals would surely help catch them. He counted on it happening. He bounced his hand on his steering wheel to the piano beat and heavy, slurry jazz tone. The beat magically matched his heart rhythm.

"Let the good people reign. Nothing will stop us."

Starting the ignition in the car, he drove smoothly through fast traffic with expert hands and back to Jess. He knew his job was difficult sometimes and she would be waiting. Derek was glad and felt lucky. They were good for each other. He knew life was precious.

She texted him that she called the book people and asked them to deliver one of the stuffed tiger toys for Ara. Jess asked for the large three-foot display animal to be delivered to Ara's hospital room. Tiger lilies were included in the bouquet from the florist. Jess believed Ara would make it and become stronger.

"Yes, she will," said Derek, catching his wife's positive thoughts. His wife's love alone would pull him through and back from death's grip. She shared that wonderful love with her friends which now included Ara and Jack.

He knew there was plenty of time to do the dance with the Snake woman. He would be ready for her and high tide.

44 All about Ara

AFTER TWO MONTHS, Ara went back to Alabama to pick up her beloved, Felidae. The zoo people, Jack, Jess, and Derek watched on the computer as she approached his cage. The small swimming pool with water had been brought in along with a beach ball, several sturdy platforms, and plants. Ara told them how to arrange everything. She had her gold chain, knife, and treats. The zoo was granted the rights to the video and she signed a form that she wouldn't sue.

Ara approached his cage because he was sleeping. She clinked her chain, and he instantly awoke and came to the door. She held out her hand and he smelled her. He made a low growl. She bowed to him and began pacing back and forth. He didn't move until she gave him the release command and then he matched her every step. She gave him a treat. She clinked her chain twice, and she paced. The tiger sat and waited. She came back and gave him two treats.

Seeing Ara open the cage, Jack thought he was going to have a heart attack. She walked to the three platforms, and the tiger looked at the pool of water.

She clinked her knife against the chain, and he jumped on the lower platform. She pointed to the second one, the tiger moved to the second platform, and the third. She gave him more treats and rubbed his head. He was in ecstasy and rubbed against her hand. She gave him the release, and he ran over to the pool and drank a long time. Then he urinated.

She held the beach ball high over her head and called him. The tiger stood on his hind quarters, but had to come down. She came over to him and bowed. He laid down on the floor as she approached. She told him to sit up. The tiger sat up. She gave him more treats. Then she walked up close to him and looked down. The tiger put his paws on her shoulders. She talked to him. The tiger rubbed her hair.

Jack couldn't look anymore until she clinked her chain. She had told him about that part.

Then she clinked her chain and the cat sat. She threw the beach ball to him, he jumped at it, and she let him play with the ball until it popped. Then he got another drink and urinated, moving slowly toward the cage. She continued to talk to him until he was inside, and then she closed his cage door.

The zoo people came in and fed him because that was Ara's routine. She left her sweet tiger boy whose tail was beating a happy tune. The tiger would be tranquilized for his flight to Los Angeles. Ara would make sure when he arrived that he was taken care of and visited him twice a week at the small Los Angeles area zoo. Then she told Jack she must say goodbye to Scott.

XXXXXX

Their flight landed, and their limo arrived. The limousine pulled up to the polo horse estate and Ara went to the front door. Scott had gotten his old girlfriend out of the house. Jack stayed in the limo. If she needed him, he would be there.

Ara walked into the living room and Scott enveloped Ara into his arms. She always felt and smelled good. He slowly kissed her, and she pulled away.

"I'm sorry that I hurt you when I fled. My world at that time was way too complicated and confusing. You are the person who is good. I didn't feel that way about me until now. I will remember our time together and love you for the person who does care about me. But there is someone else that I need very much."

Scott answered, "I know those facts. It is the older gentleman in the car?"

Ara replied, "Yes."

"Did you catch the bad guy?"

"Yes, we did with some difficulty."

"You must realize that I will always love you. You're good enough for me and are a part of my heart. I want to remain your friend," said Scott.

"I would like that very much. I need good friends with heart."

Scott already knew who Jack was in her life because Jack had called him when Ara was in the hospital. He called him four times. They both talked about Ara a long time. Jack also informed Scott when they would arrive. It was so Ara could say goodbye officially. Scott would slip and call her Elizabeth, for that was whom he had known.

Scott took her hand and told her, "I'm glad you made it and will be happy."

Ara kissed him again and said, "Goodbye, Scott, please love those polo babies for me."

"Goodbye, Elizabeth. You know I will."

Scott opened the door and said, "Oh, by the way, I saw the tiger video from the zoo's website. That activity was plain crazy-dangerous."

Ara smiled, "Not any crazier than making love to a wild man in a lake."

Scott laughed. He walked her to the limousine and told Jack, "Take care of this beautiful woman now."

Jack said, "I will certainly try."

Scott wanted to know if they wanted to come to a good, old-fashioned Alabama wedding in three months.

"Sure." Ara waved again, and their limo drove them to the airport.

Jack told Ara that he thought Scott was an okay kind of guy.

45 Ara and the Psychologist

ARA STEPPED INTO the psychologist's office. She hadn't wanted to go, and Jack told her that she needed to at least try therapy so that she could find peace. Ara knew that somewhere in her life she had messed up big time. "Failure kept playing repeatedly in her head." Jack occasionally saw her sadness. He didn't want her to feel that way.

Ara didn't know how to erase the words. Besides, she occasionally had nightmares still. She read books about obsessive-compulsive behaviors. She thought maybe that was what was wrong with her. Jack told her that she must stop the self-diagnosis.

Reaching her destination, she opened the smooth, sleek door to a beautiful fifteenth floor office in downtown Los Angeles. Even the waiting room showed a massive view of the Pacific Ocean. Ara looked out at the tourists enjoying the beach and water. She wished she was down there running the wet sand.

The glamorous receptionist with red hair told her that it was now her turn. It was her turn to divulge the off-things that were a part of her life but not the true facts. Jack told her that she must not utter any names, places, or accept blame for anything. He wanted Ara to feel good within her soul again. He felt her soul was worth saving, hence, a well-known, rich psychologist was required. She didn't think anyone could help her forget her past.

Ara sat down in the comfortable white leather chair and waited until her psychologist, Rosemary Quinn, entered the modern room filled with sleek furniture. The office felt like something out of a designer's catalog. The end table looked like a piece of glass sculpture. The low black couch and exotic dripping crystal chandelier stole the show. There were no magazines in the room or garbage cans.

The view of the ocean was floor to ceiling glass. Ara thought, "Money."

She began to sweat and feel nervous. There was no tape dispenser in the room. Ara was glad there was no tape dispenser. It occurred to her that her compulsive behavior with the tape had been her way to survive. It helped her to survive a horrific hunter. She picked up the small notepad and took a piece off. She folded an origami bird out of her piece. She heard the psychologist knock on the door before stepping inside. Quickly Ara stuffed the bird and pad behind her when the woman entered the room.

Rosemary introduced herself and asked Ara why she was here.

Ara explained that sometimes she had feelings of doing good and bad things. She was confused by that. The choices were fraught with disastrous consequences. It was difficult to choose the correct path.

"Well, we all have good and bad feelings, don't we?"

Ara was stunned by her response. The psychologist moved out of her chair and went to the bar. She asked, "Do you want some?"

Ara replied, "A martini? Um, yes, that sounds okay, if you're having one."

The psychologist filled her glass and Ara's and came over and sat down with a thud.

"It's not a ginger-type drink day. Usually my flavor is water. But the flavor flips like good and evil. Yes, there is that, the evil part of a personality. Isn't it always there? It is an age-old problem. You shouldn't be upset at all. And if you are, then it's perfectly natural on the emotion side of things. It's best to let go of your fears, even though we have been told, like forever, to hide everything. Women can't break out of the predefined mode. I say to heck with that crap. You have come to a safe place. I've created this office so that my clients will feel safe. So, let's talk about the stealing and cheating. Which one is worst? It depends whether you are the victor or victim. Yes, this is the place to divulge all."

The psychologist stopped, and tears came to her eyes after looking at her large photograph. It was the only one in the room. She knew her arrogant husband didn't want her to buy this picture, but she persisted. She was glad. It reflected her personality, free, and complicated. Burnout wouldn't happen for some time. Rosemary liked that idea.

The woman hesitated and said, "I knew he was cheating on me. I had him followed. Smart move on my part. When I confronted him, he told me that he was just collaborating with her. It's the new age word for screwing someone."

The psychologist stared into her glass, totally removed from the room, and her new client.

"He's dating my receptionist," exclaimed Rosemary. "I should fire her, but she is so good. Besides, she will be out of a job soon enough."

Rosemary laughed at her inability to get rid of the known enemy immediately. There were, obviously, other things the secretary was good at. Rosemary shuddered and put her feet up on the white and black leather footstool. She was ready to get wiped out. Her husband would wipe her out. All the overtime hours she had put in to build her business were for naught.

Ara was stunned. She said the first thing that came to her mind, "When they cheat, an eruption occurs, but the afterglow is beautiful."

Rosemary seemed to center back into the room. "Sorry, where were we with your story?"

Ara knew that Rosemary was going through a crisis of some sort. "I think that I don't know how to deal with evil?"

Rosemary handed her the card for her investigator friend who was good at finding anyone.

"I can only see you three times this month, because I'm moving back to the east coast where people are more civil and friendly."

"That's all that I need, just three sessions, and I think that I will be well."

"Yes, let's hope that you make it. You do talk strange like you've been here before. I can give you a name of another psychologist friend in the business for any continuation of therapy."

Ara shook her head. The world was a mess. It just depended on what degree.

Rosemary knew that she was important for this woman's survival. She would try to help her before she left. Her experience was extensive. They could share their knowledge.

"What evil are you dealing with now?"

Ara knew that she should tell her story, but she couldn't. She played it safe and diluted things.

"A man tricked me repeatedly. Somehow, he found me. I wanted him out of my life."

Rosemary gave her a card for her shark lawyer. She misinterpreted the reason for Ara's visit. "As a woman, you need to be well-armed. You have come to the right place. You need to sue him for everything that he is worth today and the future. That is what I'm going to do, before he does it to me. I want to live in the afterglow."

Ara smiled. The woman had been listening to some of her conversation. Her mind wandered. The picture on the wall was two giant bright stars. She didn't need to read the inscription.

"The large photograph is Capella A and B. It looks good in your office. I love the wild golden obsession theme. It's two stars that look like one from our view on earth. Both are very real. It took a while for scientists to unravel the mystery."

Rosemary was surprised. "Yes, it is a photo of Capella in the constellation called Auriga. Most people wouldn't know its golden color is the same spectral G as the sun. I love this painting. It's appropriately named Charioteer."

"I know about golden things. It's been part of my obsession."

"Obsession can be good if you're careful with its power. A master trickster can be defeated," said Rosemary. "Or a quitter."

The psychologist did hear her.

"Yes, I know," said Ara.

Ara was thinking their conversation would be about Freud or Jung or some other great author in the land of psychology. Instead she pocketed the business cards the woman had given her and took a sip of her drink. She liked this person. She was impressed with the sensible woman who was coping with her own disaster. The psychologist handled the word obsession just right and didn't probe her about the comment. Ara decided that she could be friends with the woman. It was a breakthrough for her to know there were other people as obsessed. She didn't want to talk about tricksters or quitters, so she changed the subject.

"I'm acquainted with some great clothing designers. I have a new friend, Jess Wright, who is a super woman, top of the line in the couture world. I could introduce you to her so that you would have some wonderful outfits when you reach the east coast and visit the Cape to meet interesting new people. She might even be able to include some constellations in your design."

Rosemary looked at Ara. Her client had distracted her twice. She was very intuitive. She laughed. Perhaps she was in the business too long or needed to take some classes to brush up on the millennial's approach to life. The young woman was refreshing instead of depressing. It buoyed her up.

"I knew there had to be something good about this day. I'm glad you selected my business. Our time is up but I look forward to our next visit. We can talk about your new friend then."

Rosemary looked around and a panic expression hit her eyes. "My yellow pad, where is my little notes? I have to have the pad."

Ara produced the small pad that was behind her and the origami bird. She guiltily handed both items over to her psychologist.

Rosemary looked at the bird and pad of yellow paper. She put the tiny piece of art in her pocket. Smiling, Rosemary took the yellow pad and ripped the thing into two separate ones. "Here, take this one. Thank you for the rising phoenix bird. It represents regeneration or rebirth. How appropriate. I want you to come up with words that we might use in some design piece. I like the concept of magnificent clothing with constellations that we can review on your next visit. Let's call this more exercise therapy."

"Yes, I can see it as such a thing. I know lots of constellations. Let's see what we can come up with."

Rosemary let Ara out of her office. Both women smiled as if there was a shared secret.

Ara went back home to Jack feeling relieved. Therapy could work.

She knew that she was finally well. Her old story was one that had been spinning for ages in her mind. It was time to let the past rest. Jack was where she wanted to live. She had weathered the storm. There was good in her life. Ara belonged to a family of super great people. They walked on the good side. She knew the difference. She had finally chosen well.

Ara drove home watching the sunset develop into multiple scatterings of light. The warm, red-orange afterglow enveloped the coast. Jack was waiting outside for her when she drove into their drive. She knew he wasn't a trickster or quitter. She was safer than she'd ever imagined. A small twinkling of stars hit the evening sky.

46   Annabelle Visit with Hamm

HAMM WAS GLAD to get out of his cell. He hated this place. A person couldn't get a decent sandwich or cup of coffee. Even the air outside smelled bad in the prison exercise yard. Someone told him it was because of the large steer farm nearby. He didn't plan on eating the hamburgers in this joint either. They smelled like the air.

Sitting down in the chair with the caged window, he looked at the young woman who had come to visit him.

"Hello, Annabelle, what are you doing here? I told you last time I'm going to be in this stupid place for some time. You don't need to come back if you don't want to. I will understand. I'm also broke so I can't take care of you."

"I know you're broke and that doesn't matter. I like you very much and will keep visiting you. My money from my family will be sufficient. You shouldn't worry about me. I never went back to our apartment because there were police all over the place. I'm glad I didn't move in with you or I would have no clothes to wear. My brother told me to avoid your place. He didn't want me to get sucked into your theft issue."

Hamm thought about what she said. Annabelle didn't know about the possible murder wrap. He hoped his relationship with her would improve his relationship with the bad dudes. He still worried about the money he owed to the Green Stream clan.

The young woman didn't get the fact that Hamm used her. Hamm thought maybe he still could do that after all. He looked at her. She was rather plain, not the normal girls he picked. She was short and wore an older, dull hairdo. Her short legs were not model quality. In prison a man couldn't be picky.

"It really wasn't my fault that I was caught. The Wrights are to blame. They owe me money. Then there was your group of friends. They weren't nice to me. They took away my job and wouldn't let me continue the stolen car deliveries. I was willing to work off my debt. I shouldn't have to pay them all the money either. It was just a simple mistake. I'm willing to pay half. That would be fair. I'm a fair guy. You must convince them to change their minds."

"That's what I think, too. You are a nice and fair person. That is why I have come up with a plan. I did talk to my brother about you. I'm getting older, and my prospects are looking slim. I want to do the family thing and make babies. You're the first intelligent man I met that likes me."

Hamm looked at her not quite sure where this conversation was headed. He hated babies.

Annabelle looked at him and laughed. She knew Hamm didn't like children. He had told her many times. There were enough children in her family. No babies were all right with her.

Hamm didn't know if he should laugh or not. He tried to smile. He felt like a sinking pirate ship from the Wrights' sunken treasure book. He thought he was going to lose all the silver in the wooden barrels that were onboard. He noticed her eyes were on fire like the last light on the second cannon-balled ship.

She took his smile as a good sign and would lay out her proposition that was approved by her brother.

"My brother is very powerful in my family. He loves me very much. I'm his only sister and my big brother always protects me. He knows my every want and need. I like you as a partner, major big time. I tell my brother everything. I have told him about our current difficulties. My brother is on our side. He will help us with our difficulties."

Hamm heard the words, "I like you and major big time." He thought that was what was in her eyes.

"If we are married, I wouldn't have to visit you through a cage. I could touch you a lot in the family visitation room. My brother can talk to his group. If we are married, you won't be poor relation anymore. As a wedding gift, my brother would erase the debt permanently. You will also be protected in prison from then on. When you get out, there will be jobs waiting for you. Family members always receive the higher paying jobs. What do you think about my solution to our minor difficulties? Oh, and I'm all right with no children."

Hamm bent down to check his shoe. He thought fast. Geez, what illness has befallen this woman? All this marriage stuff was surreal. It was only sex. She doesn't understand sex was all he wanted.

He felt his stomach ache as if a rusty cannonball hit him. He needed to think about this new venture. It might work and save his skin at the same time. But, if he ever escaped, he would have to move some place far away to get away from the clan and the brother. Russia might be a good place to hide.

Hamm sat up straight because the guard was approaching, and he was relieved. Their time was up. Hamm smiled, "I'll think about what you told me. I like you very much, too. I appreciate the proposal and suggestion. It seems like a good plan."

He slid off the hard metal chair and went with the guard. His forehead was sweating from an oncoming fever and migraine at the thought of marriage to Annabelle.

Annabelle arose, happy once more. He appreciated her. Her suggestion was a smart plan. She knew this was going to work. She was going wedding dress shopping to pick a short-skirted one to show off her pretty legs.

"I definitely need a corsage, new shoes, marriage license, what else?"

Her brother would be happy she was finally getting married. Their family would increase by one more person. She was exhilarated just thinking about everything. Their future looked so bright. Maybe she could find a better apartment. Her waiter tips at the restaurant were improving.

Annabelle would talk to Sandra about a raise. Sandra would talk to Randy on her behalf. They would be joyous for her.

Then there was the wedding money to buy presents. She would buy Hamm a motor scooter when he was out of prison.

Annabelle Surf had so much to do. Hair appointment was that thing she forgot. She needed a shiny new color. Also, she must order an orange-colored rose lapel flower, the clip-on style, for Hamm to match his prison uniform. Her dreams were coming true.

Hamm sat in his prison cell. If he didn't marry her, he would be on the upcoming cancellation list by the clan. Bad things always happened in a prison. He looked at the ceiling for any vents. Maybe there were vents in the library. There was no hole big enough in his jail cell for him to slink away. He checked the drain pipe to the sink. There was a large cap of metal there which wouldn't budge. "They must have used cement."

He would need a miracle and he didn't believe in them. Hamm made his decision. He was not stupid. He knew he was going to be in prison a long time. There were no options unless one of the inmates had an escape plan brewing. Hamm would keep his ears open. Russia or anywhere on the map was looking better all the time. He would have to go to the library and find some small out-of-the way place where no tourists went. He could get a job at a local store delivering groceries to old folks in the country. He reminded himself to check for large vents tomorrow.

"Once I'm out, I will require a means of transportation to get to the docks. It would be easy to

jump an oil tanker ship heading to Finland. From there,
I need money for the final trek."

47 Antiquities Permanent Display

THE LONDON POLICE confiscated the contents of the bank box and found the lists of Tiger Sphinx's other accounts. The dead man's gold eagle crown and two-piece clasp were put up for sale at an auction. Jess and Derek attended the auction and purchased the items.

They flew home and took photographs for their book. The Wrights returned the original bottom part of the scepter to the owner, Constantine Olsen in Walnut Creek, California, and had a special safe installed in her home for the valuable object and jewels. They paid for her insurance policy on them.

The Wrights brought the top part of the scepter to show her how they fit together and gave her pictures of the scepter fully cloaked in the real jewels, not the borrowed jewels.

Constance was grateful for their help. The Wrights had told her before that they were donating the items they purchased in memory of the Louisa Renaliere family. The collection went to a specific museum. The old woman contacted her lawyer, because she wanted to be remembered like Louisa.

Constance thought her family could have been royalty, too. Consequently, she left the bottom portion of the gold scepter to the same museum as the Wrights with the jewels. The museum could only have the collection if the scepter was put together in all its glory like the Wrights' photograph and her family's name appeared in the display.

Constance passed away and her lawyer let the Wrights know what was in her will. She also left them her home in case they needed money for anything. They put those funds into college scholarships under her name.

It was opening day for the special gold antiquities exhibit at their favorite museum. Jess was excited and kept squeezing Derek's arm. They cut the gold ribbon and had their pictures taken with the exhibit in the background. The museum's acquisitions were beautifully displayed. Each asset was displayed in its own highly-locked case with lighting. The collection included the golden eagle scepter with emerald eyes and diamonds around its neck with a gold branch holding a large ruby. The eagle design wings spiraled to the bottom of the scepter. The gold crown with same eagle design and two-piece eagle head and wing clasp showed well in the exhibit. The diamond ring had a large magnifier on the front. A person could see the intricate same eagle design.

There was a large commemorative placard attached to the exhibit with the brief story of the Renaliere's ancestors. There were the three dedication brass plates with Louisa Renaliere, Constance Olsen, and Jess and Derek Wright inscribed as donors of the antiquities. The museum sold the eagle T-shirts that

Jess designed and placed them in their shop. They sold out in a week and she ordered a second and third batch sewn.

The book Derek and Jess wrote was published and sold out. They went to the book signings and Derek was glad when everything was over. He was ready for life to settle down. Jess and the children felt the same.

They took the motorboat out to Catalina Island for a much-needed personal vacation.

Jess cuddled up with Derek in the evening.

She asked him, "Do you remember when our great life started?"

She slowly moved her feet up his leg until he caught her foot and swept her up in his arms.

Derek put her down and hit the number 6.5 button that would play soft calypso music and held out his hand to her.

He mentally thanked Dean Crain who told him Jess's favorite songs were number six and seven. Dean recommended he try number six first. He told Derek this song had a soft piano that pulled in all the instruments one by one slowly, so slowly that it reminded a person of stealth mode. Then the sound and beat increased exponentially to an astonishing high. Jess's hits on number six song were a hundred to one. Dean told him in the poker world that might be a winning hand. Dean would bet on those odds every time.

Dean gave Derek a business card for calypso lessons. Derek took the lessons. The number six calypso song started all their annual parties and played every two hours. Everyone knew it was her song and the group all loved it. The couple had performed a dance ensemble for their group at one of their annual parties. It was a once in a lifetime special dance dedication in honor of Dean Crain.

Their group's wives made their husbands take calypso lessons with them. They wanted to dance just like them.

Jess looked at Derek with all her love in her beautiful eyes. He had the song re-recorded to the slower 6.5 number. Derek knew that look and had always waited for it. She kicked her sandals off and Derek held onto her for a second before he twirled her around the upper motorboat deck and back into his arms.

Derek replied, "I remember very well that particular evening."

He asked her if she wanted to do that again.

"Of course, always."

He led her through the intricate dance steps, guiding her back and forth like he had in the past. Derek whispered in her ear, "I love, want, and need only you."

They danced close together into the night. Their soft footsteps matching the heavy metal electric guitar and drum beats of sound. He finally stopped the music and kissed her with a long passionate kiss that showed her she was his one and only woman.

48   Vacation near Catalina Island

A COUPLE WEEKS later Derek took some days off and the Wright family went to their favorite spot again to drop anchor near Catalina Island. Jess took the children to a face or arm painting class where they had to design their own patterns. Justin helped Sami with hers, and they both came home with beautiful tiger designs.

Ripping open the small cardboard box that arrived from Italy, Jess wondered what the owners of Louisa Renaliere's old apartment sent them. She thought the finalization of the estate and real estate transaction completed months earlier.

There was a note inside stating that they renovated one of the rooms and removed a closet. Evidently, stuck in the closet was a packet of small drawings. They thought they might be important and sent them to the Wrights.

Jess opened the envelope and inside was a more fragile envelope with ten drawings. The drawings were those that Louisa's mother had drawn for her of the crown, clasp, ring, scepter, and cape. There were several close-up drawings. Jess looked at the last drawing which was the great-great-grandfather seated in his chair in full regalia. Next to the man was a golden tiger.

She called for Derek to come quickly. She showed him the address on the box and the drawings.

Derek scratched his chin. "Honey, this is amazing. Louisa's drawings are correct. The museum will be pleased. We need to copyright them first."

"Don't you see it? Louisa forgot something."

Derek looked at the drawings carefully again. "Louisa forgot the tiger."

"Yes, she did. It looks like Felidae, Ara's tiger. There's more."

Derek smiled. "It certainly does. What am I missing?"

"Look what the tiger has on its head. It is small, and the fur almost hides the gold."

"Is that a small crown? Ara asked me about a small crown in our initial meeting with the police. I didn't want to mention it to you. Now I'm sorry that I didn't."

"I wonder how Ara knew about the second crown. It is a mystery."

Derek shook his head. "We should share the image with her. Maybe she saw the small crown at some auction place and repressed it."

"Definitely. Ara talked with me about the next tiger book and may want to use this image."

He nodded, "Go ahead. I know you want to send the file."

Jess sent photos to Ara, so she could see the influence the zoo website video had upon their children from their face painting class. Also, she sent the important Renaliere photo with the tiger.

Ara was with Jack and she had just visited Felidae. She was excited about the royalty image and she very much wanted to work with them to include it in the next book. They called the Wrights back. Jack gave them his regards. Ara told them her secret. She was three months pregnant.

Jess congratulated them and sent War Julio's wife, Janet, an e-mail so she would spread the news to their group. There was a huge baby shower planned in the future.

Janet's father recently died and left the Miami businesses and his money to War Julio's wife. Janet sent pictures of their older sixty-five-foot motorboat, inherited from her father, which was moored next to his black air-boat.

Also, there were pictures of the new and wider dock by their fishing business in Curacao. The dock was perpendicular to the other two docks. The new dock would accommodate the Wrights' eighty-five-foot boat. War Julio told Derek he made the dock wide enough to accommodate a party. He was building a larger warehouse, too. Jess was glad their business was expanding, and she thought a party there would be fun.

It was two days of playing, reading, and family time together. Jess felt it was important for her husband to finally unwind. They talked about retirement. Jess recommended he go into another different private practice. He would like to do so, but would miss all the best part of his job, *catching the con artist.*

Derek talked about taking a one-year leave of absence. He thought it would be fun to go to Curacao again. Their children were older, and it would be a good educational experience. The motorboat could take its time getting there.

The children went to bed. Jess told her husband, "I have a surprise."

"Oh, really, what is it? I like your surprises. I remember your eagle midi-type T-shirt." He wanted to go there again. Taking if off had been just the start of crazy.

"You must close your eyes and wait."

"I should wait how long with my eyes partially shut?"

"No partially on the eyes. It must be totally."

"Okay, total it is."

Jess took the custom scotch bottle and glasses putting them on the counter in the bedroom. Then she quickly microwaved the oyster garlic butter and poured it on top of the gourmet oysters from Tomales Bay. She put on the champagne-colored lingerie nightie with the crossover straps and tightly fitted very low bra top. The front skirt design was the silk painting of the back of the female eagle tipping a wing toward the larger eagle, signaling her mate. It was the prettiest of her collection. The champagne color and oysters were a reminder of their date in Napa, California.

"Now you can come into our bedroom."

He wondered what she put in the microwave. He opened the door and quickly shut it.

"Honey, that's beautiful. I knew you would pick this color." He saw the other lingerie garments on the bed. Her collection had arrived.

Then he saw the custom scotch bottle with her label. He noticed the glitter and glasses. He picked up an oyster and popped it in his mouth and poured them each a small sip of the powerful stuff.

Derek smiled. "This is good."

He held an oyster out for Jess to eat and grabbed another one for himself. He sipped the scotch. She sipped hers. He picked up another oyster and downed the great morsel. Then he looked at Jess who undid the crisscross strap. She was the next morsel he wanted.

He laughed, "Come here sweet woman. You are smooth."

Jess bent to pick up the second lingerie item.

Derek gently grabbed her arm. "Later."

She looked at the amazing garment.

"Later, my love."

Jess dropped the second lingerie outfit. His message was received. It was strong and clear. She went into his waiting outstretched arms.

The last morning on their motorboat, they talked some more about their plans. Derek was thinking about purchasing a larger boat, possibly one-hundred-fifty or one-hundred-sixty-feet long. He had been looking at the newer yachts.

They could afford it. It would give them a little more room. He checked with War Julio and either size ship could be accommodated on his dock. War Julio bought the warehouse next to his in Curacao for the extra room. War Julio was interested in buying their old motorboat. He sold his wife's ship and had also been looking. He was excited, because he loved the Wrights' crazy motorboat.

"That's unreal. What in the world will our friends think of the two large ships?"

"We will have bigger parties, of course."

She remembered War Julio saying that he would love to take trips with them.

"It will be impressive mooring the two ships together. The arsenal onboard should be enough to scare the police and the bad guys." That made Derek laugh just thinking about it.

"This exchange can work well. Oh, by the way, the number six song must be left on the stereo sound system."

Jess had fits of laughter.

"We can leave all the songs and make copies for us."

Their parties seemed to be getting larger. Jess knew the guest lists had increased. She loved the idea of a large yacht. Derek would show her the brochures the companies sent him. Of, course, she would want to have some custom-made items. Jess could start looking at her fabrics and other decorative items for the yacht.

They would contact some of the ship dealers also in Fort Lauderdale and San Diego. He already checked with some of the manufacturers on all the extra gear. It would also mean a larger helicopter which would be a good idea. They would need extra crew, and he would talk to the captain about that.

Jess wanted to spend some time in Puerto Vallarta. Ara and Jack told them they would fly down and party with them on any of their trips. Jim and Mary Beth wanted to be involved in the trips, too.

Derek bounced the idea off War Julio about their arrival plans in Curacao. War Julio told him that his house was always open to family. War Julio and Janet also wanted to join them in San Diego and cruise the entire trip with them in their newly-acquired, eighty-five-foot motorboat.

Then some of the Miami and San Francisco people heard about Puerto Vallarta and voted into any future visit there.

Derek thought, "So much for being alone with my lovely wife in the place tourists called PV."

The Wrights needed to return the motorboat to Los Angeles the next morning. The motorboat would be going in for its annual check on engine systems, bottom paint, etc. It would take three weeks. The chef almost emptied the freezer and cold cooler, and he apologized for the hot dog dinner with cheesy noodles. Derek and the kids liked it when the freezer was almost empty. They told their chef they were fine. Their crew was excited to take three, paid, weeks off shortly. It was a wonderful end to a beautiful summer.

Derek picked up his glass of wine, "To the Wright family, a great team." The kids and Jess clinked their glasses.

49   Felidae and Cubs

ALONG WITH THE original purchase of Felidae, Ara was given his frozen semen. There were only three of the precious vials. She had given the third vial to the Los Angeles zoo. There were only two vials left. The third vial worked on the two-and-a-half-year-old tigress.

The zoo was pleased everything did happen, otherwise they would have to wait ninety days before trying again. It would take approximately one-hundred-twelve days before the birth happened.

The zoo would call her for the delivery in the special room they maintained for the tigress. The special room was like a cave. The cameras were installed, and they let her go in and out, so she would feel comfortable there. The zoo would do everything possible to save a cub and help it find the mother's precious teat. They wanted the cub to live because she would not mate again for two years.

The zoo told Ara that Felidae was having some urinary tract problems. The male cat was now over eighteen years old and things were slowing down. They were giving him medicine and would let her know if there were any other problems.

They reminded her that twenty years in captivity was the normal timeframe where in the wild

307

on a preserve, it was fifteen years unless the poachers or a snake or lion interfered to shorten its life.

Ara and Jack drove to the zoo and just arrived to capture the final moments before birth. After the birth and cleanup, the zookeepers were excited about there being two cubs, a male and female. They watched the tigress closely who moved to the drier area of the cave and brought her cubs close to her.

She laid down next to them to provide her warmth and nourishing vessels. It wasn't long before the wiggling cubs found the teats. The little female was last to find and master her capture of nutrients. The zookeepers were pleased that they could relax for some time.

The mother and cubs would be closely monitored. The cubs looked to be a good size, more than two pounds each. They would nurse for twenty-four weeks before they introduced small pieces of meat. The cubs would grow quickly and at six months, weigh eighty-five to one hundred ten pounds. The zookeepers would hide their food and the tigress mother would show them where to find it.

Ara and Jack hired a photographer to take pictures for Ara's book of their progress and a video photographer for the zoo's website as a gift to the zoo. Felidae's other two vials would be granted to them as well.

XXXXXX

Ara had written most of her children's book when the zoo contacted her about her tiger boy. He was fading fast and she needed to come.

Ara arrived at his internal cage. She signed the waiver documents and went inside his cage. She was six months pregnant and Jack was worried about her. She told him to wait in the outer corridor. He could watch through the special glass in the heavy door. Ara told him she would be fine. She brought a soft pillow to sit on the cement floor. The large cat lifted its head, but couldn't stand or sit up.

Ara held his head in her lap and told tiger boy her children's stories which were all about him. The cat's tailed flicked a few times. She considered his beautiful golden eyes and saw that he felt her little girl kick in its womb. She saw the two cubs in his eyes. The tiger knew about his offspring. It was all right to leave. Felidae knew he would see them someday. He would also see the Goddess child. He was content. His job while here on earth was done very well. He was protector guardian.

Jack and Ara buried him in a ten-acre parcel of land that was in one of the valleys that they owned. They wrapped him in a golden satin blanket fit for a tiger and placed his body in the earthen ground so that his spirit could roam free with his ancestors.

They planted wildflowers and trees indigenous to the area and a short drive where Ara could park and visit him. A brick pillar and wrought iron fence with gate was added to keep people out. They placed a small marble plaque in memory over the ground where his head lay.

Jack would continue to buy all the real estate land that came up for sale anywhere near the tiger's resting place, unknown to Ara. He wanted to help her build the land later if she chose. It was an investment opportunity he felt was safe due to all the development. Los Angeles was moving in an outward direction. His wise decisions would bear fruit someday. The land would be worth a fortune.

She completed her final story and it was an immense success. The royalty picture drawn by Louisa Renaliere's mother was the final page of the book. Every year, they donated the proceeds of the book to the zoo for the care of Felidae's two offspring.

The flowers bloomed in his grave field and the trees grew. It looked like a forest.

Derek paid a songwriter to work with Ara for music about her tiger boy. There were three separate sections to the arrangement of the song. Ara had cleverly placed first her tiger boy, then the tiger female cub, and then the tiger male cub as the name in the lyrics. Justin and his music teacher located another opera singer.

The recording studio and symphony ensemble were engaged by the Wrights for Justin's first recording with the opera singer. The sound was correct for the exhibit, full of mystery, and love to produce a moving operatic melody. The song because it was split into three separate songs played only once during the day.

They allowed the zoo the rights to play the short songs on their introduction to the tiger exhibit. The times of the songs were posted so people knew when to return to the exhibit to hear the dedication to tigers. Young girls loved the sound. That boosted Justin's confidence level up more than a notch. All the girls wanted to meet the young singer.

Jack called Jess, "I have a favor to ask you. I'm going to be out of town for a week. I need help with Ara because she is acting real quiet and I think she misses her beloved tiger boy. Could you possibly check on her for me?"

She told him it would be no problem. Jess would set up some time with the three children. Ara was probably having the early baby blues. It happened to most women. She was glad he called. The children would love a day off from their schoolroom.

Jess took Sami, Justin, and Maggie with Ara to touch tiger boy's plague and see his forest. They spread more fertilizer from glass jars that Jess provided. The children headed back to the car as a gentle rain descended. Jess gave Ara a bag of ping pong balls. Ara opened the bag and let the balls fall. It was a fitting gift for her tiger boy. The two women ran to the car.

Ara smiled. Her daughter would come when she was older. She would know Felidae had existed. Jess smiled back at her friend and started the car. It was a good day.

They drove to the zoo to eat hamburgers and hot dogs for lunch and then peek at the two cubs. Little Maggie was fascinated by the little creatures that came to the window and looked at her. The male cub tried to lick her, but only succeeded in smearing the glass. Ara would be happy when Jack called. She would be filled with information about their day.

Ara and Jack's sweet baby girl arrived, and he thought she looked very much like Ara. She had soft, fuzzy blonde hair. They named her, Lis Tigre Jones or French for Tiger Lily. She liked the idea of Lis, because it reminded her of Elizabeth who also was loved.

Jack was all right with that explanation. Jack called her Lis, his little Lily Tiger. When she was older, they took her to Felidae's forest and let her lay the tiger lily bouquet of flowers near his headstone, and then they went to the zoo. The male cub licked the glass, then, too.

Jack and Ara set up an online fund for donations for the zoo to build a larger tiger enclosure. There was a naming contest for the two cubs on their site which generated high attendance at the zoo. The popularity of the cub storybook helped fuel the donations higher. All their friends contributed, and enough money was received for a larger enclosure to be built.

The female was named Rena Felidae and the male cub was named Rah Felidae. The enclosure was called simply, "The Forest of Golden Tigers."

50   Decision Time

DEREK WENT TO work, and his administrative assistant brought him some papers in two folders. He looked at her and she was scowling. She pointed at the reports. He read the labels she put on the files. He looked up in alarm. She told him she would get him strong coffee and shut his office door. Derek didn't want to open the folders. The feelings of doom were creeping in. He swiveled his chair to look out his window. The day was warm, peaceful, and calm. Derek never told Jess about these two criminals. He waited until his secretary brought the coffee. Derek hadn't read the reports. He didn't need to do so because he knew what the reports would say. He told her he needed an hour alone. She was to cancel his afternoon appointments. His admin assistant nodded.

Derek called his wife and asked her if she was home.

Jess answered, "Yes, I spent the morning going through the children's clothes that don't fit and have them boxed."

She would have them check the boxes tonight and their housekeeper would drop them off at the needy thrift store. They would have to buy some new clothes.

"Why, what's up?"

"I'm leaving work for the rest of the day. I'll bring Chinese takeout for lunch."

"Great, see you soon."

Derek arrived and kissed his wife and they ate moo Shu pork for lunch. Jess loved to eat the stuff with the duck sauce.

He brought his coffee and cream to the coffee table with a latte for Jess. He sat across from Jess. Derek wanted to take her hands, but felt guilty. He should have told her about this gang a long time ago. She could tell something was seriously wrong because she knew him. His eyes became darker when there was a problem.

Jess asked, "What is it Derek, tell me."

Derek started his story about a man and woman that he had helped the police capture when he first became an investigator. He was inexperienced and new to the job. It was before he met her.

The two people were the leaders of this group called *Green Stream*. The group first started robbing small mom and pop shops. Then they moved to stealing cars and got into the disappearing act with the expensive cars. Next, they robbed banks.

The police thought the group might have murdered but couldn't prove that part in their trial. It took two years to catch them and put them in prison. The first problem was that both were being released from jail in six and a half months. Evidently, they provided revealing and important evidence for a recent case. In the agreement, they received an earlier release date.

Jess said, "You can wait until they commit another crime and send them right back to prison."

Derek did not smile. The second problem was what they threatened him when they left the courtroom that last day long ago. They said that they would kill his children when they got out.

Jess jumped up from the couch, "You believe the bad man and woman will hurt our children?"

"Yes, I do."

He explained to Jess about the snitch. He heard from a snitch in their same prison and was told, "The bad man paid money to receive the address of Derek Wright's home because the two were going through with their plan when they are released."

"What do you want to do? Can we set up a plan to catch them?" asked Jess.

"I'm taking some time off to think about how to trap them. I am worried that something bad might happen to Sami and Justin before I can put the Surfs in prison again. The school our children attend was only semi-secure. We can put our children on the motorboat, but that will also place you in harm's way."

"The solution I have in mind is to lay low and get out of Los Angeles. Then I can bring our groups together to discuss private surveillance teams and a plan to catch them."

Jess nodded her encouragement for him to continue.

"I can request a leave of absence for a year, but leave the door open so that I can come back any time. We could shut up the house and have our security company handle it. Remember our plan for a yacht in our future? I think we should proceed with the purchase quickly. We should think about selling the house and move forward. We do own property and can work with our architect later for new house plans. I will inform our friends about the names of the man and woman. We will request silence of our whereabouts once we leave for Curacao other than to our group and my contacts."

Derek finished the last container of food.

"Our group can meet in Puerto Vallarta and then later Curacao for our annual party. We have approval from War Julio to moor the yacht at his new pier. You can enroll the children in online learning and I'll help you."

"What do you think about my contingency plan?"

"Let's sell the house and do this move. It will be an adventure. We want to build a new house, and I'm all right with delaying it. The children and I can be ready in the six-month timeframe. Why don't you find us a yacht, my sweet husband? Maybe a used one would fit into our plans?"

Derek loved her. Everything was fun, even the hard stuff. She was ready to travel any ocean or fly anywhere. Jess would help him as much as she could.

"I think our children should be told."

Derek said, "Only the good stuff. The rest we can talk later with them once we are securely onboard."

Derek went to make the calls to his people. His list was a long one. He called Jim first and then War Julio. He called a custom boat builder he knew who also kept up with the used yacht market. The custom boat builder also knew about what could be done to convert a yacht and had the contacts. They arranged to talk at a boat show in San Diego that was happening soon.

The lawyer would get all the permits, licenses, and clearances started. The captain and chef would coordinate their teams and the supplies. He told everyone this was a silent mission, and everyone received the names of the bad guys.

All of them knew the routine of "run silent and deep", but this message included the words, "primary guard on the children". They all knew these former cons should be brought back to jail or put down. Their group preferred the latter.

The code name for the two people were *pollutants.*

Ara listened in on Derek's call to Jack. She knew some people to privately ask questions. They were her loyal, trusted people. She would let Derek know what she had found. Derek thanked her, but didn't want her to place herself in harm's way. Ara told Derek she dealt with these types of low life before.

Derek smiled and thanked them.

Derek called Skid Peters and asked how Maggie was doing. Skid fell in love with Stace Keats who had left him. Stace went to Curacao and died having their child, Maggie. Skid was a diver for the Wrights in Africa when they found a sunken treasure. He owned a Surf Shop near San Diego and was a single parent raising his little girl. The Wrights were good friends.

Skid told Derek his world was fine.

Derek talked to him about their plans and the reason for their departure. Derek told him the name of the cons getting out of prison. There was dead silence on the other end. Skid knew the two people and had run-ins with them. Skid didn't know they were being released. He received the same threat from them that Derek did.

"How did you get involved with them?"

"I was young, and the other analogous word is stupid. No, a person should insert a correction and add extremely idiotic onto the sentence. I went drinking one night, a long time ago, before Stace. Too much beer does crazy things to my mind. I accidentally married one of their members but quickly got a divorce when I woke up from my delusional state."

Derek asked, "Who did you accidentally marry?"

Skid said, "The woman."

"Not Amy Surf?"

Skid hated to say her name, "Yes, Amy."

Derek said, "Unbelievable."

"Amy is still pissed at me. She also is a vengeful person or was. The bad feelings that she has towards me have probably not receded. She was always like a coiled snake whenever I saw her after the divorce. That is why I became a diver so that I'm never in one place too long. The woman can't track me. I'm worried about her reaction to Maggie."

Derek talked to Jess about the conversation that he had with Skid.

"Trouble." Derek agreed.

Jess said, "We should ask them to join us. Besides, Maggie was born in Curacao. It will be fun showing her the place her mother once lived."

They could take the sub diving machine out with their children. Skid was a wonderful teacher. War Julio knew Skid and Maggie. Jess knew, "Everything will work if they protect each other."

Derek called Skid back and told him what they needed to do and invited him aboard the cruise. Skid gladly accepted. He would bring his diving gear.

Traveling great distances in a ship was not a problem. They did it before.

Jess went to start the spaghetti and dinner salad because it was their maid's day off. "Our next adventure will be a good one."

Louisa told her long ago this would occur. Derek finally told her about two people she already knew existed. She read all the newspaper articles she could find regarding the two names. She also knew the prison they were being released from. Jess was a step ahead of everyone.

Her daughter, Sami, came home with their driver. She walked into the kitchen and looked at her mother. Sami quietly helped her mother with the salad and little tomatoes. Jess was singing her favorite song. Sami knew her mother was happy about something. She loved when her parents went a little crazy. Jess tickled her. Sami told her she was glad they were traveling to Curacao. She saw the vision.

Jess smiled and thought, *magical*. She squeezed her daughter and said that she was correct. Jess hadn't told her a thing. Sami already knew. Jess hit the number six song on their recorder music machine. Jess was glad she talked to her daughter about Aphrodite and Venus, wonderful women. Jess wanted her to know she was part of life's very elite, absolute best species. Her daughter told her that she always felt their connection.

She and Sami picked up the salads as they danced into the dining room when Derek and Justin walked in.

Jess arranged online live opera lessons for Justin who loved to sing. Derek looked at her and she nodded. He knew Jess set up activities for their intelligently gifted son. They introduced Justin two years ago, to an opera female artist in the area for lessons. She would continue his lessons online.

"It's a wonderful celebration time."

The males grabbed the sauce and spaghetti bowls and followed the females into the dining room table, dancing calypso to the ascending sound. They went around the table a couple times singing the words to the magical number six song.

Justin was happy Maggie and Skid would be on their new yacht.

It was a familiar song and their children learned the beat and dance at an early age. Their children were good dancers. It was part of growing up almost normal around Jess and Derek. Derek would twirl Jess and bend her low backwards and then bring her up close holding her. Their children learned firsthand what love meant. They saw the stars in their parent's eyes. Those stars were directed their way and they felt loved.

Old Louisa had seen their family's love and felt it, too.

51   Amy and Minnow Surf

AMY HOOKED UP with Minnow Surf after breaking off with Skid Peters. Minnow was the second leader in their group called *Green Stream*. Next, the leader of their group had a run-in with the police and crashed his motorcycle and died. That's when Minnow took over.

He told Amy, "I will find your old boyfriend for you and bring him to you. Then you can do what you want with the man. You can hurt the dude. It is fine with me."

He missed his gold ring that looked like a classroom ring, only different. There was a small fish surrounded by a pond. He was given the ring by his friend who was smart about mixing strange chemical compounds.

Minnow found a blonde woman named Susan Kamar for the friend. Susan was a crazy girl Minnow dropped when Amy appeared in his life. He thought he did Susan a favor introducing her to his new friend. The ring was for a favor until his green-eyed friend could send him money. Then the chemical guy would want the ring back. He never saw his male friend again, so he kept the ring. Nor did he ever see Susan and wondered what happened to her.

That admission made Amy happy. He left someone for her and supported her anger at Skid. She and Minnow got a quickie marriage in Reno, Nevada, because it was closer. Minnow was doing a drug deal there at the same time, learning the business.

Their group kept moving up in the crime world getting larger and richer. Money worked both ways. Good people liked money as did the bad guys. It could buy stuff and people. Money meant power. The group tasted power and it became their drug of choice next to marijuana and cocaine. They still stole expensive cars and jewelry as a sideline.

In the drug trade, the game was always about which team was the smartest at conning someone out of something. Their clan started stealing cocaine from a lesser con artist. Then they accidentally killed the leader of that group and stole his drug business.

Amy and Surf made a mistake and decided to rob their last bank. A smaller bank was chosen close to their area and business because they believed things would be easy. They waited for the armored vehicle to pull up outside the bank and unload a new batch of money.

They heard that the money being delivered was two-hundred-thousand-dollars higher because the Rose Bowl parade would be happening soon. The bank needed the extra cash for all the tourists and parade people that would descend upon the town.

What the couple didn't know was there was no extra money. Nor was there very much money in the vault. The bags contained shredded money. The real money had been removed from the bank except the coins were left in the vault. All the money bags contained were the packets of shredded money in individual locked bags.

There were a few stacked and numbered pads of real bills on the vault shelf. The numbered bills had been recorded. The whole scene was a trap to catch the criminals. One of the bags contained a tracking device.

The couple robbed the bank and their quick white get-a-way van picked them up and three other white vans drove past the bank about the same time. The effort by the group was to ditch any police tails. They had taken some bags of coins because Amy wanted to take a bath with the coins and her lover, Minnow, to celebrate their winnings. She was a little kinky sometimes.

They grabbed the loose real bills, and would wait on opening the bags until they reached the house. Only the team who planned and participated in the heist would appear at the house. Minnow called his selected members to meet there. He said, "The hit is a success."

The police and Derek slowly followed the one white van to the old house in the hills. It was a rundown, older area. The houses were small. There were two cars parked out front. The white van backed into the driveway close to the single car garage. The garage door went up and four guys were in the garage. The five thugs got out of the van. The police surrounded the house. Several of the boys tried to run, but stopped when shots were fired. They were arrested, tried, and went to jail for their crimes.

Amy was the one who told Derek, "I will get your children," in the courtroom that day long ago. She was angry at being caught. Mostly, she was mad at herself. Prison was not in her plans. She wished that she never stepped foot in the bank with Minnow. It was a bad decision.

Minnow said, "I will help you. It's Mr. Wright's fault."

The two had secretly been sending messages to each other for years. Their letters to each other were opened by the police and contained nonsense. Their hidden messages were on the back of their stamps. Minnow gave Amy the Wright's address and told her they owned a large boat. He told her about Sami and Justin. He wrote to her that Skid had a daughter called Maggie and owned a surf shop. He wanted to fuel Amy's anger toward Skid, so she would know he was there for her.

They knew they were being released and could hardly wait to see each other again. Amy and Minnow set their date, time, and place to meet. His Green Stream group did well while they were in prison. He was, however, no longer the leader.

His cousin, Randy Moore, was now the leader. Randy bought a nice house for them in a good neighborhood as a favor. It was the least Randy could do for Amy and Minnow. Randy would let them work for his restaurants, too, if they were going straight with their lives and stayed out of trouble.

This pissed off Minnow big time. He was gone, but he expected Randy to step down when he was out of jail. Minnow would become angrier when he saw the two-and-a-half million-dollar house Randy and Sandra

Moore lived in and the five-hundred-thousand-dollar house he and Amy were given.

As soon as Minnow got out of prison, he would have to work on that little problem. Minnow killed before and it hadn't been hard at all. He enjoyed the experience. He felt the power of evil in his gun hand. He thought evil was as good as money.

Amy always liked Randy and that might be another problem. Minnow would have to keep his plan for Randy a silent one.

His sister was marrying a new guy. He was happy for Annabelle. He would need to see if her husband was interested in making more money when he got out. Minnow wasn't sure how long her husband would be in prison.

Randy knew his wife Sandra wasn't about to hand over her wonderful house and life to Minnow and his broad, Amy. Randy remembered Amy who always brought out images in his mind of hot. He wondered if she still looked great. His wife Sandra was always buying face creams, taking spa treatments, and getting some injections. He couldn't remember what she originally looked like. She was pushing him for more money because she wanted plastic surgery she read about in a magazine. He bet Amy didn't need any plastic surgery.

After a year in prison, Randy visited Amy.

Randy said, "I'm sorry you're in jail. I thought Minnow did not build enough layers to protect you. If I had been the leader of their group, I would have protected you and not crossed with the law. You would be out of jail. I do remember our two nights together after your divorce from Skid. I figure you didn't tell Minnow because I'm still walking around."

Amy smiled.

He told her, "I'm going to marry Sandra. She finalized her divorce. I'm glad she found me again. I want you to hear about our marriage from me."

Randy said, "Sandra is beautiful like silver and platinum, but you are precious gold."

"Stop trying to cheer me up in prison. I like Sandra and it's all right. She will be good for you."

He told her if she needed anything, "You let me know."

"I will. Thanks."

Amy thought about their conversation many times in prison.

"You bought your restaurants and they are probably one of the layers you did talk about to me. I should have listened to you."

52 Cover Complete

THEY PACKED THEIR house in boxes and the warehouse crew moved them to a secure room at the warehouse. A second room in the warehouse was easily converted to a master bedroom and bathroom for Derek.

It was their special warehouse with the library of Louisa's books. There already existed a kitchen, bathroom, and a four-bunk bedroom. Derek moved their bedroom furniture into the newly-built room. He would fly back to Los Angeles on occasion to check the investigation and would stay at their warehouse.

Their vehicles belonged to Derek's company as did the warehouse. The lawyer transferred temporarily the title to the warehouse and cars to a Miami company owned by War Julio. Derek would fly back to the warehouse when the time was ready to pursue the pollutant clan.

Their house with the rest of the furniture was placed on the market and sold quickly. The Wrights already owned a private piece of land that they would build a larger home with their own security guard gate and a helicopter pad with its own storage building. He and Jess would work with their architect on the new plans while they traveled.

The motorboat was also temporarily transferred into the same Miami company name.

Skid's surf business was put in a different Miami company name temporarily and his managers would work through a new contact who would work through Skid. The outside sign was changed to "Mo's Surfboards".

Skid's house was also put under that same company name. Skid and Maggie would be picked up at one of the San Diego piers or at their slip after they picked up the new yacht.

Derek and Jess flew to Sydney, Australia, for a few days' vacation. Then they flew to Miami for a couple days before flying to Phoenix. A private plane owned by one of the Miami friends flew the Wrights back to San Diego where they boarded the new yacht. The whole set up was to create confusion for anyone tracking them.

Derek said, "Our cover is complete. Everything is hidden from view."

They liked the sleek ships in San Diego at the Yacht Show they attended previously.

Derek and Jess drew up the paperwork and purchased the 2009 used one-hundred-sixty-foot, super yacht with larger helicopter, through the owner of a large yacht business. Their other special requirements would be added by several other companies through the same yacht business.

Derek negotiated a good price for the yacht and upgrades. They used the money from their sunken treasure find off the coast of Dakar, Senegal, Africa, and Jess's books, clothing, and perfume line. Plus, they had money from Dean's holdings to finance the rest for the twenty-million-dollar yacht.

The yacht business would deliver the boat to a special warehouse dock in San Diego if they hadn't found a slip. Their children were excited as was Maggie to walk among the sleek mega yachts. Skid was in awe at the show. He made a date with one of the single female manufacturer's representatives. The rest of Derek's group would meet on the converted yacht again in Puerto Vallarta to discuss what plans they would create and which groups were assigned surveillance of the pollutant tribe.

Their next meeting was in six to seven months when War Julio was throwing a party for their small group to celebrate his new dock in Curacao which coincided with their annual party. He told Derek to take care of his motorboat.

All the wheels were set in motion for a new con artist game to begin. There always existed the good group versus the evil one.

Right now, the scale was level and the winds or destiny would cause the scale to sway soon.